MW00463051

INDEPENDENT SOURCES

SASHA MCCANDLESS LEGAL THRILLER NO. 15

MELISSA F. MILLER

BROWN STREET BOOKS

Copyright © 2022 by Melissa F. Miller

All rights reserved.

No part of this book may be reproduced in any form or by any electronic or mechanical means, including information storage and retrieval systems, without written permission from the author, except for the use of brief quotations in a book review.

1

WACB, Pittsburgh's Most Trusted Source for News
Dressing Room of Fan Favorite Evening Anchor Maisy
Farley
Monday, 7:10 PM

Maisy dipped her fingers into the extra-large tub of Pond's Cold Cream and dug out a glob of the white stuff. She methodically worked the cream into her skin. After she massaged it into her face in small circles, she waited a few beats while it worked its magic. She rolled her shoulders, wiped the excess cream away with a cotton ball, and then peered into the mirror to examine her naked face.

She tilted her head from one side to the other, searching for any blemishes or imperfections. Finding none, she sat back satisfied and winked at her reflection. "You still got it, sugar," she reassured herself.

Just then someone rapped on the door. She winced and sent up a quick prayer that her self-affirmation hadn't been loud enough to be overheard out in the hallway.

"It's open," she called.

She swiveled around to greet her visitor as the door creaked open. The new field reporter peered into the room.

"Uh, Ms. Farley?"

Maisy scanned her mental Rolodex for the reporter's name and drew a blank.

"Don't be shy, darlin'. Come on in." She smiled broadly and waved her hand.

The reporter hesitated for a moment, then she stutter-stepped into the room and pulled the door closed behind her. She stood ramrod straight with her hands clasped together in front of her. She looked for all the world like a high schooler who'd been hauled into the principal's office.

Maisy studied the woman for a long moment, and the name finally popped into her mind. *Summer. Summer Reed.*

She'd met Summer a few weeks earlier. She'd caught the fresh-faced strawberry blonde with the startlingly bright blue eyes staring at her over a tray of bagels at an early-morning all-hands meeting. Tired, and possibly a bit cranky at being dragged into the station at five a.m. for a meeting that could have been an email, Maisy had at first dismissed the girl—*woman*, she corrected herself

—as a starstruck intern earning summer high school credit. But Summer had mustered up her courage to come over and introduce herself, gushing that Maisy was her idol. She'd grown up watching Maisy on tv with her parents.

Now Maisy turned her attention back to the young reporter, but Summer was staring at Maisy's makeup table with a puzzled expression.

"You hoo, over here. Did you need something, Summer?"

She dragged her eyes back to Maisy. "Oh, sorry. Mr. Wilson wanted me to ask you if you could stop by the conference room for a … um, brief meeting … before you leave for the evening."

Maisy suppressed a smile. The local media award winners were scheduled to be announced today. Every year, her news producer, Preston Wilson, 'surprised' the talent with cake and cheap champagne when the winners were named.

"Right. Of course."

She pulled her signature blonde curls up into a loose topknot and snapped an elastic around her hair. Then she screwed the lid back onto the jar of cold cream and grabbed her pocketbook.

She was halfway across the room before she realized Summer hadn't moved.

She craned her neck and looked over her shoulder. "You coming?"

"Yeah, of course. Can I ask you a question?"

"You certainly *may*." Maisy was loath to correct someone's grammar outright, but these young reporters butchered the English language without mercy.

"Do you use that drugstore stuff to take off your makeup?" She pointed at the tub of cleanser.

"I sure do."

Summer wrinkled her nose. "And it works?"

Maisy strode across the room, grabbed the jar, and pressed it into Summer's hands. "Try it yourself and you tell me."

"Oh, I couldn't—"

"Take it. I always have a spare jar or two in reserve. I'm telling you, sugar, once you use this stuff, you'll thank me. It'll work much better than whatever fancy French micellar water you've probably been using."

Summer stared at her for a beat, then popped the makeup remover into her shoulder bag. "Uh, thanks. Your skin *does* look great ... for your age."

Maisy pressed her lips together, pulled her shoulders back, and walked out of the room without dignifying the statement with a response. Summer trotted down the hall behind her like an eager puppy. She appeared to be clueless that she'd just insulted her idol.

Maisy stopped outside the conference room and arranged her expression into one of surprise before pulling open the door and stepping inside.

"Surprise!" a chorus of voices sang.

Livia, the station's longtime makeup artist and hair stylist, tossed a handful of confetti in Maisy's general direction.

Maisy clasped her hands to her chest and scanned the room. The entire evening crew was there, along with an assortment of weekend and daytime people who happened to be in the building. Preston gestured toward a thickly frosted sheet cake with a big grin. Maisy's co-anchor, Chet Roy, stood against the wall, stiff-backed and expressionless.

Ha. Looks like somebody didn't win ... again.

"What's the occasion?" Maisy asked.

Maisy's favorite camerawoman, Jocelyn, gave her a knowing look before popping the cork on the bubbly.

"Local Media Stars were announced today—as if you couldn't guess," she said as she handed Maisy a plastic flute of champagne.

Maisy grinned.

Once everyone had a glass, Preston raised his in Maisy's direction. "To Maisy, Pittsburgh's fan favorite media personality for the sixth year running."

"Seventh," Livia corrected him.

"For the *seventh* year running," he amended.

Maisy pushed back the swell of disappointment that rose in her chest and lifted her own glass. "Y'all know I could never do it without the best team behind me. This is a joint effort." She smiled and gestured toward Chet, pretending not to notice the grimace he tried to pass off as a smile.

The assembled group responded "cheers" and swigged their almost-chilled champagne.

Maisy took a small sip and tilted her head toward Preston while Jocelyn and the video editing intern cut and passed out the cake.

Preston clapped her heartily on the back. "Well

done, Maisy. Really. Nobody can knock you off your throne."

"Mmm. So, who won the investigative journalism award?" she asked casually.

Preston pursed his lips, then snapped his fingers at Summer. "Reed, who got the Dirt Digger Award for Investigative Work?"

Summer trotted over. "I believe that went to Troy Jones over at the *City Paper*."

"For his series on the safety lapses with the driver-less car pilot program?"

"Right, that's the one," Summer confirmed.

"Ah."

That's all she said. One noncommittal syllable. But Preston knew her well enough to hear the lengthy, unvoiced monologue that single sound carried.

"Your exposé of the corners being cut at that compounding pharmacy was stronger, Mais."

He was right. She could acknowledge that without being prideful or vain. Troy's investigation was good, but hers was better. Earth-shaking. Change-inspiring.

"Then I wonder why I didn't win," she mused.

Preston made a choking, coughing sound and shifted his gaze nervously.

"I'm sorry, I didn't quite catch that," Maisy said.

He cleared his throat. "Summer, why don't you get Maisy a slice of her cake before it's all gone?"

After she walked away, he turned back to Maisy with a pained expression. "Now, before you get mad, you have to listen to everything I have to say. Deal?"

"Of course."

He squared his shoulders and inhaled deeply. "Okay, so the station made the decision not to submit your piece in the investigative journalism category."

She lowered her chin and stared at him. "The station is a brick building, Preston. I don't think it decided anything. Who decided?"

He raised his hands as if to ward off a blow. "It wasn't me."

It better not have been. They'd sat down together, gone through all her clips, and had agreed that her 'Dangerous Doses' piece was the strongest one.

"Who?" she repeated. Her voice was dangerously soft.

"Uh … new management, Mais. They wanted to be able to promote you as the perennial fan favorite. It's a huge deal to be the most popular media personality for seven years in a row in any market, let alone one as big as ours. You're beloved by our viewers."

"I don't want to be Pittsburgh's most well-liked *personality*, Preston. I'm a journalist. I have a brain, you know."

"I know. And I'm sorry. I knew you'd be upset. That's why I didn't tell you that corporate pulled the dirt digger submission. I guess that was a mistake."

She arched one thin eyebrow. "You think?"

"Maisy, I'm truly sorry. But my hands were tied. It's not my fault that you're so darn lovable."

She sighed, then softened. Preston was many things, but a man of principle wasn't one. She knew that. She couldn't be surprised that he wilted in the face of an edict from the network.

She mustered up a smile. "I guess I *am* irresistible."

She patted Preston on the arm, avoided Summer and the slab of cake, and made her rounds quickly, laughing and joking with her colleagues. She waited until she was alone in the elevator to let her hot, bitter tears fall.

2

Sasha popped out of her seat and elbowed her law partner in the side. "There she is!" She waved frantically in the direction of the door to catch Maisy's attention through the throng of bodies crowded around the bar.

"The body check was unnecessary," Naya grumbled.

Sasha rolled her eyes. "Will you just do your thing, please?"

Naya grumped, but complied. She placed two fingers in her mouth and emitted an ear-splitting whistle that cut through the music, the laughter, and the clink of glasses.

Maisy's blonde curls bobbed and her head appeared above the crowd as she bounced up onto her tiptoes to scan the room. Sasha waved her arms overhead as if she were flagging an airplane.

"You know she can't possibly see you, right?" Naya asked before climbing up to stand on the seat of her chair and whistle again.

Sasha lowered her arms. Given her stature, or lack thereof, Naya was probably right. Her height was only one reason why Sasha hated crowds. But it was a big one. At best, she was armpit-level with most adults. And she'd learned through experience that being armpit-level in a crowded club in the middle of the summer was an assault on the olfactory system.

Maisy shimmied through the sea of sweat-slicked, gyrating bodies and emerged in front of the cramped corner table that Sasha had secured through a combination of flirtation, threats, and bribery.

"There she is—Pittsburgh's perennial fan favorite." Naya greeted her with a wide smile.

"Hi."

Maisy's voice lacked its trademark effervescence. Naya raised an eyebrow and threw Sasha a questioning look. Sasha raised her shoulders and shook her head. She had no idea why Maisy seemed so flat and somber.

"Come on, squeeze in. What do you want? I'll swim over to the bar to place our order." Sasha steeled herself for the armpits.

Maisy wrinkled her nose. "Or we could go back to my place and hang out without the cloud of body spray and the crappy music. I'm sure I have some chilled Prosecco in the fridge."

Naya was already grabbing her sweater and purse from the back of her chair. "Now you're talking."

Sasha frowned. "Are you okay?"

Maisy was an extrovert, always the first one to dive into a social scene and the last one to leave a party. She claimed loud, busy places charged her batteries and gave her energy. A quiet night at home might sound like heaven to Sasha or Naya, but it wasn't Maisy's style.

"Yeah. I just ... I'm not feeling it. Come on, let's get out of here."

Naya took the lead, cutting a path through the bar and beelining for the back door with Maisy on her heels. Sasha trailed along behind them, distracted by Maisy's out-of-character behavior but admittedly glad to be leaving the crush of people packed into the club.

Naya pushed the metal door open and inhaled deeply. "Ah, fresh air."

Sasha stepped out into the parking lot and gazed pointedly at the dumpster by the door. "More like fetid, humid air."

"Cranky, cranky," Naya admonished her. She dug out her key fob and popped the locks on her car. "I assume you walked over?"

"I did," Maisy confirmed.

"So did Mac. But I didn't buy this thing to hide it in my garage. Get in," Naya waved at her gleaming sports car.

The cherry-red Mercedes had been her first big purchase after making partner, and she babied the thing —washing, waxing, and polishing it every weekend. She also insisted on driving everywhere. She slid behind the wheel.

Sasha gestured for Maisy to take the front passenger seat.

"You sure, sugar?"

"I'm sure. The back seat is sized for someone like

me. Not a giraffe like you. If you sit back there your knees will be up by your ears," Sasha told her.

Sasha climbed over the center console and dumped herself unceremoniously into the cramped back seat.

"Graceful," Maisy told her.

"Careful, or I'll change my mind."

Sasha was relieved to hear Maisy giggle as she settled into the passenger seat. Still, it was a pale impression of her usual exuberant laughter.

The short drive from the club to Maisy's townhouse didn't present any further opportunity for Sasha to probe her friend's mood. So she pounced the moment Maisy unlocked her front door.

"What's wrong?" she demanded as she crossed the threshold into Maisy's gleaming foyer.

Maisy paused in the process of unbuckling her left pump. She braced herself against her veined marble wall and stared up at Sasha. "What?"

"Geez, Mac, let her get her shoes off first. Look at them. They're almost as absurd as the things you wear."

Sasha lowered her chin and gave Naya a pointed look. "Really? You mean to tell me you haven't noticed?" She gestured dramatically toward her extremely sensible quarter-inch kitten heels.

"I thought you looked even shorter than usual. Did Leo finally get through to you?"

"No," Sasha said mournfully, "but my orthopedic doctor did. I don't want to talk about it. It's too painful."

Naya huffed in exasperation, and Maisy smiled her megawatt smile.

Then she tossed her heels into the closet and patted

Sasha's arm. "You poor thing. Let's drown your stiletto sorrows with some bubbly."

Sasha and Naya trailed her down the hallway to the kitchen. For a moment, Maisy seemed to be herself. But once she'd popped the cork on the sparkling wine and had poured it into three flutes, her shoulders slumped and she deflated before their eyes.

"To Maisy Farley, anchor extraordinaire." Sasha raised her glass and tried to catch Maisy's eye.

"Cheers," she said with no enthusiasm.

Naya lowered her flute, pursed her lips, and furrowed her brow.

Sasha leaned over the spotless kitchen island to peer at their friend. "Seriously, what's going on with you? Come on, it's us. You don't have to put on a happy face for me and Naya."

"It's stupid. I know I should be thrilled to have won the fan favorite award again. And I am—I'm grateful that the viewers like me. I don't take it for granted for a moment."

"But?" Naya prompted.

She let out a small sigh, then said in a soft voice, "But I thought this might be the year my investigative work was finally recognized."

Maisy's misery made sudden sense.

"For your exposé of that pharmacy, right? That was a killer piece. It truly was. I'm sorry you didn't win. The judges missed the boat on that one," Sasha told her.

Naya nodded her agreement.

Maisy barked out a bitter laugh. "Can't blame the judges. The station didn't submit it."

"What?"

"Preston said management decided they really wanted me to win fan favorite again. They think I'm a bubblehead."

"He *said* that?" Naya's eyes went wide and she jutted her chin forward.

Sasha's pulse raced and she fisted her hands. The next time she saw Preston Wilson, someone was going to have to hold her back.

"Easy, tigers. Of course he didn't come right out and say it, but he didn't need to. They've never taken me seriously, and they're never going to."

Beneath her blonde bombshell/southern belle exterior, Maisy Farley was a tough-as-nails, ambitious reporter. Chasing stories and digging up the truth fulfilled her in ways that being celebrated for her beauty and charm never could. But she was right. The station had put her in a box ages ago. She'd had to fight for every scrap of respect she'd won there.

"So what are you going to do?" Naya asked softly.

Maisy cocked her head. "Do?"

"Yeah, what are you gonna do about it? Lay down and let them step all over you? March into Preston's boss's office and raise hell? Or send out a clip reel, get a job at another station? What are you going to *do* about it?"

Maisy turned toward Sasha. "Do the two of you think I should quit?"

Sasha gave Naya a warning look. "I think you need to address the issue. I'm not sure quitting should be your opening salvo. Look, you just said they're really invested in you being the fan favorite for however many years—"

"Seven," Naya provided. "Seven consecutive years."

"Right, seven. So you have leverage. Use it. They'll want to keep you happy. They won't want to lose you," Sasha told her.

"Mmm." Maisy appeared to be considering her options in a new light.

"But, sure, there's no harm in getting your resume in order and making sure you have a strong portfolio. You know, just in case."

Naya nodded her agreement. "Right. That's all I meant."

Maisy scraped her teeth across her lower lip. "Maybe I can get them to revise my contract to add a clause guaranteeing that they'll submit one of my stories in the dirt digger category next year."

"Yeah, great. Something like that," Sasha enthused.

Maisy looked at her expectantly.

"Oh, no. You don't want me to renegotiate your contract. I'm your girl if they breach your contract. I'm a deal breaker. You want Naya. She's the deal maker."

Naya chuckled and turned to Maisy. "Get me a copy of your contract. I'll make it happen."

"Great. I'll have to dig it out. Haven't read it since I signed it. Shoot, I probably didn't even read it then."

Sasha and Naya shared a knowing look. *Clients.*

"Of course, I'll pay your standard hourly rate." Maisy hurried to add, misunderstanding their silent exchange.

"The heck you will. You'll pay me back with manicures and pedicures at the Orchid Day Spa."

Maisy squealed and clapped her hands. "You're a peach, you know that, Naya? A big soft, juicy peach."

"That's me. A peach." Naya lowered her chin. "If you tell anybody, I'll kill you. And you *will* read the revised contract before you sign it—even if I have to tape your eyelids open and make you do it."

"Hey, can I get in on this mani/pedi deal? I did give you that referral, after all. I'll pass on the torture session, though," Sasha teased.

Maisy shook off her gloom, and the whole room seemed to brighten with Maisy's mood. They grabbed their drinks and padded out onto Maisy's breezy balcony to drink and giggle and watch the sun dip down behind the hills. Sasha made it a point to leave her phone on the kitchen island so she could relax and be present with her friends without the ding of distraction.

3

Milltown District Attorney's Office
Monday, 7:45 PM

Ron almost let the call go to voicemail. He was already in the hallway, briefcase in one hand, tie loosened, locking his office door when he heard the phone ringing.

He checked the time reflexively. He'd missed family dinner. Again. Julie could only hold off the boys' complaints of hunger for so long. He'd walk through the kitchen door to be greeted by a silent kitchen lit only by the light over the stove and a lone plate covered with foil. The boys would already be asleep, and Julie would be reading in bed, pretending she hadn't heard him come in.

He was already in the doghouse at home. Might as well take the call here so whoever was calling didn't track him down at home later and tip Julie's cold shoulder routine into full-fledged anger.

He turned the key in the opposite direction to reopen the door, flipped on the overhead light, and lunged across the desk to grab the handset.

"Ron Botta," he panted.

"Yes, this is State Attorney General Francis Nolan. Is District Attorney Botta available?"

Ron flopped into his desk chair and tried to slow his breathing. "Uh, Frank, it's me. Ron."

After a puzzled pause, the AG responded, "You answer your own phone?"

"At eight o'clock at night? Yeah, I do. The county doesn't have the same kind of overtime budget as you Harrisburg bigwigs do."

"Fair point. Well, as you note, it's fairly late in the evening, and I'm sure you're eager to get home to Julie and the boys, so I'll cut to the chase."

Ron nodded to himself. Nobody would ever accuse AG Nolan of beating around the bush, no matter the time of day. "What's going on?"

"I'm calling about your mess."

Ron scanned his memory, trying to identify a mess big enough to interest the commonwealth's highest officer of the court. "I'm not sure ..."

"The federal civil rights litigation, Ron."

Ron knitted his eyebrows together. "What, that prosecutorial misconduct case?"

"How many federal civil rights cases are you currently defending?"

"Okay, just the one. What about it?"

Frank laughed without humor. "You're kidding, right?"

Ron kicked off his loafers and leaned back, resting his feet on his desk. "Not at all. It's a dog of a case. Borderline frivolous, Frank."

There was a long pause. Then, "Judge Cook doesn't seem to agree."

Ron rocked forward in his chair, lowering his stocking feet to the office floor with a thud. "You talked to the judge?"

"Hell, no. Cliff Cook isn't the type of jurist who'd put up with any kind of meddling. No, nothing like that. I've got a legal assistant keeping track of the docket. She pulls all the filings and decisions for me. And I can't help but notice the judge hasn't been ruling in your favor."

Frank wasn't wrong. The federal district court judge had been uniformly unimpressed with the office's arguments. But, that didn't mean anything. Did it?

"Uh ... okay, that's true. But you know federal judges. Sometimes they give all the benefit of the doubt to the party they're ultimately gonna rule against. You know, so there's less to appeal." He frowned, second-guessing himself. "Don't they?"

"Shoot, I don't know. I don't spend any more time in federal court than you do, Ron."

Ron shrugged. He and Frank knew the common-wealth courts inside and out. They were prosecutors for the state. But federal court was a different beast. Maybe he'd been too cavalier about the scathing decisions the judge had been issuing. He unbuttoned his top collar button and tugged at the knot on his tie.

"There's no way they're going to be able to establish a pattern and practice of prosecutorial misconduct," he insisted.

"You sure about that?"

Ron bristled. "Not to be rude, Frank, but what's the commonwealth's interest here?"

He allowed himself a small smile. Unlike some states, Pennsylvania's district attorneys didn't answer to the state's attorney general. Heck, they didn't even answer to their local mayors. Ron was an elected official. He answered to the voters of Milltown, and nobody else.

Frank responded curtly. "If the state legislature or the governor decides you've gone rogue out there, you don't think they'll authorize my office to do an independent review of your procedures?"

"Well, I ... is that in play?" he stammered.

Frank shifted into a friendlier tone. "No. Not yet. But I'll be honest with you, there are whispers. Harrisburg's worried. So, I'm calling for an honest assessment of the case—prosecutor to prosecutor."

Ron closed his eyes and fervently wished he hadn't come back inside to take this particular call.

"Look, I won't deny that Sasha McCandless-Connelly has gotten some helpful rulings. The court shut down my motion to dismiss and most of my motions in limine—to be fair, though, those were all long shots. No federal judge is going to limit the evidence in a case like this. You know, not when civil rights are at stake. So I went the other direction and absolutely buried her in paper. McCandless, Volmer & Andrews is a tiny boutique firm. They don't have the staff to handle a massive discovery dump. They've got to be overwhelmed."

"I wouldn't be so sure."

"What's that supposed to mean?"

"The name partners over there all came from Prescott & Talbott. They're not exactly small-time lawyers."

Ron gritted his teeth. "So they started out at a white shoe firm. Doesn't mean they have more than twenty-four hours in a day."

"I hope, for both our sakes, that you're right."

"Again, this case doesn't involve you."

"If these plaintiffs establish a pattern of prosecutorial misconduct out of your office, you're looking at a multimillion-dollar judgment. Don't forget your office is part of the commonwealth's self-funded malpractice insurance consortium. A loss will impact every county in the consortium, which last I checked was fifty-four of the sixty-seven counties."

Of course. Now it was starting to make sense. Frank was worried about the insurance fund. It always came down to money with guys like him.

"I guess I'll just have to get a defense verdict, then. My motion for summary judgment is pending now. We've finished briefs and arguments. We're just waiting for Judge Cook to rule, and I have a good feeling about our chances."

"Still, you should make a settlement offer."

Ron lost his patience. "With a summary judgment motion pending? Do you realize how weak that would make me look? Besides, where am I supposed to come up with the money for a settlement? Are you gonna let me tap your precious consortium funds?"

Frank was silent for a long moment. When he spoke, his tone was measured. "Let's be candid. Your office did violate the plaintiffs' civil rights by ginning up those inevitable discovery exceptions. You know it. I know it. And it looks like Judge Cook knows it, too. Sure, McCandless-Connelly might view an offer as weakness or worry, but her clients won't. Sam Blank is effectively homeless, and Max Barefoot is a convicted felon—he's barely employable. They're not going to turn down a generous offer on principle."

Ron knew he was probably right. Most plaintiffs' eyes turned into cartoon dollar signs when there was real money on the table.

"You're forgetting Charlie Robinson. He's a gainfully employed college professor. And a Marxist or something, to boot. A socialist might stand on principle. And there's no point in settling with two of them only to proceed with the expense of trial with the third."

"That's true. You'll structure the offer so it's all or none. Robinson might be an anti-capitalist adjunct professor, but I suspect he'll settle if he knows failing to do so would screw over the other two."

"At this point, I'm not inclined to make a settlement offer, generous or otherwise. I appreciate your suggestion and—"

"District Attorney Botta, you've misunderstood."

Ron waited.

Frank continued, "I'm not making a suggestion, I'm telling you: offer to settle. There's a concerned citizen who's willing to put up the money to see this case go away."

Ron's surprise outweighed his irritation. "A concerned citizen?"

"Yes. A very influential, powerful private citizen who, for reasons of their own, doesn't want this case to go to a verdict. They're willing to provide up to fifteen million dollars to make it go away. That's five per plaintiff. Surely you can work with that."

Ron tried to speak and found that his ability to speak had vanished. He made a series of choking sounds, which Frank seemed to interpret correctly.

"I know. It's a highly unusual situation, and an obscenely high sum of money. But this is out of your hands, Ron. Hell, it's out of mine. You have to make an offer. Now. Before Judge Cook rules on summary judgment."

Ron managed to find his voice. "Is that an order?"

"Technically, we both know I can't order you to do squat. But, I'm telling you, for your own sake, you need to do it."

"So, not an order. Are you threatening me?"

"No, it's not a threat. Consider it a warning. If you don't make the offer and don't win summary judgment, you'll have to deal with the fallout and, to be frank with you, I don't have the clout to protect you if that happens."

A powerful, influential—and wealthy, obviously—

private citizen with the ability to pull rank on the top legal officer in the commonwealth? That was a short list.

"I don't suppose you can tell me who this concerned citizen might be. Or what interest they have in my case."

"I honestly don't know why this individual is so interested in this case. And I've been instructed not to share the person's identity unless and until the settlement is accepted. They plan to put the funds into some sort of trust vehicle that can't be traced back. The plaintiffs aren't to know anything about the funding source. So, can I count on you to play ball?"

Ron scratched the stubble on his chin. "Like you said, this is a highly unusual situation. I need to think this through."

"Don't think too long, Ron."

The line went dead as the attorney general ended the call. Ron swiveled his desk chair around to stare out at the last gasp of the setting sun and consider his options, such as they were.

4

Just one peek, Sasha promised herself when they traipsed back into the kitchen in search of snacks. While Maisy cubed the cheese and Naya rinsed the grapes, she eased her phone out of her bag and unlocked the screen with her fingerprint. When the display came to life, she nearly dropped the phone.

"Holy sh—smokes," she murmured.

"Holy smokes?" Maisy echoed.

"Fiona's apparently developed a colorful vocabulary, and Leo swears she's not getting it from him," Naya explained.

"Haha. Fiona's a real firecracker."

"Well, there's no question who she gets _that_ from."

Sasha heard their conversation as if it were taking place underwater at a distance. It was a faint, garbled sound that barely cut through the buzzing noise in her brain.

After a moment, Naya waved her hand in front of Sasha's nose. "Hello? Anyone home?"

Sasha wiped her hand across her eyes. "Sorry. I just got the strangest message."

Naya cocked her head. "Which case?"

Sasha glanced at Maisy, who had returned her attention to the block of cheddar, then stage whispered, "Botta."

Naya gaped at her. "Did Judge Cook rule on summary judgment?"

"No, but the DA's made a settlement offer. An unbelievable one."

Sasha kept one eye on Maisy. She didn't turn away from the cheeseboard, but she stood up straighter and moved the knife more slowly, quietly. As if, just maybe, she was trying to listen.

"Unbelievably good or unbelievably bad?" Naya asked.

Sasha shook her head. *Not here.* Maisy was a friend, a good friend. But client confidentiality was client confidentiality. And Maisy *was* a reporter. Snooping was her job.

Naya nodded her understanding.

Maisy turned and proffered the cheese tray. "Dinner is served. Should I open another bottle?"

"I hate to drink and run, Maisy, but something's come up in one of my cases. I need to handle it tonight."

Maisy pulled a face. "You're no fun." She turned to Naya. "You don't have to go, too, do you?"

"I can stay, but if we open another bottle of Prosecco, I'll be sleeping over."

Sasha gave each of her friends a quick hug and made her escape while they dug into their fruit and cheese. She raced down Maisy's front stairs, her head bent over her phone, rereading the email from the Milltown District Attorney. But no matter how many times she read the numbers, they didn't change.

LEO LOOKED up from the baseball game at the sound of Sasha's key in the door. He aimed the remote at the television and clicked it off as she walked into the hallway. Mocha weaved between his legs to greet her before he could.

"This dog still thinks he's the alpha." Leo leaned down to kiss his wife hello.

"He's sadly mistaken. Everyone knows Java's the boss around here." She smiled up at him.

As if he'd heard her, the cat peered down from the upstairs hallway and loudly mewed his agreement.

Sasha giggled, then covered her mouth with her hand. She pulled it away and whispered, "Are the kids asleep?"

He nodded. "After we walked you over to the club, we hit the playground and they wore themselves out on the blue slide."

"Nice. They'll sleep well tonight."

"That was the idea." He watched her kick off her shoes. She tossed them into the closet with open disdain. "You're home early."

She flopped down on the couch and patted the

cushion beside her. He settled in next to her and looped his arm around her shoulder. She rested her head on his chest and the scent of her gingery shampoo filled his nose.

"Maisy wasn't in a celebratory mood."

"Oh?"

"Yeah, I guess she was really hoping to be recognized for her journalism instead of her charm for once."

"Ah. That stinks."

"Yeah. It does. We didn't even stay at the bar. We went to her place and just hung out."

"I'm sure you and Naya cheered her up."

"I hope so. Naya's going to help her renegotiate her contract with the station. And she's probably helping her polish off another bottle of bubbly as we speak. Carl's down in Georgia visiting his uncle, so she's at loose ends."

He tilted her chin up so he could see her eyes. "You didn't have to skip out early. The kids and I were fine."

She lifted her lips to his and kissed him softly. "I know. I left because I have work to do."

She shifted to move out of his arms and off the sofa, but he wrapped his arms around her waist and held her for a moment longer.

"Now? It's after ten."

"Justice never sleeps, or something like that. At least, the DA never sleeps."

He drew his eyebrows together. "Marino?"

"No, not the Allegheny County DA. Ron Botta, the district attorney for Milltown."

"The judge ruled on summary judgment? Oh no, do you have to appeal?"

Leo wasn't entirely sure summary judgment motions were appealable. Heck, he still wasn't entirely sure what summary judgments *were*. But what he did know was this case weighed on Sasha—so much so that he wished she'd never taken it. She took the misconduct of the prosecutor's office as a personal insult. He understood that. He felt the same way about dirty law enforcement. When someone who was bound by the same rules as you blithely ignored them and destroyed innocent lives, it was impossible not to take their malfeasance to heart.

But it was consuming Sasha. It had been for months now. She wasn't sleeping enough. She wasn't eating enough. She wasn't training enough.

All she did was work and tend to their family. He and the kids were the one non-work part of her life she'd maintained. Finn and Fiona didn't have a clue that she'd been so busy. She made sure to walk them to school each day, made it home for dinner every evening, and with the exception of tonight's rare girls' night out with Maisy and Naya, had been there to tuck the twins into bed at night. It was as if the more the case ground her down, the more she insisted on maintaining a normal home life.

Something had to give, though, and soon. He almost hoped the judge *had* granted the district attorney's motion to deny relief to Sasha's clients so the grind might end. Almost. But that result would be a grave miscarriage of justice, and he knew his wife: she'd find some loophole to squeeze through to uphold the vow she'd made to Charlie Robinson, Sam Blank, and Max Barefoot. She wouldn't rest until the Milltown District Attorney's Office paid for its actions.

Sasha's wry laugh pulled him out of his wool-gathering. "No, Judge Cook didn't rule. Ron Botta made a settlement offer."

That sounded like a good thing, but her tone suggested it wasn't. He ran his thumb along his lower lip and thought. "Insultingly low?"

Another small laugh. "No, suspiciously high."

Leo shook his head. "I don't follow."

Agitated, she loosened his embrace and sprang to her feet to pace in front of the fireplace. "I'm not sure I do either, to be honest. Tonight, out of the blue, after months of telling the court at every status conference that settlement wasn't an option and that he intended to defend his office at trial and get a verdict, Botta sends me a multimillion-dollar offer."

"Multimillion dollar? Like, two?"

She wheeled around and spread her hands wide. "No, more like nine."

"He's offering to settle for nine million dollars? Three apiece for each of your clients?"

She nodded.

He stared at her. "That's good. No, that's freaking amazing. That's life-changing money."

"I know. So I need to set up a meeting with the guys for tomorrow morning."

"To convince them to take it."

She caught her lower lip between her teeth. He knew

what that gesture meant. She was about to say something she didn't want to say.

He repeated the question more slowly, "You're going to convince them to take the money. Right?"

"I don't want to. But I think I have to." Her shoulders slumped and she sagged.

"Hey, hey, come here." He had no idea why she was so disappointed about securing an actual mountain of money for the three men, but she was decidedly, undeniably unhappy.

He stood and folded his arms around her, cradling her from behind. He'd long-since noticed that sometimes Sasha found it easier to give voice to her thoughts and worries when he wasn't watching her face.

She leaned her back against his chest and let the words pour out. "Look, the offer's *too* good. Yes, Judge Cook has been ruling in our favor, pretty much a hundred percent of the time. And, yes, the guys make sympathetic plaintiffs. Especially Sam. But we're advancing a long-shot legal argument. The courts have created an almost insurmountable standard to prove a pattern and practice of prosecutorial misconduct that will give rise to civil liability. It's not a slam dunk. And even if it were a slam dunk—which, again, it's *not*—nine million dollars is too much money. Nobody opens negotiations with nine million dollars, Connelly. Nobody."

He spun her around to face him. "Maybe Botta's afraid of you. You are kind of a badass."

That earned him a smile. "I'm a good lawyer. I'm not *that* good. And this case isn't that good."

"We'll have to agree to disagree on your lawyering ability, but maybe he's afraid of something else. Could there be something even worse than the crap you know about that he's worried might come out in discovery?"

She narrowed her eyes and pursed her lips, running through some mental list, then shook her head. "Discovery's over. We've deposed all the main players. They've completed their document production. And they used the oldest trick in the book. They turned over an avalanche of information in an effort to overwhelm us. I can't imagine there's a scrap of paper in their archives or a file on a computer that I don't already have. I have two hundred and eight boxes of email messages, for Pete's sake."

"You printed all the emails? But you can just review those electronically, can't you?"

She snapped her fingers at him. "Focus."

"But—"

"I'm old school. I like paper. Sue me."

"I'll pass. So if there's nothing ugly hiding in the wings, why make such a huge offer right out of the gate?"

"Exactly. And Botta's not some first-year assistant district attorney who got overexcited and jumped the gun. He knows how negotiations work. Which means he's actually willing to settle for a higher amount."

He let out a long low whistle that perked up Mocha's ears. "Holy crow."

"Right. But here's the other thing—he doesn't have access to that much money. I know he doesn't because the Milltown DA's office participates in the Common-wealth's insurance consortium."

Leo shook his head. "Which means what?"

"The largest counties in the state, and some of the tiniest, have their own malpractice insurance policies with private companies. Just like my firm does, you know? They pay an annual per-attorney premium and the insurance carrier agrees to defend them against any malpractice claims, which would arguably include deliberate prosecutorial misconduct."

"Arguably?"

"An insurer could argue that the prosecutor's office engaged in intentional criminal behavior that falls outside the scope of coverage. But forget about that. It doesn't matter."

"It seems like a big exclusion."

"It would be, but not in this case. Most counties don't have outside malpractice insurance. They pay a small part of their yearly budget into the state's malpractice insurance fund, and the state foots the bill if they get sued. That's what Milltown does."

"And the state wouldn't make that argument?"

"My understanding of the fund is that the counties direct their own defenses and make their own settle-ment and payout decisions. The state doesn't have a say in whether they settle, and like I said, Botta has been adamant that he won't settle. But even if he had a change of heart, there's not nine million dollars avail-able to him."

"You're sure about that?"

"Positive. We got copies of Milltown's deposits into

the fund during discovery. There's an unnecessarily complicated formula based on their payments into the system and the county's tax base to determine the maximum payout in a variety of scenarios. And Milltown isn't a big county. The *most* they could have offered is shy of a million for all three plaintiffs to drop their claims."

"None of this makes sense. What if you go to trial and get a bigger judgment?"

"Milltown would have to pay it, but they'd have to scrape up the delta between what they can take from the fund and what they have to pay from somewhere else. Probably raise taxes or sell some of their police department's tanks. I don't know."

"But what you do know is Ron Botta doesn't have nine million dollars."

"Bingo."

"So who's footing the bill?"

She rose up on her toes and planted a warm kiss near the corner of his mouth. "That's the million-dollar —er, nine-million-dollar—question. And I need to try to dig up an answer before I talk to Charlie, Sam, and Max." She heaved her briefcase over her shoulder and started toward the stairs, headed for her home office. "Don't wait up for me."

"I'll put some coffee on before I go to bed."

She turned and beamed at him. "I knew I kept you around for a reason."

He raised one eyebrow. "I don't think my barista skills are the only one."

"Okay, that's fair. You do have other ... desirable skills."

He shooed her up the stairs. "You better go before I decide to distract you with some of those skills."

He walked out to the kitchen to the sound of her quiet laughter as she tiptoed up the creaky wooden stairs. He filled the coffee maker's water reservoir then scratched Mocha absently behind the ears with one hand while he waited for the coffee to brew.

Sasha's explanation settled in his gut like a stone. He never would have imagined the prospect of nine million dollars could cast a pall over an evening, but she was right: something was rotten in the county of Milltown. Rot. Evil. Darkness. It seemed no matter what they did, bad things followed them around like a storm cloud.

5

L andon Lewis smoothed the black linen napkin over his lap. It matched his dark suit pants. His host, who wore a pair of cream-colored crinkled seersucker pants with a light blue stripe, had been given a white linen napkin. The Gilt Club was the sort of establishment that paid attention to such details. He eyed his breakfast companion across the table and took a long, centering breath. And this was a man who demanded such precision.

Don't let your nerves blow this. Stay calm. He's just a man.

Landon nearly laughed aloud. While it was factually

accurate that Leith Delone was a male human being, he wasn't just any man. He was one of the four richest individuals on the planet. He bought and sold social media sites on a whim, funded political elections to seat his handpicked candidate, and somehow owned two of Jupiter's fifty-three confirmed moons.

And he'd flown Landon across the country to have breakfast with him at this ridiculously exclusive club— so ridiculously exclusive that it didn't even officially exist. The driver who'd picked Landon up at the private airfield to ferry him to this meeting had apologetically asked him to don the silk blindfold that kept him from learning the club's exact location.

He invited *you. Don't forget that,* he ordered himself, as his hands trembled.

He clasped them together on his lap to hide the tremor. When his hands stilled, he reached for the crystal goblet of mineral water that glinted in the soft morning light and took a long drink to wet his bone-dry throat.

Delone watched wordlessly.

Landon returned the glass to the table and waited for Delone to say something—anything. The room was silent save for the ice clinking as it melted in the goblets and the faint ticking of the minute hand of Delone's chunky platinum watch. *Tick. Tick. Tick.*

Three minutes passed. Sweat beaded on Landon's brow. He cleared his throat.

Delone twisted his neck to the left with a crack that echoed in the quiet room. He repeated the motion on his right.

When the billionaire finally spoke, his distinctive gravelly voice was surprisingly soft. "I appreciate your hopping on a plane to meet with me on such short notice."

"It was my pleasure. An honor, actually."

As if he'd expected to hear nothing less, Delone smiled thinly. "Before Claude returns to take our orders, why don't I tell you why I've brought you here?"

Landon nodded, somewhat distracted by the prospect of ordering breakfast without the benefit of a menu. Delone seemed to read his thoughts.

"The chef will make anything you want."

"Anything?"

Another smile, marginally warmer. "The members here expect to get what they want when they want it. Menus are for those who settle for what they're told is available."

Landon thought it likely that the people who belonged to the Gilt Club didn't limit that philosophy to their meal options. "I see."

"Now, as for why you're here. Can you guess?"

Landon had been asking himself the question for hours, ever since he'd received the midnight phone call summoning him to Malibu.

"I haven't the slightest idea," he admitted.

Delone's smile widened. "I'm buying your company."

"My ... my company?"

Of the myriad possible reasons he'd considered and rejected for this meeting, the idea that Leith Delone wanted to buy his company hadn't even crossed his mind. Probably because it wasn't for sale.

"Yes. The Joshua Group."

"There must be some confusion." Landon took care not to ascribe the confusion to the man sitting across from him.

"No."

"I'm not looking for a buyer."

"You weren't. But you'll sell after you hear my offer."

Landon squirmed in the silk brocade chair. "I'm sure whatever you have in mind is a generous price. But the Joshua Group has never been about the money. It has—I have—a higher purpose."

He steeled himself for Delone's reaction—an amused scoff or a brusque demand that Landon be realistic.

But Delone merely said, "Had."

"I beg your pardon?"

"Had. You, and, by extension, the Joshua Group, had a higher purpose: The Cesare Program. The algorithm you created to detect latent criminality after the murder of your only child, Joshua. Correct?"

Landon blinked.

"I know all about Cesare and what motivated you. And I know you entered into a consent decree with the Department of Justice to terminate the Predictive and Preventive Crime pilot program. I also know that in the months since you shut down the PPC, you've tried and failed to modify the algorithm to detect and predict abuse and misconduct in law enforcement officers."

"If you know all this, then why are you interested in the Joshua Group?"

"I believe there is a place for Cesare. But not in law enforcement."

"Espionage? I've tried to tweak it to detect intelligence officers who were likely to be vulnerable to being turned by a foreign power, but results were mixed."

"May I suggest you're thinking too small?"

"Too small?" Landon echoed, bewildered. If anything, he was setting his sights too high by trying to weed out and eliminate evil before it took root, before the wrongdoer even recognized his own latent criminality.

A discreet knock sounded at the door. Delone pressed a button concealed in the table. A moment later, the lock disengaged and the door swung open automatically.

A waiter entered the room bearing a silver tray that held a carafe of coffee, a tea service, and a pitcher of orange juice that had unmistakably been freshly squeezed. He arranged the items in a perfect row on the serving bar to the side of the table.

"Coffee? Tea? Juice? Or perhaps you gentlemen would prefer another beverage?" Claude clasped his white-gloved hands behind his back and waited attentively to serve the drinks.

"This is fine. Leave it," Delone answered.

The thought that Landon might want something else didn't seem to occur to him.

"Very good, sir. Have you settled on breakfast choices?"

"We're mid-conversation. I'll call for you when we'd like you to return."

"Of course, sir. Please forgive the intrusion."

Claude turned and slipped out of the room, closing

the door soundlessly behind him. Delone waited a beat, then used his button to reengage the lock. He waved toward the beverage station. "Help yourself."

Landon didn't move. "What did you mean, I'm thinking too small?"

"Ah, the insatiable curiosity of the scientific mind." Delone rose and strode over to the buffet.

Landon waited, his skin crawling with impatient need, as the richest man in North America fixed his cup of English breakfast tea just so. Delone's movements were unhurried and precise. There was no denying that Leith Delone was confident, brash, perhaps even arrogant. But he appeared to also be methodical and thorough.

These were qualities Landon respected, so he waited quietly as Delone dropped a sugar cube into his teacup, squeezed a burst of fresh lemon into the beverage, and stirred in a dollop of fresh cream.

Still standing beside the tea service, he raised the china teacup to his lips and sipped the liquid. He returned to his seat and took another drink of his tea, then placed the cup in its matching saucer, tented his fingers together, and leaned toward Landon.

"You think small because you view Cesare through one specific lens. You created the program to solve an unsolvable conundrum. You want it to predict who will misbehave."

Landon bristled. "It's designed to root out more than mere 'misbehavior.'"

"You misunderstand. I'm not denigrating your goal. But, at bottom, all the behaviors you've tried to detect and prevent are instances where someone might act *outside* the bounds of the social compact."

He bobbed his head from one side to the other, weighing Delone's interpretation. Eventually, he nodded. "That's true."

"It is," Delone agreed. "And you have only envisioned a governmental entity as the user."

"Of course. It would be tragic if Cesare fell into the wrong hands. The pilot program established that much."

"Ah, the Milltown Police Department debacle. Yes, it's clear the department misused your creation. But it hardly proves your point."

"I don't understand."

"A police department *is* a governmental entity, and, yet, the police turned out to be the wrong hands. Withholding Cesare from private enterprise because of the actions of one corrupt police department is illogical, not to mention short-sighted. Cesare has applications you've not dreamed of. Imagine all the good a private, nongovernmental entity might do with a tool as powerful as Cesare."

"The good you might do, you mean. That's why you want to buy the Joshua Group—to exploit Cesare for commercial purposes?"

Delone's expression hardened. "I take exception to your tone. I'm not proposing anything grubby or improper. Yes, I do want Cesare. I'm prepared to offer you a buyout of one hundred million dollars in exchange for your business's tangible and intangible property, which would, of course, include the Cesare program and all proprietary software, hardware, and intellectual property related thereto."

Delone sipped his tea as Landon's breath caught in his chest.

One hundred million dollars. His mind raced as he considered the endless possibilities. Then reality caught up with his imagination, and his mounting excitement skidded to a dead stop.

"There's a pending federal lawsuit alleging multiple violations of civil rights. The plaintiffs claim the Milltown District Attorney's Office engaged in a pattern and practice of misconduct over the course of at least a decade. The theory of the case centers on the prosecutors' misuse of an exception to some discovery rule. The Joshua Group isn't a defendant. But Cesare and the PPC *are* peripherally involved."

"I'm aware of the litigation. And, as you say, your program is only tangentially involved. The case is a blip. Nothing." Delone waved his hand as if doing so made the lawsuit disappear.

Landon shook his head. "I'm afraid it's not nothing. The named plaintiffs in the case were erroneously selected by Cesare for referral to the PPC Program. As part of my arrangement with the Department of Justice, I agreed to cooperate with the plaintiffs' attorney."

"A fair tradeoff."

"I think so. But plaintiffs' counsel intends to call me to testify at trial. Once I do, Cesare and the Joshua Group will unavoidably lose a great deal of their value. I can't in good conscience sell you an asset that might soon be worthless."

Delone laughed a raucous belly laugh. After he caught his breath, he wiped his eyes, then said, "I appreciate your candor, but your testimony won't be a problem."

"Respectfully, it might."

"My people have done their due diligence. We've turned over every rock. We know all your secrets. I'm not concerned about the case. There's not going to be a trial. You won't be called as a witness. Cesare won't be demonized in the court of public opinion."

"I don't understand."

"The case will be taken care of."

Landon stared at him uncomprehendingly.

Delone elaborated, "I'm going to make the plaintiffs an offer they can't refuse. The case will settle in short order."

"Oh."

"So, we have a deal." It was a statement, not a question. "My people will be in touch with the necessary documents and to obtain wire instructions for your bank. Now, if you'll excuse me, I have a dinner meeting in Geneva."

He pushed the button to unlock the door, returned his teacup to its saucer, and stood. Landon began to rise, too, but Delone gestured for him to sit.

"Stay. Tell Claude you want Norwegian scrambled eggs and salmon with brown cheese. It's outstanding. Afterward, one of my drivers will return you to the airfield. A pilot is standing by to fly you home."

Delone had almost reached the door before Landon

had the presence of mind to ask the question. "Wait. Leith—er, Mr. Delone," he called.

Delone turned. "Yes?"

"How *do* you plan to use Cesare? If not to predict misbehavior?"

"I'm going to change the world."

6

"Nine million dollars? That's a shit-ton of money," Max Barefoot breathed.

Beside him, Charlie Robinson threw him a warning sidelong gaze.

Max ducked his head and turned to Sasha. "Sorry," he mumbled. "I mean it's a crap-ton of money."

She smiled. "Don't worry about it, Max. It's a breathtaking sum. That much is for sure."

She paused while Charlie interpreted the exchange into Black Sign Language for the third plaintiff, Sam Blank. Although Sam could read lips pretty well, this was a critical conversation. She found herself once more grateful for Charlie's ability to communicate with the deaf man.

Sam's eyes widened and he responded to the news. Charlie chuckled.

"What'd he say?" Max asked.

"He said, sorry, Sasha, Max is right. It's a shit-ton of money."

She waited for the laughter to die before she reminded them, "The offer is for nine million total. So it would be three million apiece."

"Oh, only three? Forget it then," Max joked.

"You mean three minus your fee," Charlie interjected.

She shook her head. "I told you when we started this, I'm representing you pro bono. No fee."

"Yeah, but not if we make bank," Max protested. "You gotta get your cut."

She hated to dampen the mood. It was rare to see clients as exuberant as these three were. But, she had to do it before they got too caught up in dreams of spending their millions.

"Let's not get ahead of ourselves. The first order of business is for you to all read this settlement offer very carefully. Take your time. Circle anything you have questions about. We all need to be on the same page. Okay?"

She passed each of the men a copy of the document and a highlighter. Then she sat back and drank her fourth coffee of the morning while they each studied a sheet of paper that had the potential to change their lives. She allowed her heavy eyelids to flutter closed as she waited.

How could she be this tired? She hadn't even pulled an all-nighter. Once upon a time, she would have viewed three hours of sleep as a luxury, now it was an insufficient nap.

She felt someone watching her and snapped her eyes open. Charlie studied her with a concerned expression.

"You okay?"

"I'm fine. I was trying to remember something, that's all."

He gave her a look that suggested he was unconvinced.

She smiled and gestured at the paper. "Are you all done?"

He nodded. Max lifted his head and capped his highlighter. "I'm done, too."

Across the table, Sam nodded that he, too, had read the settlement offer.

"Great. Who has questions?"

They all had questions, which pleased her. A client who was willing to share what they didn't understand was infinitely easier to work with than one who pretended they knew what was going on, but didn't. In her experience, the pretenders tended to be mid-level management types who worked in environments where 'fake it till you make it' was the prevailing ethos and admitting ignorance was a black mark.

But, Charlie, Max, and Sam weren't hampered by such corporate constraints and they recognized the importance of the decision they were about to make. So they covered their documents with neon circles and underlining and peppered her with questions for a solid hour.

Caroline popped in with a plate of muffins, a pitcher of water, and, to Sasha's delight, a piping hot carafe of fresh coffee. After Caroline left and Sasha had a full mug in hand, she looked around the table.

"So, have we covered all your concerns?"

Charlie peeled the wrapper away from a blueberry muffin. "I just want to make sure I have this right. All three of us have to take the deal? If one of us holds out, the other two don't get their share?"

She sipped her coffee and inhaled the scent of medium roast beans. "That's right. The offer is for a complete release of all claims by all of you."

Charlie pressed his lips together. Of the three, he seemed the most likely to reject the settlement on principle. He had a secure, if underpaid, position as an adjunct college professor. He also had a healthy distrust of capitalism. But, she knew he'd be torn. Sam and Max didn't have his advantages. The money would change their lives in ways that would really matter.

She empathized with Charlie's ambivalence because she shared it. She had to encourage the three men to settle. Doing so would be in their personal best interests. She knew that, and she owed them a duty to act in their interests. She also believed with every fiber of her being that there was something drastically wrong about this settlement offer. She wanted to shout 'don't take it!'

Instead she drank her coffee and watched their faces.

Max said, "Didn't the DA tell the judge settlement wasn't an option?"

"He did. Multiple times."

Max frowned. "So why the change of heart?"

"I don't know, and I'd love to hear Mr. Botta's answer myself. With your permission, I'll ask him. But he's not obligated to share that with us, and I sincerely doubt he will."

Max rubbed his forehead and stared down at the offer.

"If you had to guess, why do you think he'd make this offer? Just give us your legal thinking. We know you can't read the guy's mind," Charlie urged her.

She placed her mug on the coaster and rested her forearms on the table. "If I had to guess, there's something that's going to come out at trial that he wants to keep buried. That would make sense. But last night after I got the offer, I combed back through all the documents they've produced and I reread the deposition transcripts. I honestly didn't see any smoking guns. Yes, our case is solid, but that's been true this entire time. So what's changed?"

Charlie eyed her. "You did all that last night? No wonder you look so tired."

"Dude, that's rude," Max hissed.

It was rude, but it was also true. She did look tired. Her mirror didn't lie. She made a mental note to pop out and buy a new concealer at lunchtime. Maybe more makeup was the answer. Then she turned back to the more pressing issue.

"There's something else that doesn't make sense.

And this is something I think the district attorney *will* have to divulge. The evidence Milltown turned over shows that the district attorney's office doesn't have nine million dollars. They have a one-million dollar annual budget to run the office, and their insurance coverage isn't even a million dollars. The math doesn't work."

Max grunted. "Something stinks."

Sam, who'd been watching without comment, tapped Charlie's arm and signed a question.

Charlie turned back to Sasha. "Sam raises a good point. Usually in a negotiation, the first number isn't the real number. Does this mean he'd actually pay us *more?*"

"Sam's right. I think we have to assume that a nine-million-dollar opening volley means there's really a higher ceiling, which again raises the question: where's it coming from? If that matters to you."

She let her words sink in. Ethically, the plaintiffs didn't have an obligation to probe the source of the settlement funds. Morally, maybe they did, but maybe they didn't. If she were in their shoes, she'd want to know. But that was easy enough for her to say. She wasn't the one being offered a crap-ton of money.

The three men looked at one another, then at her.

Again, Max spoke up. "Can you give us a minute?"

"Of course. Take all the time you need. When you're ready for me, just press the red button on the phone and it'll buzz the reception desk. Caroline will let me know."

She gathered up her notes, her phone, and her coffee and headed for the door, leaving them to discuss the enormous decision they faced.

~

SHE BUMPED into Naya on her way to Caroline's desk.

"Hey, Mac. Wow, you look rough."

"So I've been told." She peered at her friend. Naya looked well-rested and fresh. "You and Maisy didn't open that second bottle?"

"No, we did. I spent the night at her place and hit the gym this morning. Now I'm full of vim and vigor."

"Huh." Maybe instead of the makeup counter, she should spend her lunch hour at the Krav Maga studio or going for a long run.

Naya jerked her chin toward the conference room door. "Are they discussing the offer?"

"Yes, and I'll tell you, I didn't expect it to be such a tough decision."

"How much money are we talking?"

"Guess."

Naya looked off in the distance and bobbed her head from side to side, calculating the value of the claims and the economic realities of a small-town prosecutor's budget. Sasha watched with interest. Naya was known for her accuracy in valuing businesses, assessing claims, and guessing what the bill would be at lunch. If the transactional law partner thing didn't work out, Sasha figured her friend had a lucrative future as a game show contestant.

Finally, Naya nodded to herself and said with authority, "Six hundred thousand total. Two each."

Sasha snorted. "You're off by a multiple. Three each."

"Nine hundred thousand? That's more than I

thought, but I guess I can see it."

"No, you're missing a zero. Nine million. Three million each."

Naya's jaw hinged open. She gaped at Sasha for a moment, then she clamped her mouth shut and wagged a finger at Sasha. "Good one. You almost had me."

"I'm not kidding. Ron Botta offered to settle for nine million dollars."

"Holy … smokes."

"I know."

Sasha leaned against the wall. Naya leaned next to her. After a moment, she gave Sasha a sidelong glance. "So what is there to talk about?"

"I honestly don't know. I thought they'd snap it up. Who wouldn't? But those guys? I think they've had enough real-world experience to realize that if an offer seems too good to be true …" she trailed off.

Naya finished her thought with a heavy sigh. "It probably is. Yeah. What do you think Botta's up to?"

"I don't have a clue. I spent most of the night going back through all the documents and transcripts, looking for something I missed, and nothing jumped out at me."

Sasha bumped the back of her head gently against the wall as if she might jar loose a new insight.

After a moment, Naya nudged her. "Get this, Maisy found her contract."

"And?" She asked, still preoccupied with the wild settlement offer.

"And she has a bonus clause that she either forgot about or never knew about in the first place because—"

"Clients never read the docs," Sasha finished her

sentence as if they were a poor comedy act.

"She gets a bonus for winning a media award."

"Good for her, seven in a row."

"But it's double if the award is for investigative or documentary works."

"Ahhh, the plot thickens."

"Mmm-hmm. And, there's more. If they fire her, she has a one-million-dollar golden parachute."

"Seriously?"

"Yeah, I know it's chump change to your clients, but to some of us, it's real money."

Sasha jabbed her in the ribs.

"Oh. Why are your elbows so sharp?"

"I don't know, but if I were Maisy, I'd get myself fired."

"No kidding. You and me both."

"As managing partner, I feel I have to remind you: you do not have a golden parachute."

"I think I prefer the elbows," Naya told her.

Caroline rounded the corner. "Oh, there you are."

Sasha straightened up. "Are the guys ready for me?"

Caroline gave her a confused look and handed her a sheet of paper. "What? No. You just got an email that there was a new entry on the docket in this case. Judge Cook denied the defendant's motion for summary judgment."

Sasha stared at the email.

Naya eyed her. "Now what?"

"Now I guess things get interesting. Thanks, Caroline." Sasha took the printout and hurried back to the conference room.

7

Ron Botta stared at his email. He read the docket entry for a second time as if willing the words to change. They didn't, and he swore under his breath. His breakfast churned in his gut. The sausage, egg, and cheese muffin that he'd scarfed down in the car threatened to make an encore appearance. He grabbed the antacids from his top desk drawer and fumbled with the cap.

He chewed the chalky, vaguely fruit-flavored tablets and washed them down with a swig of bitter room-temperature coffee. Then he groaned and hit the speaker button on his desk phone before tapping in ten digits to make a call that he dreaded.

While the line rang, he rolled his neck and swallowed around the acid rising in his throat.

"Good morning, you've reached the Office of the Attorney General for the Commonwealth of Pennsylvania. How may I direct your call?" a pleasant female voice asked.

"Yes, this is Ron Botta calling for Mr. Nolan."

"Oh, District Attorney Botta, how are you?"

Ron tried to tamp down his impatience and reminded himself that his current predicament wasn't this faceless woman's fault. "I'm fine, thanks. Is the AG in? I really need to speak to him. It's … urgent."

"He's on another call, but I'll let him know you're on the line. Would you mind holding?"

"No, not at all. That'd be great."

She placed the call on hold, and he listened to the canned voice rattling off PSAs while he tried to come up with a good way to break the news to Frank. Just as he'd accepted that there was no good way to deliver bad news, Frank's assistant came back on the line.

"Thanks for holding, Mr. Botta. I'm putting you through now."

"Great. Thanks."

"Ron?" Frank's voice boomed through the speaker.

He inhaled deeply and gripped his stomach with one hand. "Hi, Frank. I'm sure you're busy, but I wanted you to hear this from me—"

"—Cook denied your motion for summary judgment. I know."

He blinked. "How? The order literally just came out."

"I got a call from a friend," Frank said cryptically.

Ron wanted to press him, but decided to plow through what he had to say and get the call over with. "I did make that settlement offer. I sent it to McCandless, Volmer & Andrews last night."

"And?"

"And I haven't heard from them yet. I offered nine,

so I do have some wiggle room … if you still think I should settle. I'll be honest with you, I know it looks bad. But I don't think a defense verdict is out of the question. You know jurors are always inclined to give the government the benefit of the doubt." He clenched his teeth and waited.

"Nothing's changed, Ron. You have to settle this case. Call Sasha McCandless-Connelly and tell her the number's gone up to twelve. That'll still give you some room to negotiate."

"Wait. You want me to bid against myself? They could still accept nine."

"Nine, twelve, fifteen—it doesn't matter. Don't try to pinch pennies. Get the deal done."

He shook his head. "I can't *make* them take the money," he protested.

"Figure it out, Ron. You have to settle this case. The sooner the better."

Ron fell silent.

After a beat, Frank said, "Do you understand?"

No, I don't understand at all, Ron thought.

"Yes," he said miserably. "I understand."

"Good. Now make it happen."

How? he wanted to ask.

The line went dead. Ron lowered his head into his hands and listened to his labored breathing for several minutes. Finally, he lifted his head and punched another telephone number into his phone.

Here goes nothing.

8

Maisy silently ran through her intro for the six o'clock broadcast, trying to spot any phrase that her co-anchor could possibly infuse with dirty double entendre. It was, she knew, a lost cause. No matter how anodyne, how bland, or how inoffensive her words were, Chet would somehow make them seem suggestive. The inevitable result would be a barrage of viewer emails sharing their unoriginal fantasies (and, worse, blurry closeups of their genitals) and a smattering of voicemails to the station calling her a slut. She smothered a soft sigh.

Livia was intimately familiar with Chet's shenanigans and Maisy's valiant, if doomed, efforts to avoid them. The makeup artist worked in silence while Maisy focused on the upcoming broadcast. It was the routine they always followed.

So Maisy was mildly surprised when Livia's soft cursing drew her back to the present. In all the years they'd worked together, Maisy didn't think she'd once heard the demure woman swear. "What's wrong, darlin'?" she asked with some concern.

Livia met her eyes in the mirror and whispered, "Here comes Preston. And he's in a mood."

Maisy shifted her gaze and caught the producer's reflection. Livia was right. Preston stalked across the dressing room, hands fisted, eyebrows knitted together in an angry vee, and lips pressed into a sour frown. If he were a cartoon character, steam would be pouring from his ears and a black scribble would be bobbing above his head like a storm cloud.

Maisy stifled another (not-so-soft) sigh and closed her eyes. What was that little mantra Bodhi'd taught her? *I breathe in peace; I breathe out love.* She filled her lungs, breathing in peace. She breathed out—

"Farley!" Preston barked.

Love eluded Maisy, and she started in the makeup chair, bumping the curling iron in Livia's hand in the process. Livia squeaked in dismay as the hot rod made contact with the side of Maisy's neck.

Maisy yelped as her skin sizzled.

"Sorry! I'll get you some ice." Livia waved her free hand in a distraught gesture.

"It's okay, I'm fine," Maisy tried to assure her.

But Livia was already scurrying off toward the refrigerator.

Maisy fixed a big, bright smile on Preston. "Did ya need somethin', sugar?"

When Preston was in one of his moods, she always graced him with an extra dollop of Southern sweetness, dropping her gs and laying on her accent more thickly than usual, as if she might somehow cajole him out of his funk. So far, she'd yet to succeed. But much like her efforts to keep her exchanges with Chet squeaky-clean, she kept trying. Her mama didn't raise a quitter.

Preston waved a hand at her neck. "That looks like a sucker bite."

Livia raced up with an ice cube wrapped in a dish-cloth and pressed it against the burn.

Maisy waited a beat before responding. "Well, you know that's not what it is. Besides, Livia can cover it up with makeup, can't you, Liv?"

She bobbed her head. "Of course."

Preston appraised Maisy critically, as if she were a used car he was thinking about making a lowball offer for. "Change into a high-necked blouse. That'll cover it … along with … all of that." He gestured toward Maisy's chest.

She glanced down at her blouse, genuinely confused. "All of what? I'm not showing any cleavage."

Those days were, thankfully, in her rearview mirror. She hadn't had the girls on display since her stint as the weekend weather girl. The day the station had hired a real meteorologist and set her free as a field reporter had been the happiest day of Maisy's career.

"Not your rack, Farley. Your turkey neck."

Her hand flew toward her throat of its own volition. She didn't have a turkey neck. Did she? She leaned forward and peered at her reflection.

Beside her, Livia clucked and shook her head. No.

Maisy exhaled slowly. "Thanks for the suggestion, but you know, I've found when I wear very demure clothing, it has a counterintuitive effect on the viewership."

She had no idea how popular the naughty librarian fantasy was until the first time she'd worn a turtleneck sweater on the air.

Preston rolled his eyes.

She dropped the sugary act. "What crawled up your butt and died?"

He blinked in surprise at the unaccustomed bluntness.

Well, get used to it, pal. I've about had it.

Before he could further critique her appearance, she gave a pointed look to the big digital countdown clock on the wall. "Did you need something? I'm almost ready to go on the air."

Chet was already in his anchor seat. She could see him through the closed-circuit monitor, cracking jokes —or trying to—with Jocelyn. She couldn't see the camera operator's reaction, but judging by the rigid set of her shoulders, she wasn't enjoying the banter. Shocker.

Preston sighed. "Instead of the recorded piece on the spoken word festival, I need you to do a different spot." He thrust a piece of paper toward her.

Maisy frowned as she took it.

"Brow," Livia whispered.

She smoothed her forehead and blinked at Preston. "But that poetry piece isn't just a feel-good puff piece," she protested.

"Yeah, yeah, asylum, the arts, I get it. But, it's over

and done with. We'll air it tomorrow. Management wants you to read that instead."

Despite her disappointment, Maisy's curiosity was piqued. "What's going on?"

Preston shrugged. "You can read, right? Read it. Then throw it to Summer Reed. We set her up live for a reaction shot."

"A reaction shot? For what?"

"Some big civil rights case against the Milltown district attorney."

The scene from her kitchen the night before flashed in her mind. Sasha had run out because she'd received some kind of message from Ron Botta. Maisy hadn't been *trying* to eavesdrop, she really hadn't. But it was an occupational hazard. She tried to remember exactly what Sasha and Naya had been whispering while she cubed cheese.

"Is it about the prosecutorial misconduct case?"

Preston shrugged. "I guess we'll find out together. Can I give you a word of advice?"

As if she could prevent it. "Always."

"Keep an eye on Summer. She's gunning for your chair."

Maisy's smile faltered. For all his many flaws, Preston was her producer, and she knew he valued her work. So the warning hit her in the gut. She turned away from the mirror and locked eyes with him.

"Thanks. I appreciate that."

He pressed his lips together and gave her an unreadable look before turning to Livia. "Cover up that thing on her neck and get her on the set before that camerawoman jumps across the anchor desk and throttles Chet."

Livia murmured something reassuring while Preston frowned at Chet's antics on display on the monitor.

Maisy decided to strike while the iron was hot. "Hey, Preston?"

"Hmm?"

"Can you set up a meeting for me with management? I want to talk about my contract."

He gave her a long look. "You sure this is the time?"

"Well, yeah. Didn't I just win fan favorite for the seventh year in a row?" She furrowed her forehead. Why wouldn't this be the time?

"Brow," Livia chided her.

She smoothed her forehead and checked Livia's handiwork. The burn on her neck was completely covered. The makeup blended seamlessly into her pale skin.

"You're a magician."

Livia shooed her out of the chair. "You better go."

"We'll finish this conversation later," Preston promised. "Get out there."

She waggled her fingers in a goodbye and raced to the newsroom, wishing that she'd retired her high heels along with her pushup bras when she'd moved to the anchor desk. Then she recalled Sasha's misery at her little kitten heels. Nah. She needed her armor.

As her stilettos struck the tile floor, their rhythm seemed to clack out a name: *Summer. Summer. Summer.*

Maisy took a deep breath, let it out slowly, and

pushed Preston's warning from her mind. Then she fixed a smile on her lips.

~

EIGHTEEN MINUTES LATER, she finished fake laughing at Chet's thinly veiled joke that she looked tired because she'd had a wild night out celebrating her recent award. As they went to commercial, she finally had a moment to read the script Preston had thrown at her. She scanned the page and looked up at the control room.

"Davey, is Preston in there?"

"Yeah, Maisy, I'm here," came the response in her earpiece.

"I'm not reading this."

"Maisy—"

"Attorney Sasha McCandless-Connelly is gumming up the works in a potential settlement. What could be motivating Pittsburgh's most controversial litigator …" she read off the words and flapped the page in her hand. "What is this shit?"

"Maisy!" Preston was scandalized, and with good reason. Maisy never swore at work.

"I'm serious. I won't be a part of this. It's not even sourced."

She pushed away the memory of Sasha and Naya's whispered exchange in her kitchen.

"Maisy, it came down from corporate. You can read it, or Chet can. Your choice. Read it and then throw to Summer for a reaction shot. And we're back in five."

Chet turned to her with a Cheshire Cat grin and

held his hand out for the paper. She narrowed her eyes at him and turned to the main camera.

"… two, one."

She smiled and ad-libbed. "Now for a developing story, we're going live to reporter Summer Reed, who has an update about a big case involving the Milltown District Attorney's Office."

Summer appeared on the monitor. Could she really be trying to steal Maisy's job? She looked so innocent. Innocent and young. Maisy pushed the thought out of her mind and focused. Summer was standing outside Sasha's office. Summer froze, waiting for Maisy to say the words that Maisy dang well wasn't going to say. Finally she gathered her wits and started talking:

"Thanks, Maisy. I'm here in Shadyside hoping to get a reaction from Attorney Sasha McCandless. With any luck, she'll be out momentarily."

Any moment, Maisy corrected Summer in her head. Momentarily means she'll be coming out *for* a moment, not *in* a moment. The distinction, lost in the modern vernacular, drove Maisy to distraction.

She said, "Her name's Attorney McCandless-Connelly, actually. A reaction to what, Summer?"

Summer looked stricken.

Chet craned his neck and peered at the sheet that Maisy had dropped to the floor. He intoned, "Well, Maisy, there's some speculation that Attorney Sasha McCandless-Connelly is gumming up the works in a potential settlement. You remember that high-profile civil rights case her office filed back in 2019. What could be motivating Pittsburgh's most controversial litigator to tank a deal?"

Maisy blinked in disbelief.

On the screen, Summer smiled, her relief splashed all over her face.

"That's right, Chet. The firm in question is McCandless, Volmer & Andrews. That's a name viewers may recognize from Attorney McCandless's many high-profile cases and, well, scrapes with the law."

Chet slid Maisy a sidelong look.

"McCandless-Connelly," she repeated as if in a daze. Then, Naya's explanation of her contract rang in her ears. She was virtually unfireable.

"Summer, do you know how WACB came to learn about this possible settlement?"

"Um ..." Summer hesitated. "Not at this time."

"As you know, Summer, our policy is to confirm all reporting with an independent source. Why don't you explain for our viewers how we did that in this case?"

Summer froze and blinked slowly. Maisy wasn't positive, but she might have been blinking out 'SOS' in Morse code.

In the control booth, Preston shrieked, "Cut, cut, go to commercial and cue up the outro graphics."

The technical director switched on the intercom and called down from the control room. "Going to credits in three. Chet, you take the outro and make sure to remind the viewers how excited we are about Maisy's award. Graphics has a picture of Maisy and the award to cue up when the theme music starts to play."

"Got it," Chet answered in a tight voice.

"Make sure you mention this is the seventh year in a row that I've won," Maisy added.

He gritted his teeth. "Of course."

Two, one.

Maisy smiled at the camera while Chet sang her praises in a tone that suggested they were best pals.

"That's a wrap," Jocelyn told them.

Maisy dumped her mic pack on the desk and stormed off the set.

9

"She's gone." Jordana turned away from the window and let the louvered blinds fall back against the window.

Sasha looked up from her keyboard and eyed her intern in confusion.

"Who's gone?"

"The reporter," Jordana said slowly, exaggerating each syllable.

Sasha put her monitor to sleep and gave Jordana her full attention. She'd been in the zone, concentrating so intently, that the intern's words had been bouncing off her.

"I'm sorry. Tell me again."

"Some dumb-ass …" Jordana sighed and tucked a strand of hair (pink, this week) behind her ear. "Sorry, dumb-butt. Some dumb-butt reporter from WACB."

"Not WACB," Sasha told her. "Maisy would've warned me."

Jordana shrugged. "I dunno. That's what was on the

card she gave Caroline before Naya tossed her out of the office. Summer something. Anyway, remember how you asked me on Monday to arrange a prep session with Mr. Lewis?" She wrinkled her nose just in case Sasha had forgotten how distasteful Jordana found the man.

"Yep. Did you put it on the calendar?"

"Nope."

Sasha blinked at her, the reporter forgotten. "Is there a problem?"

"I don't know. I've left him two voicemail messages. I sent him two emails. I can see that they were received and read, but he didn't respond. So, this morning I texted him."

Sasha opened her mouth to tell Jordana that lawyers didn't text their clients, then she remembered that this was the twenty-first century and stopped herself.

Jordana went on, her indignation rising, "And he read that, too—right away. But he didn't answer. Shouldn't a tech genius who created an evil algorithm have a basic understanding of electronic communication? He has to know I can see that he got my messages." She huffed out a breath that ruffled her long bangs. "Anyway, what should I do?"

Sasha tapped her fingernails on her desk and thought. Maybe Jordan's disgust for Landon Lewis had leaked through in her communications and she'd offended him. Sasha doubted it, though. Jordana was fiery and opinionated and changed her hair color on the regular, but she understood professionalism.

It was possible that Lewis felt slighted that Sasha had

delegated the scheduling to a senior in college rather than asking a legal assistant to handle it or contacting him personally. He was a prickly, proper guy. Maybe that was it.

"Tell you what. I'll reach out to him myself." As if she didn't have enough to do.

Jordana protested, "I'm not trying to get out of doing it, Sasha. I just don't know what to do next. Write a letter and have it messengered to him? Tie a note to the leg of a carrier pigeon? Try to summon him from the dark side with a magic spell?"

Sasha laughed. "Look, I appreciate that you're not trying to dump him in my lap. But he's going to be an important witness for us if Sam, Charlie, and Max's case does go to trial, so let me have a crack at him. It might be an ego thing."

Jordana pulled a face as if she was certain that was the problem. "Okay, if you're sure."

"I'm sure. If I can't get an answer out of him, I'll let you know to find a pigeon. Or a spell."

Jordana flashed a smile. She turned to leave, then turned back. "You said if."

"If?" Sasha echoed, unsure where this was headed.

"If the case goes to trial. You're not trying to convince them to settle, are you?"

Sasha answered carefully, "It's not my decision. It's theirs. The attorney's job is to explain the settlement offer and its terms thoroughly and to answer any questions the client has. But it's up to the client, not the lawyer."

"But—"

Sasha held up a hand. "Let me finish. Whether I think they should take the offer or not doesn't matter. I can tell them what I think and advise them of the possible outcomes of taking and not taking the offer, but I can't decide for them."

"They have to get justice. Not just for themselves, for everybody else whose rights the DA violated. It's a matter of principle." Jordana's nostrils flared and her voice shook.

"For you and me, maybe. But think about them. That money could change their lives, all of their lives. But especially Sam and Max's."

"But—"

"Don't get ahead of yourself. They haven't decided yet."

"I guess," Jordana said sullenly.

"But, Jordana?"

"Yeah."

"You should prepare yourself for the possibility that they will take the offer. Four million dollars apiece is a lot of money."

"You mean three."

"Nope. I mean four. After the summary judgment decision came out, Botta called and increased the offer from nine million to twelve."

"It's blood money," Jordana shrieked.

Sasha felt for the younger woman. Did she ever.

"Be that as it may, it's their decision."

"Professor Robinson is an anti-capitalist!"

"Even anti-capitalists have bills to pay, my friend."

Jordana frowned, unconvinced.

"I hope you never lose that fire in your belly," Sasha told her. "But try to have some grace for people who aren't quite as committed to the cause as you are."

That advice apparently didn't warrant a response. Jordana simply nodded and left.

Sasha shook her head and jotted down a note to call Maisy and ask her what was up with the paparazzi in the parking lot. Before she had a chance, Naya swept through what had apparently become a revolving door.

"Did you watch the news?"

Sasha gave her a look. "Do you see a tv in here?"

"You might have streamed it. I don't know. Is that a no?"

"Yes. It's a no."

"WACB reported that you're trying to torpedo a settlement in the Botta case. Maisy cleaned it up the best she could, but it looks like someone in Botta's shop is talking to the press."

Sasha rubbed her left temple as pain began to pulsate behind her eyes. "That doesn't make sense. He's desperate to settle, and even Ron Botta knows that trying to force my hand publicly would backfire. It also might set off Judge Cook, who's already fed up. No, Botta wouldn't do that."

"Someone did it. It wasn't anyone here. So who?"

She shook her head. "I don't know."

Naya gave her a closer look. "Are you okay?"

"I need some coffee."

"It's almost seven o'clock."

"I have—"

Naya cut her off, "Pack up your crap and I'll drive

you home. After you have dinner with your family, if you want to stay up all night, make a pot of coffee there. But why don't you just shut it down for tonight. The court just granted summary judgment. Your clients are, for reasons that escape me, struggling with the difficult decision of whether they want to be multimillionaires. It's not like anything's going to happen in the case before morning."

"Thanks."

Naya was right. The case was on hold, she might as well get some rest.

10

Maisy didn't even bother taking off her makeup before she beelined to Preston's office. She pushed open the door without knocking and found him sitting with his head in his hands, staring at the old Penguins hockey poster that the sports director had gotten the team to autograph for Preston's fortieth birthday.

"What the devil was that?" she demanded.

He turned toward her with a sickly expression. "I told you, corporate sent that story."

"Since when do we air unsourced, un-fact-checked propaganda?" she said in a milder tone.

He exhaled heavily. "I didn't have a choice."

"Mmm."

"Are you just here to berate me or do you need something?"

"I told you, I want you to set up a meeting for me."

"To talk about your contract."

"Right."

He rubbed his eyes. "Is this about the investigative journalism thing?"

"What do you think?"

"What I think is you ought to be careful. You did just tank the evening news and hang a reporter out to dry on live television."

Fortified by what Naya had explained about her contract, Maisy looked at him calmly. "Are you gonna fire me?"

He sighed. "Of course not. But, listen, The station's under new ownership, and you're the most expensive on-air talent in the entire stable."

This tidbit was news to Maisy, but she played it off. "Are you suggesting budget cuts are coming down the pike?"

WACB had been sold four times—each time to an increasingly larger media conglomerate, and, each time, the new owners imposed new, increasingly draconian budget cuts. If they were sold again, Maisy figured she'd have to start bringing her own toilet paper from home.

"I haven't heard anything yet. But you know the drill, it's just a matter of time."

She shook her head, sending her curls bouncing wildly. "I thought the new company's owned by one of those eccentric billionaires. The one with all the spaceships?"

"No, it's the one who owns the moons. But how do you think those guys got so rich? Not by spending money, that much is for sure."

"Whatever. I've paid my dues. The station owes me this." She made her eyes go wide and hopeful.

Preston stared back at her, unmoved. Then he leaned closer. "Wait—what color are your eyes?"

"What?"

"I could've sworn they were blue. But they aren't, are they? Are they … purple?"

She waved a hand. "They change depending on the season and what colors I'm wearing. Sometimes they're blue, sometimes they're violet. And sometimes, when it's one of those steamy summer days when the heat shimmers off the pavement, they look green."

"Seriously? I had no idea. Are you a witch?"

Yes, Preston, I'm a witch. A witch who's discovered that magical potion known as colored contact lenses.

"I think we're getting off topic. How about this? I won't push for a meeting right now, if you'll promise the next tip that comes in on the tip line is mine."

"Most of those tips are garbage," he protested.

"It's my time I'll be wasting," she countered.

He shrugged. "Have it your way."

"Say it. Say you promise."

"Oh, come on, Maisy."

"Preston, say it."

He shot her a put-upon look, but intoned dutifully, "I promise the next garbage tip that comes in is all yours."

She gave him her brightest smile. "Thanks, Preston, you're a gem."

"Yeah, yeah." He waved her toward the door and turned back to staring at his poster.

"But I'm not going to forget about that meeting. I won't be put off forever."

"Understood."

She started toward the door. "One more thing."

He groaned. "What?"

"Is Summer really gunning for my job?"

He looked over his shoulder. "That's what I heard. But I wouldn't worry too much about it now. You're riding high on your seventh award, and she'll be lucky to keep her own job after that piss-poor display tonight."

"Really?"

"You know as well as I do that this is an unforgiving business."

"Yeah, it is." She tried to summon up some sympathy for the rookie reporter, but she couldn't quite manage it. She knew she had a hand in Summer's disastrous showing, but some lessons were best learned the hard way.

"You could have just let Chet read the piece. You didn't have to burn her on the air."

"She did go to J-school, right?"

"Yeah, Columbia."

"Then she should have known better, shouldn't she?"

"When did you become such a ballbuster?"

"Didn't you know? Ball-busting comes with the turkey neck. It's a two-for-one deal."

She swept out of his gloomy office on the strength of her parting shot.

"Close that door behind you," he shouted.

She ignored the demand and left him to his sulking.

11

The offices of Prescott & Talbott,
Pittsburgh, Pennsylvania
Tuesday evening

Charles Anderson Prescott the Fifth—Cinco to his friends and his enemies alike—pressed his hands hard against his thighs to keep all four appendages from shaking. He was beyond grateful that this particular meeting was taking place via videoconference. Even from the other side of the globe, his prospective new client was intimidating.

The billionaire on his computer monitor lifted one eyebrow. "Well?"

Say no.

*Wait. Don't **just** say no.*

Say you're flattered—honored—that he's chosen the firm

for this important work, but Prescott & Talbott doesn't have the bandwidth to take on the case.

No. *Don't say that, it makes you look weak.*

Say yes. This is literally the opportunity of a lifetime. If you win this case, for this guy, everything changes. You have a duty to the firm to take the case.

You don't even know what the case is about.

What if you lose? Then what?

Leith Delone's vindictive streak was the stuff of legend. He could ruin Cinco and the firm with the flick of a finger, the swipe of a pen. His impatience was almost as well known as his vengefulness. He wasn't going to wait much longer for an answer.

Say something. Anything.

Cinco had to manage a reply before his overloaded brain short-circuited entirely. He cleared his throat. "We'd love to work with you—"

"For me."

He winced at the correction. "Of course, for you. I do need just a bit more information about the case. I'll need to run a conflicts check to make sure we don't represent any other entities in the litigation and …"

He trailed off as his would-be client sliced a hand through the air. "You don't. I've already checked. And so we're clear, I'll be writing the checks, but you won't be representing me. And you are absolutely not authorized to make my involvement public."

Oh.

The nervous excitement drained from Cinco. What was the value in working for this man if he couldn't trumpet the fact to the world? Money, of course.

But Prescott & Talbott—and, by extension, Cinco—wasn't hurting for money. He had all the money he needed. He wanted glory. And glory, not more money, was what he'd promised the Management Committee when he told them about Delone.

Delone hadn't gotten where he was by being dense. He sensed Cinco's dilemma. He leaned forward and peered into the camera.

"If you successfully defend this client, I will, of course, add your firm to the select stable of firms that perform work for my many holdings."

Cinco didn't appreciate being talked about as if he, or the firm, were a workhorse. But the prestige being dangled in front of him was a tempting carrot.

"I see. Still, I will need the client's name to check for conflicts."

The man's hard mouth stretched into an approximation of a smile. Cinco realized he'd never seen a photo or video of the man smiling, and he suddenly understood why. The effect was gruesome.

"As I've said, I've already checked and there are no conflicts of interest. But if you insist ..."

"I'm afraid I must. There are rules."

"Fine. The client is Ronald Botta—in both his personal capacity and his capacity as the chief prosecutor for Milltown."

A fuzzy picture of a squat balding man formed in Cinco's mind. He and the district attorney attended the same church, but Cinco doubted they'd ever exchanged more than a dozen words. They didn't run in the same circles.

What possible interest could this man have in Ron Botta or the Milltown District Attorney's Office?

"You're no doubt wondering why I care about Mr. Botta or his office."

Cinco suppressed a shiver at the ease with which this man seemed to guess his thoughts.

"A bit," he admitted.

"To be perfectly frank, I don't. I do, however, care a great deal about a very important piece of software that will be impacted if the civil rights lawsuit against the Milltown prosecutor succeeds. For that reason, the suit must fail. Do you understand?"

No, not really.

"Yes."

"Excellent." The thin lips creased into another terrifying smile.

Cinco decided to take advantage of the apparent good mood to admit his ignorance. "I'll confess I'm not familiar with the lawsuit in question."

"Approximately two years ago, a complaint alleging various violations of civil rights by the Milltown District Attorney's office was filed in the U.S. District Court for the Western District of Pennsylvania. I expect that it will settle in short order. Actually, I expected it to have already settled. But evidently, plaintiffs' counsel is playing hardball. That's why I want to retain your firm. I don't think Mr. Botta's up to the challenge of managing his opponent."

"Ah, I see." He did see.

In his view, prosecutors, as a group, had a tendency to grow complacent. Lazy, even. They became accustomed to getting the benefit of the doubt. They forgot what it meant to fight.

Cinco went on, "I assure you, we are up to that challenge."

"I expect nothing less. To be very clear, your job is to convince the plaintiffs to take the settlement offer. This case cannot proceed to trial."

"What's the current procedural posture?"

"Earlier today, the judge denied the district attorney's motion for summary judgment. There's a conference next week before the judge to set a trial date and, critically, to discuss the settlement offer."

"Oh, that complicates things. The plaintiffs are playing from a strong position with summary judgment out of the picture. Is there room to move on the settlement figure?"

"There is, but that's not the problem. Plaintiffs' counsel seems to believe it's suspect for a third party—me—to fund the district attorney's settlement offer."

"You're personally funding the settlement?" That was ... odd.

"Yes. The current offer is twelve million dollars split equally among the three plaintiffs, but I'm willing to go up to five apiece."

"Fifteen million dollars?"

"Correct. But, make no mistake, I do not wish for my involvement in the settlement to become a matter of public record. That would be unacceptable. The settlement funds will come from a trust that can't be tied back to me."

"They haven't said yes to twelve? That's madness."

"As I've said, their attorney is suspicious. I have begun to apply pressure to the plaintiffs' firm through, shall we say, more public means. That might help. Time will tell."

Cinco felt his left eye begin to twitch. An involuntary reaction to extreme stress, according to his ophthalmologist. He considered asking about this public pressure and decided he'd rather not know.

"So, you'd like me to convince the plaintiffs to settle before trial for some amount between twelve and fifteen million dollars and also convince the court that there's no need for it or the plaintiffs to know the source of the funds?"

"Precisely. Are you still sure you're up for the challenge?"

He stiffened at the faintly mocking tone. "Of course. Do you happen to know who's representing the plaintiffs?"

With any luck, he could solve this whole mess with a simple phone call or a round of golf.

"Yes, I do. I understand you're acquainted with the plaintiffs' counsel." Delone steepled his fingers and tapped them together. "It's the law firm of McCandless, Volmer & Andrews. An attorney named McCandless-Connelly, specifically."

Cinco's stomach dropped.

Sasha. Crap.

The billionaire studied him through narrowed eyes for a reaction.

Cinco pushed down the churning feeling in his gut

that said he was making a huge mistake and smiled weakly at the computer screen. "Fabulous."

"Good. I have to cut this short. I'm about to land in Geneva. My people will be in touch with the retainer and any other information you might need." Delone reached up and switched off the video feed.

Cinco sank back in his chair. His right eye decided this was a good time to join the left in twitching. He wheeled himself over to the bar on his credenza and poured himself a stiff Scotch.

It was just his luck that Sasha would turn up like a bad penny in the middle of a case that could be a phenomenal opportunity for him. He tipped his head back and drained the glass in one long swallow. He closed his twitching eyes and let the alcohol burn away the tension.

12

E leanor Anderson Prescott—Six behind her back, but not without her knowledge— flipped her phone camera around and checked her reflection. The bright, white overhead lighting that Prescott & Talbott had recently installed because it was scientifically proven to increase productivity might make the worker bees lawyer faster and longer, but it did her no favors. She looked pallid and sickly.

She looked like what she was—an office drone who toiled in a sealed environment for too many hours a day. But she'd promised herself not to stand up another date this month, so she dug through her top desk drawer and unearthed a tube of red tint that the woman at the makeup counter had promised could do double-duty as lipstick and cheek stain. She rubbed her fore-finger across the berry-colored makeup and smoothed it onto her cheeks. She repeated the gesture and smeared the color over her lips. She blotted her lips on a napkin left over from her sad desk dinner and smiled at her reflection.

She looked alive, at least. She ran her fingers through her short blonde hair and traded her demure pearl stud earrings for a pair of long dangly ones made up of shimmering discs that would brush her bare shoulders once she ditched the suit jacket. There, now she looked fun. Or at least less corporate. It would do for a Tuesday night date.

She shoved the pile of cases scattered across her desk into some semblance of order and reached over to power down her laptop. That's when the shadow fell across her frosted office door. She glanced at the shape standing in the hall and moaned. She was about to cancel on yet another date.

"Come in," she called before her father's fist even made contact with the door.

"Eleanor, what are you doing here so late?" he asked as he entered her office.

"Oh, you know, just finishing up these interrogatories for Kevin. Did you need something?"

She held her breath, hoping against hope that he just wanted to say good night. Or remind her that her cousin Emily Ann's bridal shower was this weekend. Or anything other than give her an assignment.

"As a matter of fact, I do. I have the opportunity of a lifetime for you, Ellie."

She doubted that. Scut work, and lots of it, was the lot of a first-year associate—even one who was the daughter of a name partner, or maybe *especially* one who was the daughter of a name partner. She'd had plenty of time to second-guess her decision to join her father's law firm. She knew the other associates sneered behind her back about nepotism, and she knew some of the partners came down extra hard on her to prove they weren't favoring her.

It's not like she hadn't had other offers. She'd had her pick of several of Pittsburgh's top firms. Or she could have gone to Philly, where her name wouldn't follow her. But the truth was, Prescott & Talbott was the best large law firm in the city, and one of the best in the world. It would've been criminally stupid to turn down an offer that would provide top-notch training and open doors all over the world just because one of the other hundreds of lawyers there had once changed her diapers. Wouldn't it have?

Well, it was too late to do anything about it now. So she grabbed the nearest legal pad and a pen and smiled brightly at her dad.

"Great. What's the case?"

He tilted his head and took in the fresh makeup and the party-ready earrings. "Oh. You had plans."

She reached up and removed the earrings, placed the backs on them, and dropped them in her desk drawer. "Nothing I can't reschedule. Especially for the opportunity of a lifetime."

He flashed a rare smile. "Spoken like a Prescott." He dropped into her guest chair and crossed his legs.

"So tell me about the case? Who else is on the team?"

If her dad was personally involved, there would be a large team with layers of management. She just hoped whatever mid-level associate she reported to wouldn't haze her too badly.

He gave her a piercing look. "We're it. You and I are the team. At least for now."

She gnawed at her lower lip. So much for no nepotism. "Really?"

"Yes, Ellie. This matter is highly sensitive and extremely confidential. Nobody can know what we're working on, aside from the Management Committee, of course."

Her eyebrows crawled up her forehead. "Dad, I have to ask—are you putting me on this case because I'm your daughter?"

He spread his palms wide, like a supplicant seeking understanding. "Well, yes. I need someone I can trust completely. Your work is stellar, but so is the work of the rest of your class. Unlike them, though, you alone offer the most important thing: complete loyalty."

At least he was honest. "Okay, so who's the client?"

"Nominally, our client is the Milltown District Attorney's Office." He paused dramatically. "But the true client—the one calling the shots and footing the bill—is Leith Delone."

Ellie's pen clattered to the desk. "Holy cannoli," she breathed.

"Indeed."

She scrabbled to pick up the pen. "What's the case about?"

Her father picked some nonexistent lint from his argyle dress sock. "Evidently, the district attorney has been sued in federal court."

"Not the Vaughn Tabor shooting? That case went to trial last year."

"Not the shooting," he confirmed. "But I imagine it's related in some way. Three plaintiffs have sued Ron Botta's office alleging a pattern and practice of prosecutorial misconduct that violated their civil rights."

"Barefoot," she breathed.

"Pardon?"

"The case is *Maxwell Barefoot, Samuel Blank, and Charles Robinson v. Ronald Botta, Jr., and the Commonwealth Malpractice Insurance Consortium.* I've been following it ever since it was filed two years ago. I wrote my law review comment on it, remember?"

She caught the shadow of guilt that crossed his face before he smiled. "Of course, I remember. That's just one more reason why you're the perfect associate for this case."

Mmm-hmm.

She let the obvious lie go unchallenged. She'd long suspected he'd never read her note. In truth, the note had been a small act of rebellion. A minor pushback against the Prescott name. After its publication, she'd waited and waited for him to call and ask her why she'd written a note glorifying a novel legal theory that bordered on the progressive. But the call had never come.

"How's Leith Delone involved?"

"It's not completely clear, to be honest. His people reached out to me late this afternoon and arranged a videoconference. He was en route to Geneva, but he wanted to speak right away. I just finished talking to him. He has an interest in a piece of software or a computer algorithm of some sort that might be involved in the case. He didn't provide any details about that. But he was adamant that the case needs to settle before trial."

She snorted. "Good luck with that. Judge Cook has yet to rule in the DA's favor. In fact, just today, he issued a blistering opinion denying Mr. Botta's motion for summary judgment."

He blinked in surprise. "You've read it?"

She shrugged. "Yeah."

"My, you *have* taken an interest in this case."

She didn't respond. She couldn't very well say that her legal hero had filed the case. For one thing, she figured her dad assumed *he* was her legal hero. For another, he'd never been shy about sharing his opinion of the attorney in question: Sasha McCandless-Connelly, the only associate to ever turn down partner-ship at Prescott & Talbott, had gone on to forge her own path at the helm of Pittsburgh's most successful boutique law firm.

Ellie had been fascinated with the tiny litigator ever since she'd met her at a summer picnic. It was the summer before Sasha had been offered, and refused, her elevation to partner.

Ellie'd been fourteen, about to turn fifteen, and was beyond annoyed at being dragged to yet another firm event. She wanted to spend her day at the pool at her parents' club, hanging out with her friends and trying to find someone old enough to drive them into the city. Instead, she'd been forced to put on a pink and green sundress so she could be trotted out as an example of the sort of shiny, perfect, Ivy League-bound children that Prescott & Talbott attorneys could expect to have.

She'd run into Sasha McCandless (not yet hyphenated) at the ice cream sundae bar. Nico DeAngeles, Marco's son, had dared her to steal a canister of whipped cream. At the time, she hadn't realized why he wanted it. But Sasha spotted Ellie trying to palm the metal container.

Instead of calling her out, Sasha had grabbed a bowl of ice cream from the sundae station and turned to her with a wide smile.

"Hi, I'm Sasha. You must be Ellie. Your dad talks about you all the time."

Ellie remembered staring down at her, trying not to break out into a sweat. Even as a high school sophomore, she'd towered over the lawyer. She'd mumbled something indistinct.

Sasha laughed as if Ellie had been the wittiest kid ever, then pointed to the whipped cream. "Can I use that when you're done with it?"

Trapped, she reached for a bowl of ice cream that she didn't want, doused it with the whipped cream, and handed over the canister. "Here."

"Thanks." Sasha sprayed the stuff over her own ice cream then returned the can to the table.

As she walked away, she leaned over and whispered, "I hate these events, too, kid. But whippets aren't something to mess with. You can't grow up and kick ass if you're brain-damaged or worse, dead, from abusing nox."

Ellie had no idea she was talking about, but she'd looked it up later. After she'd cussed out Nico, she played over the brief encounter in her mind. Sasha could have busted her, told her *dad, or just ignored her. But she didn't. She made Ellie feel like she mattered. Like she could grow up and kick ass.*

A year later, when Ellie announced her decision to pick a college that had a good pre-law program and then go to law school, her dad had acted like it was her destiny—a foregone conclusion. But the truth was, she hadn't had the slightest interest until Sasha's name started hitting the papers.

Somehow, she didn't think this was the time to come clean.

Her father continued, "Mr. Delone has committed to secretly fund a fifteen-million-dollar settlement to make the case go away. Botta made a generous settlement offer, but for some reason, the plaintiffs haven't snapped it up. In fact, their attorney seems committed to tanking settlement talks."

"So, we're going to defend the district attorney's office if the plaintiffs don't settle?"

He shook his head. "No. We're going to jam a settlement down the plaintiffs' throats, no matter what it takes."

"How are we supposed to do that?"

"As I just said, we'll do whatever it takes. I wonder if the attorney's failure to get the clients on board with settlement could be construed as a violation of her ethical obligation to act in their best interest," he mused.

"Her being Sasha McCandless-Connelly?"

"Correct."

"Didn't she used to work here?"

"Briefly." His terse tone made it clear that he wasn't interested in a trip down this particular memory lane.

"So at this point what should I be doing?

"Prepare papers substituting us as counsel. We'll talk to Ron Botta in the morning, he'll withdraw as counsel, and we'll enter our appearances. We'll decide how best to proceed after we meet with Botta."

She scrawled a note to herself.

He continued, "I don't need to tell you this is an important case. We can't let Leith Delone down. That's why your loyalty is so crucial. Do you understand?"

"Yes, I get it."

"And you're prepared to do whatever it takes?"

Her stomach churned. She tried to swallow, but her mouth was too dry.

She worked up some saliva and tried again. "Whatever it takes within the bounds of our ethical obligation, you mean."

Her father didn't respond.

13

Wednesday morning

Ron stumbled into the kitchen in his boxer shorts and robe and shuffled toward the coffeemaker. Julie looked up from her social media feed and blinked in surprise.

"I'd say good morning, but it doesn't look like you're having one. Rough night?"

He grunted and poured a mug of coffee. He dumped too much creamer into it and gave it a half-hearted stir. He shook a fistful of antacids out of the container that lived on the windowsill over the sink and washed them down with a big gulp of coffee.

Only then did he join his wife at the kitchen banquette. He lowered himself heavily to the cheerful yellow bench.

"This case is gonna kill me yet," he announced.

Julie frowned and flipped her phone over, resting it

facedown on the woven placemat in front of her. "The Barefoot case?"

"What else?"

"I thought you were settling that case."

"So did I. But the plaintiffs haven't gotten back to me, and the judge denied summary judgment. Now it's all a big, fat hairy mess."

She covered his hand with hers. "I'm worried, Ron. You're popping antacids like they're candy. You're barely ever home anymore. When you are, you hardly sleep. You haven't made it to a single one of the boys' baseball or soccer games. The recycling's overflowing with beer bottles. And … we haven't made love in months." She dropped her eyes to the table. "I miss my husband."

"Aw, come on. Don't cry."

She stared down wordlessly as two fat tears fell onto the placemat.

Ron sighed. "Look at me, Julie."

She raised her eyes and sniffled.

"Things are rough at the office right now. There's no denying that. But we both knew when I ran for office that there would be tough times. It'll pass. I promise." He squeezed her hand.

She wiped her cheeks with her free hand. "Ron, the things the plaintiffs say … that the prosecutors did bad things, broke the law … that's not true, is it?"

He blinked. "Julie, what are you asking me?"

"I know you would never. But, did other people? Most of the stuff they say happened, that was before you won the election. Right?"

He wasn't gonna sugarcoat it for her. "Most of it. But not all of it. The plaintiffs' theory is that there was a widespread culture of misconduct in the office. That it went on for years and it was accepted and expected."

"But that's not true."

He released her hand and ran his hand through what was left of his hair. Then he took a swig of coffee. Finally he said, "You can't believe what the plaintiffs say. They're criminals. Don't forget that."

She frowned. "Then why are you trying to settle with them? Why not go to trial and prove that your office did nothing wrong? Defend yourself and your people. Defend your reputation and your family. Did you know the boys get teased every day on the bus? The other kids call you Bad Botta."

His head snapped back. "Is that true? They haven't said anything to me about it."

"If you were ever here, maybe they would."

He ignored the sting of the remark. "The settlement situation is complicated. Some of the decisions are out of my hands."

"Out of your hands? How? You're the chief prosecutor for the county. You're the decider."

Before he could respond, the house phone rang. Julie walked over to the little desk she used to write out the checks for the bills and do her scrapbooking. She picked up the cordless handset.

"Botta residence." She listened for a moment, then caught Ron's eye and gave him a puzzled look. "I'm well, Frank. And you and Nancy? Have you been to any Senators games? I know she loves to watch them play."

Nolan.

Ron gestured to Julie, pointing first to himself and then to the front of the house to indicate he'd take the call in the study. She nodded her understanding, and he headed down the hallway, stopping to refill his coffee mug on the way.

"Yes, you've caught him before he left. He's in the study, actually. He likes to get a few hours of solid work in before he goes into the office. You know how it is— everyone needs the boss's ear for a moment, and before you know it, the morning's gone." She laughed easily.

Ron shook his head. Bless Julie, if there was one thing she could do, it was BS with the best of them. He always thought she should've gone to law school instead of him.

He kicked the study door closed behind him, tightened the belt of his robe as if it were a suit of armor and not a piece of terrycloth, and picked up the phone on his desk.

"I've got it, honey. Frank, you there?"

"Ron, sorry to bother you at home," Frank said in a genial voice.

They waited until they heard the soft click of Julie returning the phone to its base.

"I'm almost afraid to ask, but what now?" Ron asked grimly.

Frank's voice lost its charm. "Last night, I had the dubious pleasure of updating the concerned citizen about the status of your case. They were, to put it bluntly, displeased."

Ron huffed, "I'm pretty displeased myself. How

about you drop the cloak and dagger act and tell me who this very influential private citizen is? Eventually, I'm going to have to tell Judge Cook. Even if I can convince him to let me tell him *in camera* and keep it out of the record, if Sasha keeps agitating about it, he's gonna want to know."

"That's part of the reason I'm calling. The person who funded the settlement is Leith Delone."

Ron's stomach dropped to somewhere around his knees. He'd expected to hear a name he recognized. A major business person. Maybe someone tied to a political action committee. Possibly a Harrisburg lobbyist.

He never imagined that a legitimate billionaire was behind the money. And not just any billionaire: Leith Delone.

"Ron, are you still there?"

He cleared his throat. "Yeah, I'm here. Delone? Wow, that's … wild."

"It's something," Frank said. "He was livid. And I'm sorry to be the one to have to tell you this, but he's taking over."

"What does that mean? He's taking over?" The last time he checked, being a billionaire, even an especially powerful one, didn't give a person the ability to take over the district attorney's office.

"Calm down. It's not as bad as it sounds."

Frank's tone told him it was going to be every bit as bad as it sounded. "Okay. So what is it?"

"He's retained a law firm to represent you in the litigation going forward."

"To represent me? I'm representing me. I mean, I

represent the office. I'm the chief lawyer for the county, for crying out loud." Ron knew he was shouting, but he frankly didn't care.

"Well, Ron, you know what they say about an attorney who represents himself. He has an idiot for a client."

"How dare you suggest—"

"Just listen. Think it through. You don't practice in federal court. You're a highly regarded, extremely successful prosecutor. But you *prosecute* cases, you don't defend them. And you definitely don't do it in the federal arena. You're hamstrung there, while McCandless-Connelly knows the judges, knows the system, knows the little secrets, knows all the ins and outs. You don't."

"And Delone thinks he knows his way around a federal court better than I do?"

"Of course not." Frank adopted a placating tone. "He's not a fool. He's retained a very good firm, the best firm in Pittsburgh, to represent the office. They can work on the defense, and you can focus on your job, prosecuting criminals in the state system. It's a gift, Ron. The only reason nobody suggested you secure private counsel in the first place was the cost. A firm like the one Delone hired would chew through your budget in less than a week."

Ron smirked. "Then he must've hired Prescott & Talbott."

"Bingo. And Cinco himself is running the defense."

"Huh."

"What?"

Ron wondered if Frank knew about the history between Sasha McCandless and Cinco Prescott. The Pittsburgh legal community had been abuzz when she told him where to stick his partnership. But that had been at least a decade ago, and maybe it wasn't the sort of news that would make its way out to the middle of the state.

"Oh, nothing. I'm just surprised that Cinco's getting his hands dirty. He hasn't tried a case in years, as far as I know."

"I'm sure Delone insisted he handle it personally."

"Yeah, that makes sense." Cinco probably tripped over his tongue in his eagerness to lick Delone's boots.

"You're okay with this, right, Ron?"

"So long as I'm not footing the bill. Besides, it doesn't sound like I have a choice."

"You don't," Frank confirmed.

"Then I guess that's how it'll be."

"Can I count on you to play ball?"

"Meaning?"

"Delone's still insisting the case has to settle."

"That's not gonna happen."

"Maybe not, but if it doesn't, it'll be Prescott's problem. Not yours. And not mine."

For the first time since Monday, the knot in Ron's gut lessened. "When you put it that way, what's not to like?"

"Good. Then, uh, you have a meeting with Cinco at his office in forty minutes."

"Thanks for the notice," he deadpanned.

"Look. Just go meet with his team. Give them what

they need. Cooperate fully so we can put the mess to bed already, would you?"

"Sure thing, Frank."

"Thanks, Ron. I knew you'd come around."

Ron emerged from the study and walked through the hallway with a spring in his step. The millstone had been removed from his neck, and he couldn't wait to hang it around Cinco's.

14

L eo swiveled left, dodging two racing children, one dog, and a cat as they barreled along the upstairs hallway headed for the stairs.

"Don't run!" he yelled toward their disappearing backs.

In response, they squealed something at a pitch reserved for bats, or maybe dogs.

He made his way to the kitchen to find his wife heating the cast-iron griddle.

"I was going to ask where the fire was, but now that I see you're cooking, I'm afraid you'll take it the wrong way."

Sasha's culinary skills—or lack thereof—were an open secret in their family, but sometimes she got touchy if he teased her about it.

She grinned at him. "Good morning to you, too. I just brewed a pot of coffee if you're interested."

"Am I interested? Always."

He stopped to drop a kiss on the crown of her head

before getting himself a mug. "Mom's making pancakes!" Fiona informed him.

"With chocolate chips!" Finn added.

Leo turned and gave his wife a questioning look over his coffee mug before turning back to the twins. "Your mom? The same Sasha McCandless-Connelly who claims adding chocolate chips to pancakes turns breakfast into dessert? *That* Sasha McCandless-Connelly?"

They giggled wildly. "Yes, yes!"

He walked across the kitchen and peered down into the batter. Sure enough, it was studded with chocolate chips. Lots of them.

"What are you hiding in there? Wheat germ? Flaxseed? Both?"

She swatted him with a dish towel. "Will you grab the whipped cream?"

He turned to the kids and widened his eyes, then mouthed 'chocolate chips *and* whipped cream?' before opening the refrigerator and poking his head inside to scan the shelves.

Behind him, Fiona and Finn dissolved into a fresh round of laughter. He emerged with a full canister of whipped cream.

"When did we even buy this?" he wondered aloud. He did almost all the cooking and baking, and he preferred to whip his own fresh cream.

"It was our contribution to the end-of-the-year sundae party at school. Ms. Dombroski asked for four, but they only used three. So she sent this one back home. I figured we might as well use it."

"Huh. For breakfast?"

"Yep."

"Sure, okay."

She smiled reassuringly. "I'm fine."

"I didn't say you weren't."

"You didn't have to." She nodded to the kids. "Why don't you two set the dining room table? Dad will pour the waters and bring them in."

They raced off.

"Waters? You sure you don't want to give them juice? Or, I don't know, a big glass of maple syrup?"

"Oh, come on. It's a one-time treat. A little sugar's not going to hurt them."

"*I* know that. You're the one who goes on and on about sugar being poison. Did you hit your head?"

She turned away from the griddle to face him. "Look, I know I've been distracted lately. I'm stretched too thin at work. I know that. I've done everything I can to make sure my stress hasn't spilled over at home—"

"—And you succeeded," he reassured her.

"I appreciate that. But I know I haven't exactly been a barrel of laughs. So for one day, and one day only, I'm being the fun parent, okay? Don't worry. Tomorrow, I'll go back to counting the sugar grams in their snacks and you can reclaim your title as the fun one."

"I'm holding you to that," he told her.

"That's fine."

He paused to drink her in. Her hair was pulled up in a messy bun. She had pancake batter on one cheek and a dusting of flour covered the t-shirt and shorts she'd slept in. But her green eyes were bright and lively. He'd missed that sparkle.

He pulled her close. "So you're the fun one until, what, midnight?"

"Sure." She looked up at him, and her eyes softened, almost seeming to turn liquid.

"So, maybe we could see if the kids want to sleep over at your parents' place tonight?" He lowered his mouth to hers and brushed her lips with a feather-soft kiss.

The color rose in her cheeks and she breathed out her answer in a low, throaty voice. "We could definitely do that."

She dropped the spatula to the counter with a clatter and wrapped her arms around his neck. He leaned in to devour her. Out of the corner of his eyes, he spotted smoke. The edges of her pancakes were crisping up, just beginning to burn.

"Pancake!" he yelped.

She freed herself from his embrace and hurried to flip the pancakes. Then she gave him a long look over her shoulder. "Pour the water and get out of my kitchen, would you? You're distracting me."

He winked at her, then filled the water glasses. As he carried them into the dining room, he found himself offering up a silent prayer to the universe: Please, let her have this. Give her one happy, no-stress day.

~

MAISY WOKE up with the sun, rolled out of bed, and pulled on her shoes in one motion. She'd learned a long time ago that the best way—the only way—to get her workout in was to go to the gym on autopilot, before she was even fully awake. Being there when the doors opened meant a sparse crowd. Fewer run-ins with autograph seekers, fewer people to see her barefaced and sweaty.

As a bonus, her favorite cycling class—the one with the retired Steeler turned cycling coach, who cajoled, cheered, and sometimes sang—was scheduled for six-thirty, a wholly uncivilized time, but one that suited her. She had time to stretch, warm up, and even lift weights for a bit before Garth turned on the pulsing music, donned his microphone headset, and hopped on his bike to get the party rolling, as he put it.

Maisy snagged a bike in the first row, said a quick hello to her neighbors, and started pedaling. As always, once she got underway, the music and Garth's banter seemed to fade and she got lost in her own thoughts. This morning, all she could think about was the Summer fiasco.

She giggled at the memory of Summer stammering into the camera. She'd left before Summer returned to the station yesterday—if she'd even had the nerve to show up. Maisy knew that the crew would poke fun at the reporter mercilessly. She tried again to access some sympathy for Summer, but Preston's warning echoed in her brain. It was hard to feel sorry for someone who wanted her job.

As Maisy pedaled faster, her mind started to turn faster, too.

What if Summer *hadn't* crashed and burned on live television? According to Preston it was the faceless, nameless 'management' who'd sent her to stand outside Sasha's office and, what, ambush her if she'd been stupid enough to come outside? What was the plan there, and why was some corporate flack determining coverage?

And why Sasha? Did someone have it out for her? Or was it just a coincidence? Sasha *had* made news plenty of times over the past ten or so years. It was sort of what she did. But this felt different. She hadn't done anything particularly newsworthy. Had she?

She flashed back to the script that she'd refused to read: *There's some speculation that Attorney Sasha McCandless-Connelly is gumming up the works in a potential settlement. What could be motivating Pittsburgh's most controversial litigator to tank a deal?*

There *had* been a settlement offer in the civil rights litigation. She'd heard Sasha say so in her very own kitchen. Who would be motivated to push Sasha to make a comment about it? And why would they try to use her?

She pedaled faster still. And even faster. Her heart thudded like it might explode. Her feet slipped out of the clips that held them to the pedals. She pedaled harder, rocking the bike from side to side, as her hair worked its way out of its ponytail and bobbed wildly around her shoulders. She pedaled as if she might outride an ugly truth.

Garth, the Steeler/cycling coach, eyed her. "Hey, are you okay?"

She nodded, but kept pedaling and panting.

When the class ended, she was spent. She pressed a chilled bottle of water to her forehead, leaned against the wall, and tried to slow her heartbeat. Her fitness watch vibrated nonstop to let her know her heart rate was way too high, out of the safe zone.

Didn't her dumb smartwatch think she knew that already? But, deep down, Maisy knew her heart was racing as much from her rising worry as from the exertion. She needed to warn Sasha.

15

Sasha stood barefoot on the front porch and waved goodbye as Connelly and their two sugar-fueled children headed down the street. This week's summer break activity was a slime camp at the community center not far from the twins' school.

Connelly had been skeptical about paying for the kids to attend slime camp. He'd correctly, if naively, pointed out that all they needed was borax, food coloring, and water and they could make their own slime. One very long weekend spent trying to get dried slime out of the playroom carpet had changed his tune, and he'd signed them up himself. She laughed softly at the memory.

She closed her eyes, dug her toes into the bare wood underfoot, and let the sound of the birds singing in the trees wash over her. After a moment, she inhaled deeply and opened her eyes. It was going to be another blazingly hot day. The sky was already hazy and the air was heavy.

She glanced down at her phone. It wasn't even seven-thirty yet. The promise of dessert for breakfast had lured the kids out of their beds earlier than usual, and the anticipation of slime camp had made breakfast a short affair. She had time to go for a run. It wasn't *that* hot. Not yet. She should go for a run.

Or she could get into the office early and find someone to bounce her idea off. Last night she'd spent some time researching old common law cases discussing champerty, maintenance, and barratry. Really old cases. Cases from the eighteen hundreds. Cases that, if she were looking for them back in her distant associate days, would have been unearthed in the dusty basement of the county law library from a stack of musty books. In contrast, last night she read them on her laptop from the comfort of her couch, curled up with a cat and a glass of wine.

Whether it appeared in a mildewed legal reporter or in an array of pixels on a sleek computer, the law was the law. And as her partner Will was fond of telling associates, old law was good law. In fact, sometimes old law was the best law. Sometimes a legal principle remained good precedent, but fell out of fashion and wasn't cited anymore. That meant it hadn't been chipped away at, weakened by exceptions, or, worst of all, overruled. She was pretty sure she'd found just such an animal during her pajama party/research session. But she wanted to get a second opinion.

That decided it. She'd skip the run and head into the office. The earlier she got in, the earlier she could get out and the earlier her much-needed date night with

Connelly could kick off. She hurried back into the house to get ready.

Twenty minutes later, she'd showered and had traded her messy bun for a sleek knot at the nape of her neck and her flour-covered pjs for a pale pink sheath dress, a light gray cardigan, and the stupid, cursed kitten heels. She scooped up her research and dumped it into her laptop bag, said goodbye to Java and Mocha, and headed out the door with a travel mug of coffee in her hand.

As she was locking the front door, someone called her name. She turned to see Maisy standing on the sidewalk. She'd clearly come straight from her gym. She was slick with sweat, her hair was up in a high ponytail, and she was wearing workout clothes. She looked … distraught.

Uh-oh.

"Hi, Maisy." She waved as she jogged down the front steps to join her on the sidewalk.

MAISY SHIELDED her eyes from the sun with one hand as she stared up at Sasha, who was very clearly on her way to work. Maybe this had been a dumb idea.

Sasha hurried down the stairs and studied her with a worried expression.

"Are you all right?"

"Yeah," she breathed. "I was at my cycling class, and I suddenly got it in my head that I had to talk to you. But, I probably should have just called. It's not that urgent."

"Well, it must be pretty important because here you are. I have a few minutes. Come on." Sasha piloted her up the steps to the porch and sat her down on the porch swing. She sat down next to Maisy and pushed off the porch with her feet, so that the swing swayed softly, back and forth, back and forth.

After several cycles of back and forth, Maisy said, "I need to tell you something. It's probably nothing, but …"

"Is it about the idiot reporter who was staking out my office last night?"

"Summer, yeah."

"You want to come inside for a bit? I have coffee and leftover pancakes."

She shook her head no.

"Water?"

"No. Thanks, but no."

"Okay. So what's up?"

"I'm not sure. Did you watch yesterday evening's broadcast?"

"I was working. Naya gave me the highlights."

"Right before we went on the air, Preston handed me a script. Someone from the station—management, not anyone in editorial or the news department—tried to get me to say you were throwing a wrench into settlement talks in the case against the Milltown District Attorney's office."

"I heard." Sasha glanced at her. "I also heard you didn't do it. Thanks for that."

Maisy nodded. "Someone has it out for you."

She laughed. "Is that a warning? Oh, Mais, someone always has it out for me. You know that."

"This is different, Sasha. The way this went down, that doesn't happen. We're a news organization. We follow best practices, which means we require two independent sources to confirm major facts. What we absolutely don't do is run unsourced rumors. And that's what this was. For that script to have landed in my lap means someone pulled some major strings."

Sasha cocked her head, and her green eyes clouded with concern. Maisy was glad to see it because she needed Sasha to take her seriously.

"Any idea who could have done it?"

She shook her head. "No. I'll poke around. I need to ask Summer who sent her to your office."

"Can you trust her?"

"Honestly? Probably not. She's a twenty-two-year-old strawberry blonde with perfect perky boobs and clear skin who's apparently gunning for my job."

Sasha wrinkled her nose. "Ugh. Hey, thank you for pushing back on the story. You didn't need to do that."

She waved a hand. "Didn't Naya tell you? I'm pretty much bullet-proof."

"I'm serious. You stuck your neck out for me. I appreciate it."

"About my neck?"

"Um, what about it?"

"Do I have a turkey neck?"

"What? No! Get out of here." Sasha swatted her on the shoulder.

"You'd tell me, though?"

"Maisy, I swear I'd tell you."

She exhaled. "Whew, okay. Thanks." She kicked her feet off the porch, and the swing restarted. "Maybe, as a show of thanks, you could give me an exclusive?"

"I thought the turkey neck question was out of left field, but now you've really lost me. An exclusive about what?"

"Are you really gonna play dumb? With me? The settlement in your case against the Milltown DA's Office."

"There *is* no settlement," Sasha told her.

"There's an offer, though. I heard you tell Naya in my kitchen." Maisy stopped, then hurriedly added, "I wasn't trying to listen. I promise."

"But you heard."

"Yeah."

Sasha sighed. "Maisy, that settlement offer was confidential client information, and I shouldn't have said anything to Naya in front of you—or behind you, to be completely accurate. That was my mistake."

"But there is an offer, and you don't want your clients to take it. Why? Tell me your side."

"I don't have a side. I conveyed the offer to my clients. They're considering it. There's no there there."

Maisy shook her head. There was a story here. She could feel it. "Someone thinks you're trying to torpedo the settlement. They take it seriously enough that they tried to place a piece on the local news to pressure you. They must have a reason."

Sasha blew out a long breath. "Look, this is off the record. Understand?"

Maisy pouted.

"I mean it."

"Fine. Off the record."

"Ron Botta's settlement offer was significant. It came out of the blue. The timing was weird. And he was borderline desperate for my clients to give him a quick answer."

"Okay. So, he really wants to settle. He should, shouldn't he? His office is dirty through and through."

"Sure, but until Monday, he had no interest in settlement. None. All of a sudden, he offers a huge number even though we both know there's a summary judgment decision coming down any day. And in fact, the judge ruled yesterday morning. We got the decision while I was meeting with my guys to discuss the offer. And do you know what Ron Botta does next?"

Maisy shook her head, eager to hear what happened next.

"He calls and increases the offer. My clients hadn't even rejected the original offer, they were still considering it. Nobody does that. *Nobody*."

"Okay, but even more money? That's good."

"Is it, though?"

Maisy stopped the swing with her foot. "No," she said slowly. "You're right. It's weird."

"And even weirder now that someone has apparently decided to try to pressure me by intimating that I'm playing games."

"Whoever it is, they don't know you very well. That much is for sure."

"Meaning?"

"Meaning you've never been one to bow to pressure."

Sasha smiled at that, then she checked the time. "Shoot. I gotta get to work."

"One last question, still off the record: *are* your clients going to settle?"

"I honestly don't know. I don't even know which way they're leaning. If they make a decision either way, and they're okay with me sharing that fact, you'll be the first to know. Deal?"

"Deal."

Sasha gave her a quick hug and hopped off the swing.

As Maisy watched her hurry away, she kicked her legs to get the porch swing going again. She felt weightless, carefree, and alive as she swung back and forth. She wanted to hang on to that joyful feeling just a while longer.

16

Ellie surveyed the conference room. Coffee, check. Tea, check. Sugar, assorted creamers, and lemon slices, check. Bagels and spreads, check. Bowl of fresh fruit, check. Everything appeared to be in order. So why was she so nervous? Anyway, she was a lawyer, not a caterer. She let out a long breath.

The woman standing at her side patted her arm, "You'll do fine."

She turned to face her secretary. Lettie Conrad was a legend around Prescott & Talbott. She knew everyone. She knew everything. And she had the magical ability to anticipate what Ellie needed before Ellie herself even knew.

Take this morning. She'd asked Lettie to reserve a conference room, but it hadn't even occurred to her to order a breakfast service. Lettie had just done it. Thank heaven for Lettie.

"Thanks, Lettie."

Lettie smiled. "Don't be so nervous. You've got this, Ellie."

Even though Lettie had known her literally since she'd been in diapers, she was one of the handful of people around the office who treated her like an adult, like a full-fledged attorney.

"I'm going to go through my notes one more time. Will you let me know when Mr. Botta arrives?"

"Sure will. And I'll get your dad while you go to reception to greet Mr. Botta and bring him up. Give you a few minutes to introduce yourself first."

By first, Lettie meant 'before your dad embarrasses you in front of him by talking you up.' Her dad's fatherly pride had been a recurrent problem, and it hadn't helped her standing among the other associates. But she cringed at the thought of him bragging about her to a client.

"That's a great idea."

"I'm full of them," Lettie told her, pointing to a plate covered by a lid. "I know you're not a big bagel eater, so there's an omelet on the credenza for you. Lots of protein, right?"

Ellie had learned the hard way that a heavy, carbohydrate-filled breakfast left her sleepy and slow. After Wes from the mailroom had busted her resting her head on her desk after one extra-long breakfast meeting, she'd sworn off the bagels and muffins. Protein fueled her, kept her sharp and full of energy, and maybe even gave her a tiny edge against all her bagel-dulled colleagues.

"Right. I can't eat the rest of that stuff. Thanks a lot."

Lettie gave her a strange, almost bemused look.

"What?"

"It's funny. I never realized how much you remind me of someone."

"Let me guess. My dad?"

She shook her head and mused, "No. An attorney who worked here a long time ago." She glanced down at her watch. "Oh, he'll be here any minute."

Then she hustled out of the conference room without another word.

Ellie fixed herself a cup of tea with lots of cream and lemon. She'd never developed a taste for coffee, and she marveled at people who drank that stuff black. She shuddered at the thought, then pulled out a chair and sat down. She sipped her tea as she flipped through the articles, pleadings, and other materials she'd spent most of the night gathering and taking notes on after her dad had left her office.

She didn't look up until the intercom buzzed on the star-shaped phone centered on the table.

"Mr. Botta's here. I'll let Mr. Prescott know."

"Thanks, Lettie."

She closed her folder and grabbed her keycard. As she walked down to the reception area to fetch the district attorney, she reminded herself that *he* wasn't the super-powerful billionaire. He was just a lawyer, like her. An important lawyer with a big, elected position, but still just a regular guy.

He was standing in the middle of the lobby, gaping open-mouthed at the collection of modern art that her dad had insisted the firm put on display. He tilted his head to take in a sculpture that Ellie privately suspected had been installed upside-down. Judging by Mr. Botta's expression, he seemed to share her view.

"Mr. Botta?"

He turned and blinked at her as she strode across the room with her hand outstretched.

"I'm Eleanor Prescott, sir. I'll show you to the conference room."

"Hi." He pumped her hand and furrowed his brow. Then he snapped his fingers. "Ellie? Ellie Prescott? I haven't seen you since you were, gosh, in middle school."

She looked at him blankly.

"Saint Edmund's? We attend the same church. Or at least your parents and I do."

"Oh, right. Of course." She feigned recognition. She had stopped going to church regularly not long after her confirmation. So it had been at least a dozen years. And, whether Mr. Botta realized it or not, thirteen-year-old Ellie hadn't paid much attention to random adults in the congregation.

"I didn't know you worked here. Guess it pays to know the hiring partner, eh?" He winked.

It also pays to graduate second in your class from Yale, you douche.

She forced a fake laugh. "Guess so. Let's not keep Mr. Prescott waiting." She refused to call him Dad to anyone else in the office, and calling him Cinco or Charles was just awkward.

She led Mr. Botta away from the weird sculpture and to the elevator bank. They waited in silence for an elevator for a moment, and then he turned toward her with a pained smile.

"I'll confess this meeting was sprung on me at the last minute. I'm not sure I'm going to be very helpful."

At that moment, she realized he was more nervous than she was. She tried to imagine the situation from his perspective. He was a beleaguered small-town DA, running a scandal-plagued prosecutors' office on a shoestring budget. He'd been thrust into a major civil rights case, and now some big, fancy-schmancy law firm that took up its own building full of high-priced lawyers and terrible art had swooped in to take over. It's no wonder he was intimidated.

The elevator bell dinged, the doors opened, and she ushered him inside the elevator car. As they began to rise, she addressed his reflection in the shiny doors and reassured him. "We're really only looking for background at this meeting. It's probably all stuff you could rattle off in your sleep, Mr. Botta."

An expression of pure relief flashed across his face. "That's good to know. And seeing as how you're all grown up, you should call me Ron. All right?"

"All right, Ron."

Her dad was sitting at the conference table picking apart a bagel with his fingers when they walked into the room. He nibbled the piece of bagel, brushed the crumbs off his fingers, then stood to greet them.

"Thanks for accommodating us on such short notice, Ron. I see you've already met Ms. Prescott."

Ron shook his outstretched hand. "Hi, Cinco. I didn't know your kid worked here."

"Yes, Eleanor graduated with honors from Yale Law. She had her pick of clerkships or associateships, so we were delighted when she chose to make Prescott & Talbott her legal home." Her dad beamed at her. Ellie wished in vain for the marble floor to open up and swallow one of them—him, preferably.

After an uncomfortable moment, she waved a hand at the food. "Ron, please help yourself to something to eat and drink, and then we can get started."

Ron made a beeline for the bagels, and her dad resumed picking at his cinnamon raisin bagel. She grabbed the omelet from the credenza and they got down to business.

"As you probably know, Ron, Prescott & Talbott was only retained last night. So, if you could bring us up to speed on the procedural posture of the case, it would be helpful."

Ron nodded and swallowed, then wiped his lips. "I don't want to waste your time with a lot of background, but I'm not sure how much you know about the case."

"I know very little. Eleanor here has a better grasp of the details. In fact, she wrote a law review article about the issues in your case."

The district attorney's eyes widened with surprise. "You did? You wrote about Milltown?"

He sounded flattered, which meant he'd be disappointed if he ever read it. "Plaintiffs' counsel's argument that your office's ... um ... heavy reliance on the inevitable discovery exception was tantamount to prosecutorial misconduct is quite novel. So most of my focus was on that—the plaintiffs' cause of action."

His face fell. "Oh. I suppose novel is one word for it. I'll tell you plainly, I thought Sasha McCandless-Connelly really dropped the ball when she filed that complaint. Do you know how impossibly high the bar is for her to establish a claim like that?"

"Quite high," Ellie agreed.

Before she went on, she glanced at her dad to see if he wanted to weigh in. He was doodling on his notepad. From her angle, it appeared that he was drawing either a very short giraffe or an unusually tall dog. She hoped Ron didn't have a clear view of the page.

It was an open secret at Prescott & Talbott that Cinco Prescott passionately hated being a lawyer, hated everything about it. He abhorred practicing law and running a large law firm in equal measure, and he always had. Ellie had known her entire life that her dad had wanted to be an artist but had been forced to follow in his father's and his father's father's footsteps, stretching all the way back to Uno Prescott.

While most law partners had lavish home offices where they could work at home with all the creature and technological comforts of the office, Cinco had a large, light-filled art studio with drop cloths, easels, and gleaming white floor-to-ceiling shelving bursting with paints, brushes, oil crayons, sketch pads, charcoal pencils—every imaginable supply. A stack of stretched canvases stood neatly in a corner. He spent every free moment there. Meanwhile his home office was an old laptop shoved onto a card table in the basement and an ancient dot matrix printer balanced on a rickety stand that threatened to collapse under the printer's weight.

Ellie could count on the fingers of one hand how many times she'd seen her dad in his 'home office.'

But open secret or not, how could he check out during a meeting for *the* single most important client the firm would ever have and leave a twenty-five-year-old first year to run it? What was wrong with him?

She wasted a few seconds fuming, then decided to grab the opportunity. She turned back to Ron and said as tactfully as she could manage, "Even though the bar is high and the argument is unusual, it seems as if Judge Cook believes the plaintiffs have a case. Wouldn't you agree?"

The district attorney puffed out his cheeks and narrowed his eyes. After a beat, he blew out a long breath. "Well, I'll tell you since this is all covered by attorney-client privilege: you've signed up to defend an absolute dog of a case."

She raised her eyebrows. "Go on."

"I've argued vigorously that absolute prosecutorial immunity to a Section 1983 civil rights lawsuit should apply to the actions of my lawyers, but Judge Cook has made clear that he agrees with Ms. McCandless-Connelly, who feels the proper standard is qualified immunity."

"Because the prosecutors participated in the police investigations, right? Under the Supreme Court's decision in *Buckley*, absolute immunity applies to the prosecutor's behavior at trial as an advocate. But if the prosecutor takes part in the pre-trial investigation, either by advising the police or by fabricating evidence or something similar, then qualified immunity kicks in."

Ron nodded, impressed. "No flies on this one, Cinco."

CINCO HEARD his name and started. He glanced up from his sketch. Ron Botta was looking at him, waiting for some sort of response. Unfortunately for Cinco he hadn't the foggiest idea what Ron had said.

He made a throat-clearing noise and threw Ellie a look that told her to step in so he could return to his drawing.

She got the message and pulled Ron's attention back to her. "She's right, though, isn't she? Your office, um, collaborated with the police to backfill warrantless searches by fabricating inevitable discovery exceptions, didn't it?"

Cinco hid a smile. Being diplomatic was no easy feat, but Ellie was doing a fine job of tiptoeing through the minefield of bad behavior by the Milltown District Attorney's Office.

"Aha! Exactly," Ron slapped his hand down on the table, pleased.

She blinked at the intensity of his reaction, and even Cinco felt a stir of mild curiosity.

"Can you elaborate?" she asked.

Ron pitched forward, excitement shining in his eyes. "My novel defense is that yes, the prosecutors in my office did this bad thing. They did it a lot, frequently. I'll even say they did it all the time. Okay. So? You said it yourself. They backfilled. They didn't tell the police beforehand, hey, go do an illegal search and we'll take care of it later. No, they received the evidence from the police, realized it would be excluded, and found creative exceptions. That's just good lawyering." He leaned back, triumphant.

Ellie sat motionless for a beat.

Cinco shrugged.

Ron looked back and forth between the two of them, waiting for a response.

Cinco gestured for his daughter to take this one. She jumped right in. He returned to his drawing.

"But isn't the crux of the plaintiffs' pattern and practice argument the notion that your office routinely fabri —found these exceptions? The police didn't have to conspire with you beforehand because they knew the prosecutors would get the evidence admitted."

"So say you. So says Sasha McCandless-Connelly. I say the facts make it clear my team didn't collaborate with the police pretrial. They merely played the hands they were dealt. That's what I argued in my summary judgment motion. Guess the court didn't see it my way, though."

"Guess not."

Cinco glanced up at the edge in Eleanor's tone. The mental gymnastics a person would need to perform to wrap their brain around Ron's proposed defense were, frankly, dizzying. But there was zero point in arguing with him. Their job was to settle the case, not defend it. He gave her a warning frown.

Ron went on, unperturbed, "The reason the case is a dog, if you were wondering, is the sheer number of incidents where the police found evidence in the course of an illegal search that my team later got admitted under the inevitable discovery rule. There were a lot of cases. I mean, between you, me, and the lamppost, I think McCandless-Connelly should have sued the PD. They were the ones doing all the warrantless searches. Talk about a pattern and practice."

"Huh." She responded as noncommittally as possible.

Out of boredom and a desire to wrap up this interminable meeting, Cinco roused himself to contribute to the conversation. "So, how does all this play into the settlement situation? As I'm sure you know Mr. Delone is eager for this case to settle before trial." He emphasized Delone's name to remind everyone whose opinion counted—it was the only one that really mattered here.

"If by eager you mean hell-bent, then yeah, I'm aware. Well, like I was just explaining, Judge Cook seems inclined to agree with the plaintiffs' interpretation. If he's gonna find pattern and practice and use that to bootstrap an argument for qualified immunity, my goose is cooked. Personally, I wouldn't settle. If it were up to me—and, unfortunately, it's not—I'd play out the string, build my case for appeal, and suffer through the trial. I think we'd win at the appellate level."

"Hmm." Cinco's response was designed to make Ron wonder if he agreed or disagreed with his assessment. Cinco had discovered that he could get a lot of mileage out of just making people second-guess themselves without having to advance an actual opinion.

Ron gave him a confused look, then went on, "I had no intention of making a settlement offer and the plaintiffs and the court knew that. I made it clear at every status conference. So, by forcing me to make a ridiculously high settlement offer when everyone knew Judge Cook would be handing down a summary judgment decision in a matter of days, Frank Nolan—or, I guess, Leith Delone—just made me look weak and got Sasha's antenna up."

Putting Sasha McCandless-Connelly on alert *had* been a mistake. Ron was right about that much, at least.

"So you made the offer when?" Ellie prompted.

"As soon as Nolan ordered me to do it. Monday night."

"And the summary judgment decision came down the next morning?"

"Yep. She hadn't gotten back to me yet when the decision hit our in-boxes. I called up the Attorney General to let him know."

"How'd he take the news?"

Ron speared a grape on to his fork and popped it into his mouth before answering. "About how you'd expect. He was pissed. Pissed and also irrational."

"Irrational in what way?" Cinco pressed him.

Ron looked queasy at the prospect of criticizing the commonwealth's attorney general, but he forged ahead. "He somehow expected me to jam the offer down their throats despite the order. Now, in retrospect, what I did next was a mistake."

Cinco put down his pen and propped his hands on his chin. He loathed lawyering, but he *loved* hearing about other people's strategic or legal screwups. If there had been an 'America's Funniest Lawyer

Mishaps' show, Cinco Prescott would have been an avid viewer.

"What happened?" Ellie asked.

"I guess I panicked. First, I called Sasha and upped the offer."

"Before they'd even rejected the original one? What were you thinking?" Cinco asked with genuine interest.

"I don't know. Frank Nolan got me rattled. He said Delone was going to apply some kind of public pressure to her, so I thought I'd give it a shot."

"Nothing ventured, nothing gained," Cinco observed.

"Something like that. So I called her up and told her to forget about the existing offer, that the new number was twelve million."

"Oh, your second mistake," Cinco crowed.

"Yeah. That really set her off. She told me she knew from our discovery responses that we didn't have access to that much money."

"Ouch," Cinco said, making little effort to hide his glee.

From the corner of his eye, he saw Eleanor shaking her head. She'd learn soon enough. In this profession, you took your joy where you could find it.

"So I told her I'd secured funding from a third party."

"Let me guess. She demanded that you reveal where the money is coming from, which, of course, Mr. Delone forbids you to do," Cinco said.

"Right," Ron said, shaking his head miserably.

"It's quite a predicament," Cinco observed.

The district attorney brightened. "Yeah. But, hey, at

least it's not my problem. Not anymore. Now, it's your problem. On Monday, at that status conference, she's going to tell the judge I can't possibly be negotiating in good faith. I know she is. And you two will need to convince the judge that the settlement offer is legitimate without divulging the source. But even if you get Judge Cook on board, that still doesn't mean the plaintiffs will take it."

Ellie cocked her head. "Surely the plaintiffs will settle. If not for twelve million, then the full fifteen. That's an obscene amount of money."

Ron looked at her with a pitying expression. "You don't know Sasha McCandless-Connelly."

Cinco's stomach tightened and his smile faded. Suddenly, this situation was considerably less entertaining.

17

L andon's fingers shook as he punched in the number that Leith Delone's assistant had given him. *Relax*, he told himself. *Delone said to reach out if there were any issues.* And he needed to get some clarity.

Sasha's intern was relentless. She apparently brought the same enthusiasm and energy to administrative work as she did to her protesting and social justice warrior activities. While her diligence was admirable, it made him anxious. He couldn't ignore her forever.

As the line rang and he waited for someone to pick up the call, he admitted to himself that he felt uneasy and vaguely dirty about what his arrangement with Delone would mean for Sasha's case. He didn't feel any particular loyalty to her clients, but he did owe her.

He'd never claimed Cesare was infallible, and the responsibility for her clients' situation rested largely with the Milltown Police. All the same, the PPC pilot program had been swept up into the larger corruption in Milltown, and he had allowed himself to be carried away by his zeal. It occurred to him that perhaps Jordana wasn't the only one who allowed their passions to get the better of them.

When he'd entered into the consent decree with the Department of Justice, he'd also agreed to testify for Sasha in the civil rights case. Now, he was about to back out of his commitment, and he didn't like how that made him feel. He'd always been a man of principle.

A polished female voice interrupted his rumination. "Good morning. You've reached Pinpoint Partners. How may I direct your call?"

Pinpoint Partners?

He stammered, "I … may have the wrong number. This is Landon Lewis from the Joshua Group. I'm trying to reach Leith Delone, or someone on his acquisitions team."

She chirped, "You've reached the right place, Mr. Lewis. Mr. Delone is one of our founders. I'll put you through to Brian Rosen."

"And who is he?"

"He's our chief data tracking evangelist and application integration specialist."

"Um … okay."

Even Landon, who was well-acquainted with Silicon Valley's inane titles, had no clue what that meant. He imagined the opacity was by design. After all, investors don't like to admit ignorance. Better to just write the check or transfer the cryptocurrency than to ask what exactly all the buzzwords meant.

Within seconds, Brian Rosen boomed in his ear, "Landon, bro, what's up at the Joshua Group?"

His voice had the easygoing cadence of an aging surfer. Landon pictured him. Hair, just a little too long and shaggy, brushing his neck. A short-sleeved collared camp shirt in a colorful floral or dizzying geometric pattern and loose linen pants instead of anything approaching business wear. But he also knew the laid-back persona would've been carefully crafted by a stylist. In his heart, Brian Rosen was almost certainly a buttoned-up finance type.

"Hi, Brian. I'm calling to see if we have a closing date yet."

"Oh, man, we're close. Real close. Do you need me to arrange for bridge funding or a float to get through?"

Yep, a finance guy.

"No, my concern isn't financial."

"Just in a hurry to consummate the wedding, huh?" He chuckled at his own joke.

Other than being vaguely dirty, the comment added nothing to the conversation, so Landon ignored it.

"I don't know if Mr. Delone mentioned this, but the Joshua Group's main asset—"

"Cesare, right?"

"Right, Cesare. Cesare is at issue in a federal civil rights lawsuit. Only tangentially, but still, I'm expected to testify if the case goes to trial and—"

"Landon, no worries, amigo. Leith's taking care of that."

"So I've been told. But the thing is, the plaintiffs' attorney keeps trying to get me to commit to a date to go over my testimony. I've been ignoring her office, but I can't put her off indefinitely, so I was hoping to pinpoint a date."

"Haha, I see what you did there. Pinpoint a date. Pinpoint Partners. Good one." Brian laughed heartily at Landon's unintentional pun.

"Yes, well, do you know when this transaction will close? Or do you have any thoughts about what I should tell Ms. McCandless-Connelly?"

"Tell you what. Let me round up with Leith, and we'll circle back with you later today. Cool?"

"Um, yes, cool."

"Excellent. Good talking to you, Landon."

Before Brian could tell him to hang loose, Landon's curiosity got the better of him. "Hey, Brian, by the way, what exactly does Pinpoint Partners do? I assume you're the business unit that'll be absorbing Cesare?"

"Yeah, that's right. Give me a sec ..."

Computer keys clacked on Brian's end of the call. Landon waited.

"So, it looks like you've signed your nondisclosure agreement."

"I did," Landon confirmed. Delone's NDA was only slightly more draconian than others he'd signed.

"Cool. I'll lay it all out for you in broad strokes. We gobble up all the crumbs of consumer data that people drop as they meander through cyberspace on their phones or computers. Then we synthesize the data to create an integrated digital representation of the person. Like an actual avatar, you follow?"

"I do. But that's not exactly groundbreaking is it? Mr. Delone said this project will change the world."

"He's right. Sure, other companies broker that data, but not the way we will. We've been buying up loads of apps and programs that contain what you might think of as a person's virtual DNA. And the ones we can't buy outright, we license. We have an incredible amount of data that we integrate with a growing suite of algorithms and AI products—one of which will be Cesare. This whole network will function as a hive mind. Ultimately, we'll be able to pinpoint a particular person and predict what they will need to buy, where they will go, who they'll see there, what they'll eat, everything— before they even know. We'll know more about their life than they will."

Brian paused to let that sink in.

Landon took his silence as an opportunity to ask the ultimate question, "And you'll sell that avatar to retailers or ...?"

"No, no, nothing like that. End users don't like to feel like retailers are spying on them. It turns out that tailored advertising rubs most people the wrong way."

He could see that. It was moderately creepy to tell one's spouse you were out of detergent, then go online a minute later to find a social media feed flooded with detergent advertisements. It felt like an invasion of privacy.

"Then what's the avatar for?"

"Uh, well, while we won't sell a copy of a person's entire digital footprint, we will license discrete strands of data to, you know, agencies or entities that might be interested in it. You follow?"

"Not entirely. He didn't go into detail when we spoke, but Mr. Delone said he envisions using Cesare for private enterprise, not government agencies. I understand that Pinpoint Partners isn't a government agency, but it sounds like you intend to contract with the government to sell this data. Do I have that right?"

"Eventually. That's down the road. Our immediate use cases are private."

"Such as?"

"Okay, say you're a parent and you've installed a monitoring app on your teenager's phone. That app collects tons of background information that mom and dad never see and don't care about. But if teenage Kayleigh visits a clinic, picks up vitamins at the local pharmacy, and then buys some slouchy sweatpants, well, looks like somebody's expecting. Perhaps an adoption agency wants to reach out to her. Big money, my friend."

"You don't need Cesare for that. Existing data capture already does that. That's the targeted advertising you just said customers don't like."

"El wrongo. Existing data capture is primitive. Clunky. We'll tweak Cesare to predict the probability that Kayleigh's pregnant and feed it all that data plus the other data that we can harvest that other programs can't —texts between her and her boyfriend, the pic of her positive pee stick on her phone's camera roll, the fact that her smartwatch has recorded her sleeping more— and, cha-ching, pregnancy prediction. There are all sorts of applications—whether a kid's going to get into the college that he's applied to, whether the dad having the midlife crisis is going to get a mistress or a motorcycle, whether a middle-aged mom is gonna lose that weight through her dieting app or if she's going to tip over from prediabetic to diabetic thanks to her meal delivery orders and her wine of the month club. Her insurance company would love to know before they calculate her next year's premiums. Cha-ching, cha-ching, and cha-ching! You see where I'm going with this, right, Landon?"

Oh, he did.

"I do," he confirmed grimly. Pinpoint Partners was going to take targeted advertising to a whole new level of privacy invasion.

"We'll be working our cajones off tweaking Cesare and you'll be swimming in your bathtub full of gold," Brian said cheerfully. "A million Benjamins, man. That's bank."

Brian was right. One hundred million dollars *was* bank. Was that the price of Landon's soul? His vow that Josh's murder wouldn't be without meaning? Would he trade his life's work for a hundred million dollars so these boneheads could expose pregnant teens, cheating husbands, and menopausal women who eat too many cookies? Before he could answer that question, the dude-bro on the other end of the phone answered it for him.

Misinterpreting his silence, Brian assured him, "Don't you worry, amigo. The deal is inked even though we haven't wired the money yet. We're all locked in.

Even if the plaintiffs for some bonkers reason don't settle, and you have to testify, you'll still get paid. We want Cesare no matter what. At worst, we'll have to do some public relations cleanup. Maybe obfuscate the connection between Cesare and Mjölnir."

"Mjölnir? Thor's hammer?"

"Yeah. The new name's not set in stone, but that's what Leith is leaning toward. Because Cesare's going to take in all that data and hammer out an answer. Pretty cool, huh?"

"Um, yes. Cool. You'll check about the witness prep, though, and let me know?"

Landon needed to end this call before he lost his breakfast. Because Brian was right. He was already locked into his deal with the devil—or, in this case, the billionaire.

"You've got it, my man."

Landon ended the call and dropped his head into his hands. How could he have been so naïve?

18

As soon as she got to the office, Sasha buttonholed her partner Will Volmer on his way back from the break room and forced him to listen to her ideas about champerty, barratry, and maintenance and how the musty old common law principles dovetailed with the current state of third-party litigation financing. Will, always a good sport, peppered her with insightful questions and what ifs, helping her hone her theory.

Then Caroline rounded the corner. Her mouth was a slash, a thin line, and her eyes were grim.

"Uh-oh," Will said. "I really hope she's not looking for me."

Caroline, who was beelining toward them, heard him over the clack of her heels against the tile and shook her head. "Not you. You," she said to Sasha.

"Great."

When she reached their corner, Caroline gave Sasha

a sad smile. "Which do you want first—the bad news or the other bad news?"

"Oh, let's get the bad news out of the way, first." She steeled herself.

"There's been a substitution of counsel in the Botta case."

"Really? Ron finally wised up and retained outside counsel?"

"He did, indeed." Caroline's gaze shifted away over to Will then back to Sasha. "He's retained our former place of employment."

All three of them had escaped from the clutches of Pittsburgh's most prestigious—and arguably most toxic —law firm.

"He hired P&T?" Will said. "With his budget?"

"Oh, I'll bet his mystery citizen is funding that, too," Sasha said sourly.

Will nodded. "That makes sense."

Sasha sighed and eyed Caroline. "What's the other bad news?"

"The attorneys who entered their appearances are Cinco and Six."

Sasha couldn't hide her surprise. Cinco trying a case was a rarity. She glanced at Will, whose face registered his own shock.

"Wow, Cinco himself," Will said in a rare display of sarcasm. Then almost immediately, he looked abashed. "I don't mean to be unkind, but he's hardly a lion of the litigation bar."

"He doesn't much care for trial work," Caroline agreed.

"But who's Six? Please tell me Cinco hasn't cloned himself."

Sasha kept in touch with a handful of Prescott & Talbott attorneys, but she wasn't sufficiently plugged into the culture to know the new nicknames.

Caroline laughed. "It's what the other first years call Eleanor Prescott."

"Eleanor? Wait, you're not trying to tell me Ellie Prescott is an attorney. She's a teenager—she can't even be old enough to drink!"

"Ah, Sasha, the inexorable march of time. You've been gone from P&T for more than a decade. You don't think Ellie was preserved in amber the day you quit, do you? She's a practicing attorney, and, from what I've heard, a good one."

Naya, who had stopped on her way to the copy room to catch the scuttlebutt about their old firm, interjected drily, "It must skip a generation."

That earned her a chuckle from Caroline and a mildly rebuking look from Will.

"What, Will? Word on the street is her dad isn't exactly the lion of the litigation bar."

Will flushed. "Touché."

Naya snorted and was about to walk away, but Sasha put a hand on her arm.

"Wait."

Naya stopped.

Sasha surveyed McCandless, Volmer & Andrews' first three employees. Along with her, they were the original team, all of whom had cut their teeth at

Prescott & Talbott. "Do I need to be worried about Cinco?"

"You mean because you humiliated him in a move that made you a local legal legend?" Naya countered. "What do you think?"

Sasha felt her neck and shoulder muscles bunch up with tension. "Great."

But Caroline shook her head slowly. "I don't think Cinco is the problem. He is nursing a grudge against you, true. But on a very basic level, he's going to want to do as little actual work as possible. Making you pay for snubbing him would require too much effort. He'd rather expend his energy painting or sketching."

Sasha relaxed her shoulders. Caroline had been Cinco's secretary for years. If any of them understood his psyche or his motivation, it was Caroline. "Okay, good."

"But," Caroline went on, "Ellie's smart, and ambitious. The other attorneys might call her Six behind her back to try to convince themselves that it's not her drive but her bloodline that's got her this far, but do you know what your former secretary calls her?"

"Lettie?"

"Yes, Lettie. She works for Ellie now."

Lettie was a fixture at P&T. She was a wealth of knowledge who had her finger on the firm's pulse. Sasha knew she could take Lettie's opinion of Ellie as gospel. "So, what does Lettie call her?"

Caroline twisted her lips into a wry smile. "Sasha 2.0."

Naya groaned, "Oh, you're screwed, Mac. So, so screwed."

19

Ellie stared at her father. She didn't think she'd ever seen him so … contorted. His face was scrunched up and red as if he were a toddler about to throw an epic tantrum. She banished the thought from her mind and stood, expressionless, with her hands clasped together behind her back.

She was about to get chewed out mercilessly, and she had to make the most of it.

When her father had appeared unannounced to talk about her memo rather than summoning her to his inner sanctum, she'd seen her opening. After she ushered him into her office, she'd been sure to leave the door ajar. Now she just had to hope someone walking by would hear the commotion and spread the word.

"I'm disappointed in you," he snapped as his opening salvo.

"I'm sorry to hear that."

"You should be. What the devil is this supposed to

be?" He waved her memo wildly then squeezed his hand around it.

"Did I misunderstand the assignment?" she asked mildly.

He sputtered, "What?"

"You want to force Sasha's hand, make her settle. Don't you?"

"Correct."

She gestured toward the now-crumpled memo. "That's what this does."

"This? *This?* Are you out of your mind?" His voice rose, louder and higher.

Outside in the hallway, she heard someone saying, "Come here, fast. Cinco is reaming Six out."

Despite the speaker's unconcealed glee, Ellie felt a rush of triumph. The research was going to anger her father no matter what. She might as well use the tongue-lashing she was destined to receive to change her reputation, even a little. The others might still grumble about her, but they couldn't claim she received more favorable treatment.

"Right, this," she confirmed in her calmest, most reasonable tone as if he really were a tantrumming toddler.

"Eleanor. You want the district attorney's office to admit wrongdoing. The whole point of giving the other side money is to make the thing go away without admitting wrongdoing. What did they teach you at that overpriced diploma factory?"

"How to win."

Out in the hallway, someone whispered, "Oh, snap"

in a loud voice. Her father's attention shifted to the door. She followed his gaze and spotted a cluster of first years and summer associates huddled near Lettie's desk.

"Close that," he demanded.

She crossed the room and pulled the door shut, making sure her audience got a clear view of her stricken expression in the process. After she shut the door, she turned to see him pacing and fuming in front of her bookcase. Now that she'd achieved her goal, it was time to talk him down.

"Listen, Ron glossed over this earlier, but I've done the research. The whole inevitable discovery thing? It was SOP at the DA's office—"

"—SOP?"

"Standard operating procedure."

"I'm familiar with the acronym, Eleanor. Is that your opinion, or is it literally standard procedure?"

"Dad, it's in the manual!" She realized belatedly that she'd slipped and called him Dad, but he didn't seem to notice.

"The manual."

"Yes, Mr. Botta turned it over to the plaintiffs. And they attached it as an exhibit to their opposition to summary judgment. It reads, in pertinent part, 'if a case is referred to the office and the supporting evidence was obtained through a warrantless search and thus is vulnerable to exclusion, the preferred course of action is to identify and advance evidence that supports an inevitable discovery exception. If such an exception is unavailable, consider whether the independent source exception might apply.'" She lowered her chin. "Dad, it's in their training materials."

He groaned. "They put it in the freaking manual. Twelve million is a bargain."

"Exactly! So, if all we need to do is settle, lead with your chin. Or Botta's chin, more accurately."

He considered the idea. "I don't like it. It looks weak."

Was he being serious right now?

"What? Like bidding up the offer from nine to twelve million *sua sponte* was a sign of strength? Botta was right about one thing. This case barks. It's a dog."

She realized halfway through that she'd lost him. He'd wandered over to her window and was gazing out, his hands clasped behind his back. She stood up and joined him. In a weird, mind-meld moment, she followed the trajectory of his gaze and knew exactly what he was thinking.

He was focused on Point State Park and the people frolicking in the fountain, their shoes in hand and their pants rolled up to their knees. The fountain sprayed up, whitecaps and water. The rivers rolled by in the background, the houses and trees up on the hill bore witness to a carefree summer scene that conveyed light, and ease, and freedom—all things her father believed were inaccessible to him in his prison of achievement.

And she knew exactly what he was doing. He was searing it into his memory so that he might paint it later in his home studio, trying to capture with his brush the feeling so unavailable to him in his life. At that moment,

Eleanor felt she'd never understood her father better and had never pitied him more.

She vowed she wouldn't end up like him—chained to a law firm that kept her from her dreams. She promised herself she'd do whatever it took not to live that life.

Maisy arrived at the station early, humming happily under her breath. After swinging on Sasha's porch swing for a good while, she'd gone home and had a long shower, followed by a leisurely solo lunch on the outdoor patio of one of her favorite restaurants with a novel for company. She felt rejuvenated, recharged, and ready for the evening's broadcast.

She greeted everyone she passed with a smile and a kind word. She weaved through the bullpen where the field reporters worked and located Summer's work station in the maze of carousels. Summer sat with her head bent over a script, scribbling notes. She wore big over-the-ear headphones rather than the usual discreet earbuds the young reporters favored. A clear signal that she wanted to be left alone.

Summer had probably received enough verbal abuse from her coworkers to last the rest of her career. Maisy sighed. She only hoped the rookie hadn't been naïve enough to check her email and voicemail messages. Even if she was working to unseat Maisy from the anchor's desk, she needed a friend. Or, at the very least, a friendly word.

She tapped Summer's left shoulder. The younger woman froze. Then her shoulders sagged and she swiveled around in her chair to confront the person who'd ignored the giant 'do not disturb' sign she was displaying. When she saw who it was, her eyes widened, and she yanked the headphones down.

"Um, hi."

Maisy could hear Summer's music playing from the headphones that dangled around her neck, but it was too faint to make out what she was listening to.

"You holding up okay, hon?"

To Maisy's horrified surprise, tears brimmed in Summer's big blue eyes. It was apparent that this wasn't Summer's first crying jag of the day. Her eyes were swollen and red-rimmed.

"That bad, huh?"

Wordlessly, Summer reached forward and tapped her mouse to pull her email in-box up on her computer monitor.

"Oh, no, sugar. You didn't read these, did you?"

Summer's shaking shoulders answered that question in the affirmative. Maisy shook her head and plucked a tissue out of the box on Summer's desk. She pressed it into Summer's hand.

"Listen to me. Go to the restroom and pull yourself together. Splash some water on your face. Go see Livia. Tell her I said you need some hemorrhoid cream."

That instruction managed to shake Summer's voice loose. "H-h-hemorrhoid cream?" She hiccupped thickly.

"Trust me. It'll take away the redness and depuff your eyes. I mean, don't use it on the regular, but in an emergency, it works."

"Really?"

Maisy lowered her head and leaned in close. She spoke in a low voice, "Summer, no matter what any of these other monsters may tell you, you're not the first reporter to ever blow it on the air. We've all been there."

"I looked like an idiot on live tv."

To her credit, Summer didn't say '*you* made me look like an idiot.' Maisy gave her points for owning her screwup.

"You know where you messed up, right?"

She nodded, her lower lip quivering. "Preston told me to go to that law firm, but I didn't have anything but a rumor. I should've sourced the story. It was a stupid mistake."

"You got overexcited. It happens. And, sometimes, even if you *don't* bomb, the viewers will decide they hate your new haircut or the color of your lipstick and your in-box will blow up with so much venom you'll think the poison might actually kill you."

"Even ... even you?"

"Even me." She gently pushed Summer out of the chair. "Now, go. I'm gonna delete this hate mail so you don't obsess over the messages. And, whatever you do, don't listen to your voicemails."

Summer managed a tremulous smile and dabbed at her eyes with the tissue. "Thank you."

Maisy nodded. "Go. And hold your head up when you walk through the newsroom."

Summer took a breath and squared her shoulders. "Oh, by the way, thanks for that face cream stuff. It really works."

Maisy smiled. "Stick with me for more cutting-edge beauty tips like grandma's face cream and Preparation H under your eyes."

Summer giggled as she walked out into the jungle that was the newsroom. Maisy watched her go and tried to remember ever being that young and vulnerable. She knew she had been once upon a time, but two decades of television journalism had sharpened her elbows and her edges. Whether that was entirely good was a question for another time.

She turned back to Summer's computer and checked to confirm that all the read, unfiled messages in the email in-box were related to her on-screen meltdown. A quick scan of the subject lines confirmed that Pittsburgh's news viewers had indulged their worst impulses at Summer's expense. What on earth had Summer kept them for? Was she gonna start a 'mean emails from viewers' folder?

Maisy moused over to 'select all' and clicked the button to delete the messages. Not a second after the messages disappeared a new unread message popped.

"For crying out loud, people. Have some compassion," she muttered as she selected the new message to add to the trash. When she read the subject line, her hand froze in mid-air and hovered just above the mouse: **Milltown DA Settlement Funding Scandal?**

Maisy's heart thudded and her eyes darted around the room. Nobody was paying a whit of attention to her. She clicked the arrow beside the message. Now all she had to do was move the thing to the trash unread.

Or.

Her heart sped up from a controlled canter to a wild gallop. She swallowed. She dragged the mouse halfway toward the trash can icon then stopped. She released her hand, closed her eyes, and breathed.

A moment later, Maisy opened her eyes, selected the message, hit 'forward,' and typed in her own email address. Then she trashed the message on Summer's desktop and emptied the trash for good measure. She picked her purse up from the top of Summer's filing cabinet and stood. She walked through the bullpen, down the long hallway, and into her private office on shaking legs.

21

L andon gripped the phone. Despite his promise, Brian Rosen hadn't called him back. Instead, Delone himself returned the call. On the one hand, Landon was pleased not to have to suffer through another rambling, lingo-laden conversation with Brian. On the other, Delone had apparently been on his best behavior at the Gilt Club. Now, he was brusque to the point of rudeness and intimidating to the point of threatening.

Delone wasted no time telling Landon to string Sasha along. "Keep pushing her off. The settlement is going to happen, make no mistake."

"But on the off-chance it doesn't, what then?" Landon persisted.

Delone's impatience blasted through the phone. "In the event that happens, you'll go forward with the meeting and be as unhelpful as you can without making it obvious. And to forestall your next question, if the case somehow goes to trial, you'll lie on the stand if that's what it comes to."

Landon wasn't sure which part was twisting his gut: the instruction to commit perjury if necessary or the idea that he could play Sasha McCandless-Connelly for a fool. She was not stupid. And she was ferocious. She'd once threatened to cut his throat with a shard of porcelain. Who knew what she might be capable of if she realized he was stringing her along?

"Do you have the clarity you need now?"

Delone's disdain sparked a dormant ember of courage buried deep with Landon, and he spoke before he could second-guess himself. "Yes, I'm clear about my marching orders. I remain fuzzy on how you're going to change the world."

"What?"

"You said you plan to use Cesare to change the world. But after chatting with your integration sherpa or whatever Brian Rosen calls himself, it sounds to me as if you plan to use it to turn privacy invasion into a high art."

Delone barked, "What I ultimately do with Cesare isn't your concern. You get your money, and I get the program. It's that simple." Unable to stop there, the billionaire—motivated by ego, Landon surmised—continued, "But rest assured, Landon, once I retool Cesare, it will change the world."

"As Mjölnir."

"Precisely. Mjölnir will cut its teeth on the commercial applications. It's artificial intelligence, but it can only learn what it's taught. Right?"

"Well, that's a gross oversimplification, but yes."

"You've used a limited dataset to teach Cesare to predict latent criminal behavior. That's why you had limited success. I'll use a vast, growing, interconnected neural network of algorithms and AI applications to expand Cesare's understanding of the full range of human behavior."

Despite himself, Landon's curiosity spiked. "To what end?"

"As Mjölnir, Cesare will observe the diversity of human misbehaviors that fall short of crimes. Minor daily infractions like anonymous online trolling, pettiness like wearing a dress then returning it. Lying to one's spouse. All of this data will flesh out the digital avatars we create. Once Mjölnir has a robust understanding of human nature, *then* we'll turn to law enforcement applications."

"But you can't. The consent decree that the Joshua Group and I entered into with the Justice Department forbids the use of the algorithm to predict criminal behavior."

"No, *you* can't."

Frustrated, Landon insisted, "It doesn't matter whether you call it Cesare or Mjölnir. What you're proposing would violate the consent decree."

"You misunderstand. Mjölnir won't predict that a *person* will commit a crime, it will use a person's virtual footprint to predict what their digital avatar would do."

"I'm not sure I see the distinction," he confessed.

"I'm not sure you need to. But in short, let's say you

use a fasting app, and the data you input suggests that you observe Ramadan."

"Okay."

"The map app on your phone places you at the same location at the same time every week, and that location happens to be a mosque. Then your shopping app shows a purchase of ammunition."

Landon's chest tightened like a band squeezing the breath from his diaphragm. "That's all legal behavior," he pointed out carefully.

"It is. So is this: you ditch your car and take the subway, which is not your ordinary routine. Our program notes that. You exit one stop away from a government office building. And you do the same thing, a week later. Now, red flags are popping up, alarms are pinging, but, as you say, this hypothetical 'you' hasn't broken any laws. You haven't posted on any known extremist message boards. You're not making threats. You don't have a criminal record." Delone paused to take a breath.

Landon used the opportunity to interject. "So, you can't do anything with this information."

"False. The alphabet agencies—ICE, DHS, CIA, FBI, NSA, AFT—they can't do anything at this point because digital Landon's activities might be suspect, but in meat space, Landon's a law-abiding citizen."

And that's where Cesare comes in, Landon thought as a wave of dread washed over him.

"And that's where Cesare comes in," Delone said. "Cesare, connected to the rest of the Mjölnir neural network, will use the enormous dataset of online behaviors to analyze digital Landon's behavior and compare that avatar to your database of criminality. Pinpoint Partners won't say that the real person is likely to commit a crime, but if Cesare predicts that the avatar would commit the crime, we can sell that prediction to the relevant law enforcement entities. And that, my friend, is how I will change the world."

Despite Delone's obvious pride in this idea, it seemed to Landon that Pinpoint Partners was making a distinction without a difference.

But was it really his concern? He'd sold the technology. It was out of his hands. He closed his eyes and envisioned one hundred stacks, each comprising one hundred one-hundred-dollar bills. One hundred stacks of one hundred one hundreds filling a titanium hard case. Then he imagined one hundred of those cases lined up in ten rows of ten. One hundred million dollars. The image was soothing in its symmetry and its size.

His ex-wife had been right, after all. Deanne had tried to convince him that when his thoughts turned to Josh's brutal murder he could soothe himself by picturing something pleasant. In that instance, she'd meant a happy memory of a time spent with Josh. But in this particular instance, big, beautiful mountains of money did the trick.

He opened his eyes and swallowed. "Thank you. I appreciate the walkthrough more than you know."

Delone seemed to soften. "Of course. I recognize that Cesare was a passion project for you. I understand your interest, and I assure you, Mjölnir will do things Cesare could only dream of."

Landon believed him. Unfortunately, that was precisely what he was afraid of.

"I have no doubt," he managed to say.

"All you have to do is stave off the attorney for a little while longer. I have faith in you."

Delone ended the call, and Landon stared at the phone in his hand, his mind racing. What had he done? Was there any way to stop what he'd unwittingly unleashed on the world?

Eventually, his breathing slowed, and he moved to return his cell phone to the charging station on his desk. As he did so, the phone chirped in his hand and he nearly dropped the thing.

Sasha tapped her pen against her teeth as she waited for Landon Lewis to answer his cell phone. She'd briefly considered texting him, but she didn't want to give him the opportunity to ignore her the way he had Jordana.

"Hello?" He answered the call on the first ring in a breathy, cautious voice.

She dropped the pen to her desk. "Landon, it's Sasha McCandless-Connelly."

"Oh." His tone became guarded. "How odd. Your office number didn't come up on my phone."

"That *is* odd."

In reality, it wasn't the least bit odd, considering that

she'd blocked caller ID before she'd placed the call. She wasn't a college-aged intern. She knew the drill.

"Well, no matter. In fact, I was just picking up the phone to call you."

"Really?"

"Well, Jordana, actually. But I assume you're calling for the same reason."

"You assume correctly. Jordana's been trying to get in touch with you to schedule your witness prep session."

"Yes, I know. I'm sorry I've been hard to pin down. I had to go out of town for a bit."

"Business or pleasure?" She didn't particularly care, but Landon was going to be a key witness at trial, so she could invest a few minutes in idle chit chat to keep their relationship amiable.

"Uh ... well, I suppose it was a bit of both. I got a call about a ... business opportunity in Malibu and I hopped on a plane on short notice and flew out there for a few days."

"Did you just get back?"

"Last night."

"Hope the time change and jet lag aren't too bad."

"I actually was fortunate enough to fly on a private jet. It was more like a day of rest and relaxation than a slog of travel."

"How nice for you."

"It was." He coughed. "But there's no excuse for my delay in responding to Jordana. Will you convey my apology?"

"I will," she promised. She would, if only for the

entertainment of watching Jordana roll her eyes with dramatic flair.

"And how have you been? I trust Agent Connelly and the children are well?"

"Leo and the twins are great. They're at slime camp this week—Finn and Fiona that is, not Leo." She nearly burst into laughter at the thought of Leo up to his elbows in electric-blue slime. She bit her lip.

"Slime camp?" He echoed her words as if she were speaking a foreign language that he didn't understand.

In a way, she supposed she was. Landon's only child had been murdered fifteen years ago. Slime had only slithered onto the scene about six years ago. Landon probably had no clue what she was talking about. As always happened when Sasha was reminded of Landon's tragic story, her heart squeezed in sympathy. Landon Lewis might be—no, was—an aloof, arrogant person who'd created a dangerous, biased program. He was a zealot, to the point of being obsessed. And, she reminded herself, he'd abducted her off the street and held her in a cage to protect his work. He was, in short, a terrible human.

But.

But she always came back to his son's murder. She'd seen how her brother's death had changed her parents, changed her and her brothers. Losing a child rips a hole in the fabric of a family. And Landon Lewis' life had been destroyed by Josh's murder. She felt for him. How could she not?

Still, he could have devoted his energy and resources to gun reform or crime reform or a foundation to provide mental health resources for families who'd lost a child, something constructive. Instead, he'd set out to create an algorithm that would lock up potential criminals before they committed a crime. The idea was chilling. The reality was even worse: his thought crime program was racially biased. So while she could empathize with him, she didn't like him.

"Slime is … it's similar to oobleck. Do you know what that is?"

"Of course. Oobleck is a non-newtonian fluid," he sniffed.

"Exactly, and so are slime, gak, and foam," she told him, trying not to laugh at the words. "The kids concoct all sorts of non-newtonian fluids and mix in things like glitter, styrofoam balls, and food coloring. They call it all slime. So Finn and Fiona are basically spending a week at a very messy chemistry camp for little ones."

"I see." He still sounded baffled.

"Moving on from my mad scientists, I need to ask you to block out, at minimum, four hours to go over your testimony. Please take a look at your calendar and let me know some good times."

"I'm afraid I was calling to tell you my schedule is quite full. There is no good time for me to devote half a day to this any time soon. I simply can't."

She pinched the bridge of her nose between her thumb and forefinger in an attempt to ward off the instant headache that Landon was giving her.

After a long pause, she said, "I'm very flexible. We can do it on a weekend or in the evening if that would suit your schedule better." She waited a beat, then added firmly, "But we *are* doing it, Landon. So it's time to bite the bullet and put it on your calendar."

"There's still no chance this matter will settle?"

The words sent a prickle of suspicion through her, and the back of her neck tingled. The question itself was innocuous. He'd asked it several times during the course of the case, always in a wistful, hopeful tone. But the way he asked it now, it sounds as if he *knew* something.

She answered the question with one of her own. "Has the Milltown District Attorney's Office contacted you?"

"No, of course not."

It was possible he'd seen the live coverage on WACB that suggested there was a settlement offer and that she was gumming up the works. Regardless of what prompted the question, there was no point in lying about it.

"As a matter of fact, the district attorney recently made an unexpected settlement offer."

"Oh? Are your clients going to take it?"

"I can't discuss that with you, Landon. What I can tell you is that Sam, Charlie, and Max are considering the offer but haven't made a decision. That means we need to continue to move forward in our trial preparation. If anything changes, I promise you'll be one of the first people I tell. So, let's just get a date on the calendar, okay?"

She heard rustling, as if he was flipping through the pages of a desk calendar. After a long pause, he said, "I'm very sorry. I simply can't commit right now.

But if my schedule changes, you'll be the first to know."

She stiffened at the way he turned her words around on her. Landon could be prickly, but he wasn't usually rude. A sudden thought came to her with the force of a gut punch. "Did someone get to you?"

"I … what?" he stammered.

"If Ron Botta or the new law firm he hired approached you, it's witness tampering, it's improper, and I need to know."

"I assure you I haven't spoken to Mr. Botta or any other lawyers about this case, and I take exception to the suggestion that I would."

"I'm not accusing you of anything, Landon. There seems to be a campaign afoot to pressure me to get my clients to settle. If you haven't been contacted, you may be yet. I need you to let me know right away if that happens."

"I will," he promised.

"So if you haven't been talking to defense counsel, do you mind telling me why you're suddenly so unco-operative?"

"I'm busy. That's all. I have a business transaction that's about to close. Once it does, my schedule should free up, and then I'll get in touch. You have my word."

She ended the call because she wasn't getting anywhere. After they exchanged goodbyes, she replayed the conversation in her mind, searching it for holes and weak spots. One thing was clear: Landon Lewis was lying to her.

22

Maisy sat motionless in front of her computer, the forwarded email still unread. She stared at the screen unblinkingly.

This is stupid, you've been staring at this thing for nearly an hour, she told herself. *Either read it or trash it. But don't just sit here like a statue.*

She'd delete it. She never should have given into the temptation to forward it to herself in the first place. But she could still make things right. Just delete the thing. That's what she'd do. She thought the words, but her hand apparently didn't get the message as it didn't reach for the mouse.

A moment later, there was a quick, loud rap at her door. "Knock, knock," Preston called as he eased the door open.

Maisy scrambled to close her email program and pulled up the weather.

"Who's there?" she sang out as she swung around to smile at Preston. She made a mental note to rearrange her tiny office so that her monitor didn't face the door.

He looked at her blankly.

"You can't initiate a knock-knock joke and not follow through," she told him.

He pursed his lips and thought. "Uh, okay. Let's start over. Knock knock."

"Who's there?"

"Tip line."

"Tip line who?"

He dropped a piece of paper from his hand. It fluttered down to her desk. "Tip line has two alien sightings and one Elvis sighting. Are you regretting your choices yet?"

Maisy gave him an unamused look. "Come on."

He blinked innocently. "We had a deal. You said if I promised you the next tip to come in, you'd stop agitating for a meeting. I upheld my end. More than upheld. I'm giving you three tips."

She narrowed her eyes, grabbed the page, and rolled it into a ball. She tossed it over her shoulder and into the recycling bin without looking.

"Nice shot."

"Thanks. Now go away. I'm working." She smiled sweetly and pointed to the door.

"But we're square now, right?"

"Preston."

"Maisy."

"I'm not chasing down alien life forms or sad aging

mechanics who bear a passing resemblance to Elvis circa the peanut butter and bacon sandwich years."

"That's awfully specific."

"Eduardo Garcia from Greenfield. He spots Elvis every time he gets his oil changed. I mean, he's not wrong about the likeness, but that mechanic can't carry a tune in a bucket."

Preston was cackling. "You've chased that tip before?"

"A million years ago, when I was a bright-eyed weekend weather girl looking for a break. Probably younger than Summer. But like I said, that was a million years ago. Now I'm a grizzled veteran with a turkey neck."

"The turkey neck line was out of line, and I apologize."

She raised both eyebrows. "Apology necessary and accepted."

"Will you please just play nice? New owners, Maisy. New owners. They weren't amused by your stunt yesterday."

"By stunt, do you mean my adherence to the station's articulated best practices regarding independent sourcing and unbiased reporting?"

"Gah, Maisy, *I* don't mean anything, okay? I'm delivering a message from our shared corporate overlords."

She smiled her most saccharine smile. "Be a doll and deliver this message for me, will you? I want to talk to corporate about renegotiating my contract. I'll be bringing my lawyer."

"Uh-uh, Maisy, I don't think I like where this is going."

She waggled her fingers at him. "Bye-bye, sugar. Now, go get me my meeting."

"Be careful what you wish for," he warned.

She just stared levelly until he shook his head and left the office, closing the door behind him with enough force to rattle the pictures on the wall.

"Temper, temper," she called.

Out in the hall, he grumbled something she chose not to bother deciphering.

She put Preston and management out of her mind, took another deep, deep breath, and eyed her computer. Preston's visit had clarified her thinking about the email that sat in her in-box like an undetonated grenade. He hadn't been wrong last night when he'd insisted the tip line was garbage. Most of the tips that came into the tip box were worthless except for their comedic value.

A lot of Maisy's past investigative work had stemmed from her own contacts—cases that Sasha or Bodhi or another friend had told her about. The rest had been tips sent directly to her, not routed through the tip line. Those emails had been the seeds of two of her most-watched exposés: her recent series about the compounding pharmacy that cut corners by using expired ingredients and mailing the prescriptions out without the requisite temperature control measures and a piece she'd done a few years ago about corruption at the Consumer Protection Safety Commission.

Personal contacts were the gold standard. The tip

line was a flipping joke. And emails directed to a specific reporter fell somewhere in the middle. They required a bit more thought than the junk mail that came into the tip line. For one thing, the sender chose to contact that reporter for some reason. She clicked on her email program and reread the subject line: **Milltown DA Settlement Funding Scandal?**

She told herself the email had come to Summer, not her, because the rookie had just talked about the case during her memorable on-air meltdown. But wasn't she, an experienced journalist who also happened to know plaintiffs' counsel, better qualified to assess the tip?

Maybe you can't be unbiased.

It was a valid concern. Sasha was one of her best friends. In the past, she'd covered some of Sasha's escapades, but, in some cases, Preston determined she had a conflict of interest. And at least once—when Sasha had nearly died after a stabbing—she'd begged off covering the story because it was too emotional.

She could sit here and argue with herself all afternoon. But for all she knew, this tip was complete rubbish. Why not read the blessed thing before she tied herself into knots about it? Yes, that was the way to go. Just read it.

She clicked on the subject line and opened the message:

————— Forwarded message—————-

From: seissez@burnermail.com
  To: summer.reed@wacb.com
  Date: July 27, 2022
  The Milltown District Attorney is desperate to settle the civil rights litigation pending before Judge Cook. After months of stonewalling and insisting that the claims were trash, Ron Botta offered a multimillion-dollar settlement. The District Attorney doesn't have that kind of money. I know where he's getting it. Would you like to know, too?

Yes. Yes, she would.

She studied the email again, wrestling her conscience into submission. The barebones email was short on details, but what it did say squared with everything Sasha had told her. And if the writer knew where Botta was getting the money, that was news.

Really, she'd be doing Sasha a favor if she dug into this story. Hadn't Sasha said one of the holdups with the settlement was the fact that they didn't know where the money was coming from? If Maisy's reporting broke a story that shined a light on the funding source, that could only help Sasha's clients.

Maisy's justifications felt thin and flimsy, even to

her. But she wasn't about to let Summer Reed or some other twenty-something do real investigative work while she listened to a mechanic croon "Blue Suede Shoes" into a socket wrench microphone. Sasha would understand.

She typed in a brief reply, carefully skirting the issue of how an email addressed to Summer came to her attention:

Ms. Reed isn't able to investigate this matter at this time. *(True, as far as it went. Preston wouldn't let Summer touch anything juicier than a long line at the zoo for at least a month.)* Your message has been forwarded to me. *(Also technically true.)* I'd like to meet to discuss this in more detail and learn the identity of the party funding the settlement. If you have any proof that would establish identity, I would love to see that, too. I will, of course, agree to speak to you on background and without attribution. Please let me know if you're willing to meet with me, and when it would be convenient for you to do so.

```
        Many thanks,
        Maisy Farley
```

Maisy read over her response, ignored the misgivings that manifested as a swarm of butterflies in her stomach, and hit send.

23

L eo had just enough time to go for a jog before he picked the twins up from slime camp. He traded his golf shirt and khaki shorts—or his dad uniform, as Sasha liked to call it—for a worn t-shirt and a pair of gym shorts. He laced up his shoes and let himself out of the house through the kitchen. He jogged through the backyard and vaulted one-handed over the fence rather than use the gate.

As he rounded the corner to exit the alley, he had a choice to make: he could head uphill and run toward either Squirrel Hill or Oakland or keep it relatively flat and loop through the neighborhood. If he followed the flat route, he could duck into the grocery store and pick up dinner before he had to get the kids. That factor decided it for him. While Leo wasn't afraid of a cardio challenge, he was a fan of efficiency. Picking up groceries won out over getting his heart rate up. He'd make up for the terrain by increasing his pace.

He ran up Negley Avenue to Center Avenue at a

moderate pace, stretching his legs and warming up his muscles. When he hit Center, he poured on the speed. The hot afternoon air was heavy with humidity and the smell of gasoline and diesel from the passing cars and buses. He filled his lungs with it anyway and sprinted. He ran past the upscale organic market and, then a few blocks later, its scrappy lower-cost competitor. When he reversed his route, he'd try to do the bulk of dinner shopping at Trader Joe's and pick up the finishing touches from the Whole Foods Market. He made a note to get two bouquets of flowers—one for his night in with his wife; the other for Valentina. His mother-in-law had readily agreed to have the kids for a sleepover even though Pat was out of town fishing with Ryan.

He glanced at his stopwatch. He was pleased with his pace, and he still had a bit left in his tank, so he looped through Bakery Square. He passed by the storefronts, cafes, and offices without issue. But as he ran behind the big gym where Maisy took that cycling class she was always trying to talk the rest of them into, he stumbled. His heart skipped a beat. He threw his arms out just in time to wrap his hand around an iron fence and caught himself before he fell.

He frowned and scoured the ground behind him, looking for broken concrete or a piece of trash—some explanation for why he'd lost his footing. He saw nothing. He pushed off from the fence and glanced ahead and saw the warehouse. That's when it hit him. His heart hadn't skipped because he tripped. He tripped because his heart had palpitated. His body knew where he was, even before his brain had registered the fact:

this was the facility behind the PPC office space where Landon Lewis had run his off-the-books prison, where he'd held Sasha captive. His heart rate spiked again.

He leaned against the black iron fence and wrestled with his reaction. It had been nearly three years since he'd found Sasha's car abandoned on the side of the road, her scarf dangling in a tree, and blood spattered on the ground. It was the worst experience of his life— and to be clear, it had a lot of worthy competitors. But nothing had ever knocked him off-balance the way that scene had. The blood on the road, the car, the scarf turned up in his nightmares time and again. The crushing feeling that she was gone, really gone, hit him in the chest all over again. He gripped the iron spears that topped the fence and pushed back against the feeling.

She isn't lost. She's safe. She's at work.

He repeated the three short sentences over and over until they finally penetrated the noise in his mind.

LANDON PACED BACK and forth across the bamboo floor of his airy office. He couldn't seem to settle his nerves. If anything, his anxiety was only growing. The call with Brian Rosen had been unsettling. The follow-up call with Leith Delone had left him horrified. And the call with Sasha was the chef's kiss of misery. She could tell he was lying. He knew she could.

A mere two days ago, Landon had been unable to believe his good fortune. A literal fortune had fallen into his lap. And now, the money felt like a weight on his chest, pressing him down. He was certain he'd never before felt so out of control and helpless—at least not since the days just after Josh's murder when the world was dark and grim. Even then, though, there was an order to events.

Identify Josh's body. Meet with the police. Pick out a casket. Clean out Josh's apartment.

Now, all Landon could do was worry. Worry and wait for the other shoe to drop. Would Sasha's clients settle? Would Leith Delone destroy the concept of privacy and use Landon's life's work to monetize a new surveillance state? Would Cesare's ability to predict criminal behavior improve once it was hooked into Delone's neural network or would it only grow more biased as it grew more powerful?

He was going to drive himself mad worrying and wondering. He stopped pacing and pressed his head against the cool glass of the window that overlooked the parking lot and the warehouse behind it. When the PPC program had moved into the space, the broker had been surprised to learn Landon chose an office in the back of the building for himself rather than the large corner office with a view of the bustling retail square, the al fresco diners on the restaurant patios, and the backyard games, concerts, and other events that popped up on the lawn.

Bella, the real estate broker, had glanced out the very window where Landon was now resting his head and wrinkled her nose at the eyesore of the warehouse. Of course, it was the warehouse that Landon most cared about. In particular, the dank, cold subterranean spaces where he retrofitted cages and interrogation rooms to support Cesare's efforts to root out and destroy crime.

And now, the PPC itself had been destroyed and Cesare was basically being dismantled for its parts. He snorted at the poetic justice of it all and raised his head from the pane of glass.

As he lifted his head, his gaze fell on a hulking figure. A large man stood in the alleyway between the office and the parking lot. His upper arm muscles bulged as he gripped the bars of the coated cast-iron fence. Landon watched transfixed, half-expecting the man to bend the metal like a movie superhero. Instead, he threw his head back, eyes toward the sky, an expression of anguish and rage splashed across his face.

Landon began to shake when he recognized the man in the alley. He would know him anywhere. Leo Connelly was staring up at his office like the angel of death. Had Sasha sent him? What was he planning? What did he know?

Before he could question the wisdom of his decision, Landon ran out of his office and careened down the stairs, bursting through the metal fire door and out into the alley. As the door swung closed with a clang, Leo Connelly turned in the direction of the sound and locked eyes with Landon.

Landon swallowed with some difficulty and forced his legs to begin to move. He approached Leo slowly, cautiously, as one might approach a rabid beast. Leo stared unblinkingly at Landon as he closed the distance and came to stand in front of him at the fence.

"Leo?" he croaked.

~

LEO STARED AT LANDON LEWIS. He'd crashed through the fire door as if he'd been chased. In fact, for a moment, Leo had watched the door, waiting to see a pursuer emerge. But if Landon was being chased, it was by a ghost. And judging from the man's expression, Leo thought that might be a possibility.

He looked terrified. His eyes were wide, his pupils were dilated, and his mouth was twisted into a rictus of fear. He shook as he lurched toward Leo, then rasped out Leo's name.

Leo tucked his pain and anger away in an instant and his instincts kicked in. It was clear Landon was in distress, if not danger. He scanned the alley for anything out of place. Saw no threat. He glanced up at the building Landon had emerged from and scanned the windows for activity. No shadowy figures. No licking flames of fire. So he turned his attention back to the man in front of him and searched for wounds or other injuries.

"What is it, Landon? Are you hurt?"

"Are you here for me?" Landon answered his question with one of his own.

"What? No. I was out for a run. Are you sick?"

He could be drugged, Leo thought. His behavior was erratic enough that Leo would believe it.

"I didn't know. I couldn't have known."

"Okay," Leo said in a calm and even voice. "You didn't know."

He kept his gaze pinned on the man in front of him through superhuman effort. His new operating theory was that Landon had hurt—or killed—someone in the building. That would explain his affect.

"I swear I didn't."

"Did you hurt someone, Landon?"

"I didn't mean to. You have to believe me," Landon begged.

Leo mentally cursed himself for ending up in an alley, unarmed, facing down an unhinged, desperate man. He could, if he had to, overpower Landon. But adrenaline was an unpredictable beast, and if the hormone was surging through Landon's body right now, Leo might not be able to bring him down without hurting him.

"Is the person inside?"

Landon whipped his head toward the office building, then back around to gape at Leo. "Who?"

"The person you hurt."

"No, it's everyone. I hurt everyone." He dropped to his knees, gravel digging through the fabric of his navy blue suit pants.

Drugs, Leo decided. Definitely drugs. He stole a glance at his watch. He didn't have time for this. But he couldn't very well walk away and leave the man in this condition. He sighed and crouched beside Landon, resting his elbows on his thighs.

"Is there someone I can call for you?"

Landon shook his head. "No."

Leo rocked back on his heels, thinking. Landon wasn't in quite bad enough shape to justify a psych hold. But it was close.

Landon gripped Leo's forearm. "What you can do for me is tell Sasha I'm sorry."

Leo searched his face. "For?"

"Everything."

They could go around like this for hours. Leo had to make a decision and act. "Landon, listen. I'm not sure what's going on with you. I'll be honest. It seems like you need some help. And I don't know if it's safe to leave you alone or what. So can you talk to me so we can work through this together?"

The request seemed to spur Landon to pull himself together. He released Leo's arm, staggered to his feet, and brushed the dirt off his pant legs. He tucked his shirt back in and smoothed his tie.

"I'm fine. You just caught me at a low moment. I saw you through the window and I panicked. I thought you were here for me."

While the explanation didn't make perfect sense, it was the most coherent Landon had been during their exchange. So Leo was encouraged.

"You'll be okay if I leave you here? You're sure?"

"Positive. Things are really trending up for me, in fact. I guess a man has to hit the bottom before he can soar to new heights."

"Uh, yeah. I guess."

Leo stuck his hand out and Landon shook it limply.

"Take care, Agent Connelly."

"You, too, Landon."

Leo held his gaze for a long moment. Landon looked back impassively, like a man who had found sudden peace. Leo turned and began to jog away, toward the intersection of the alley and the square.

"Don't forget to give Sasha my message!" Landon shouted.

Leo raised one hand and waved to let him know he'd heard, but he didn't turn around. If he skipped the grocery store and ran his fastest mile ever, he just might make it to camp before Finn and Fiona started racking up the dollar a minute late charges (times two), charged in minimum ten-minute increments. Apparently, lawyers had nothing on camp directors when it came to billing by the minute.

He hit the square and started sprinting.

24

Sasha crouched in the hallway of her parents' home with Finn and Fiona on either side of her.

"I love you. Be good for Grandma Val, and have fun. Daddy or I will pick you up early tomorrow morning for slime camp."

They both threw their arms around her neck to hug her, pulling her backward in the process. She landed on the tile with a laugh and tugged them onto her lap. They both still fit, mostly.

"Slime camp?" Her mother turned to Connelly and uttered the words with horror that may have been mock, but may not have.

Sasha delivered two kisses to two freshly shampooed heads and raised her arm over her head.

"A little help?"

Connelly pulled her to her feet, then handed Finn and Fiona their backpacks (his orange, hers red) and repeated the goodbye hugs and kisses.

"Slime camp is ..." Sasha began to explain to her

mother, then thought better of it. "You know what? I'll let the kids tell you."

Connelly rose to his feet. "They've had dinner and baths."

Sasha's mom turned toward the twins. "I hope you haven't had dessert yet. I thought we could bake brownies together. And you can tell me all about this slimy camp of yours."

"No, Grandma! Camp isn't slimy. Eww!" Finn roared with laughter while Fiona raced into the kitchen to claim the baking stool before he had a chance.

"That one, always playing an angle." Sasha jutted her chin toward the kitchen, where Fiona stood with her feet planted on the stool, washing her hands at the kitchen sink.

Valentina raised a silver eyebrow, and Sasha could hear her thoughts as clearly as if she'd articulated them. *Wonder where she got that?*

Sasha pursed her lips. *Her father.*

"If you two are done pretending you're in a silent film, we should get going." Leo leaned in for Valentina's doubled-cheeked kiss.

"See you in the morning, Mom." Sasha gave her a hug.

Then Finn tugged at the hem of his grandmother's blouse, and the pair walked off to the kitchen hand-in-hand.

Sasha grabbed Connelly's hand and they walked out of the house together. He stopped on the porch and looked back at the front door. "Your mom locks her door at night, right?"

"Of course. Why?"

He shook his head. "Just something weird happened today."

"Well, you can tell me all about it over dinner."

"Right. Dinner. I'd planned to stop at the grocery store after my run but I didn't have time. I barely made it to pick-up before the meter started ticking." He mimed wiping sweat off his brow.

She laughed at his dramatic retelling of camp pick-up, but the race against the clock was real.

"So, you get to choose the restaurant," he told her as they walked to the car

"Or we could grab takeout. It sounds like you had a hectic day."

"Thai?"

She grinned. Thai takeout had a special place in their hearts. There was some debate over whether the first time they'd had it together *truly* counted as an official first date seeing as how they'd eaten their food standing up while keeping an eye on the contract killer tied to Sasha's favorite reading chair. Regardless, they both enjoyed a good curry.

"I'll call and order. You drive." She tossed him the keys and pulled out her cell phone.

"Place the order and then put that thing on airplane mode for the rest of our date night," he said as he slid into the driver's seat. "I'm watching you."

"You know I can't do that. My mom might need something. But I promise, no work calls."

"Cross your heart?"

"Cross my heart. I finally got in touch with Lewis today, and the guys want some more time to discuss the settlement, so unless Prescott & Talbott pokes its gruesome head up, tonight should be quiet on the work front."

"Lewis? Landon Lewis?"

She side-eyed him. She'd expected a reaction from him when she mentioned Prescott & Talbott, but the urgency in his voice with regard to Landon was off the charts. "Yes, Landon Lewis. Are you okay?"

He sped through a yellow light then pulled over to the side of the street right in front of a Greek Orthodox Church and parked. He twisted in his seat to look at her.

"When did you speak to him?"

"I don't know. Connelly, you can't park here."

He shook his head. "Please, focus. What time was it when you talked to Landon Lewis?"

She let out a big whoosh of breath that ruffled her hair and scrolled through her phone log. "I placed the call at two-thirty on the dot. Happy? Can I call in our order now?"

She looked up. No, the expression on his face was not one of happiness.

"Connelly, what's going on?"

"I'm not sure. I did some work in the morning, and then after lunch I re-oiled all the deck furniture."

"Why? Had you already reorganized your sock drawer?"

He shook his head. "Sasha, you have to oil it twice a year or it peels and fades."

"Some people pay a lot of money for that weathered look. We can get it for free."

"Sometimes I'm not sure if you're joking. Anyway, I still had some time to kill, so I figured I could go for a run, swing by the store, then get the kids from camp."

"You went for a midday run in the middle of July? No wonder you barely made it to pick-up."

"That's not why. I ran through Bakery Square and I stopped in the alley behind PPC."

Although his expression was neutral, she heard the tightness in his voice. He thought she didn't know about his nightmares, but she did.

"That was a long time ago. And everything turned out fine. Better than fine, really. Landon's going to be my star witness if this case goes to trial," she said brightly.

"Yeah, right. Everything turned out fine." His voice was thick with emotion. He paused, cleared his throat, then said, "I was standing in the alley, thinking about everything that happened, and out of nowhere, Landon comes running out of the building."

She blinked. "Really?"

"Yes, really. It was wild. At first, I thought someone was chasing him. He was so freaked out. Then he asked if I was there for him. He was wild-eyed, paranoid."

"Like he was on drugs?"

"The thought crossed my mind. He said he hadn't meant to hurt anyone. I thought maybe he, you know, hurt somebody inside the building, but he said no. He was barely coherent. But he kept begging me to tell you that he was sorry. That he didn't mean for it to happen."

"Didn't mean for what to happen?"

He shook his head. "I don't know. I checked my watch and saw that it was ten after three. Twenty minutes until pick-up. I needed to go. I asked if he wanted me to call anyone to stay with him or if he needed medical help or anything. That's when it got really weird. He said things were going to turn around for him soon. And then the last thing he said to me was to make sure I told you he was sorry."

They sat in heavy silence for a long moment. Sasha rubbed her arms in a failed attempt to get rid of the goosebumps rising on her flesh.

"He said he was sorry?"

"Yeah. Any idea what that was all about?"

She thought. "Maybe. He's been dodging Jordana all week. She's been trying to set up a witness prep session, and he won't call her back. So I blocked caller ID on my phone and called him myself. He might have been sorry because he knew it was a jerk move to ignore her."

"Well played with the caller ID. But, I don't know, this seemed more serious than failing to return a phone call."

She bobbed her head from side to side. "He did also refuse to give me a time to meet."

"What do you mean?"

"He answered my call because he didn't know it was me. But he wouldn't agree to set up a time. He wanted to know if the case might settle and said he was too busy with a business transaction to meet with me. To tell you the truth, I wondered if Botta didn't get to him and tell him to stiff-arm me."

"That might be what he's sorry about," Connelly mused.

"Maybe. I'll tell you this much. He was lying about not having time to meet me. It was obvious."

"Hmm. Do you think—"

Whatever he was about to say was lost to the sound of a beat cop rapping his nightstick on Sasha's window. She yelped and jumped. Out of the corner of her eye, she was gratified to see Connelly flinch, too. He buzzed down her window and leaned across the seat. Hot, steamy air poured into the car.

"Hi, there, officer," he said.

The patrolman arced his flashlight's beam over them. Sasha squinted at the onslaught of light and tried not to laugh.

"Uh…" the officer began.

He'd clearly expected to find a half-naked pair of undergrads from Pitt or Carnegie Mellon making out. Instead, he'd stumbled on a middle-aged married couple deep in conversation.

Connelly smiled. "We just dropped the kids off at her parents. Twins. You know how it is. Haven't been able to hear ourselves think for about eight years. Just pulled over to enjoy a quiet moment."

"Well, uh, you can't park here. The church doesn't like it."

"Sure. We'll be on our way."

Connelly started to buzz the window back up, but the officer stuck his baton in the window to stop it. Sasha's heart ticked up a beat. Connelly put his hand over hers and squeezed.

"Is there a problem, officer?" he asked levelly.

"I got a kid. Only one. But he makes enough noise for a barrel full. My sister takes him Tuesday nights, sleepovers with his cousins. My wife and I, we found a little Asian restaurant right around the corner from here. During the week it isn't overrun with college kids. Quiet."

"It sounds great," Sasha told him. "Is it a Thai place, by chance?"

He shook his head. "Chinese."

Sasha and Connelly shrugged at one another. "Chinese might be a nice change of pace," she said.

"Thanks, officer," Connelly waved.

The officer withdrew his stick and Connelly hit the window button just as the radio on the officer's belt crackled to life with "all units in the vicinity" and a voice spouted a series of meaningless numbers and letters followed by a street address that made Sasha's goosebumps get goosebumps.

Connelly depressed the button and the window stopped three-fourths of the way. The officer thumbed a button and said he was en route, then waved goodbye to Connelly and Sasha in a distracted manner.

Connelly rolled the window back up.

"I know that address," she said.

He nodded.

"But I don't know what the codes mean."

He didn't respond.

"Connelly."

He exhaled through his nose. "Suspected suicide. Subject dead on the scene. Proceed without sirens."

She flicked her eyes toward him. "That's Landon's address. Well, the address of the office building where the PPC used to be headquartered, at least."

"He was there today."

They stared at one another in speechless dread.

Finally, she said, "Well, we both know we're going there, so let's go."

"Worst date night ever," he mumbled as he shifted the car into drive.

"Remains to be seen," she told him. "There are some strong contenders." And then, because there were only two choices, and crying sucked, she started to laugh.

After a moment, Connelly joined in.

25

They got as far as the parking garage for the big box store with the bull's eye logo before the black and whites detoured them away from the square. Rather than argue, Leo parked on the ground floor of the garage. Before he could tuck the parking ticket in his wallet, Sasha plucked it out of his hand and raced into the store.

She emerged three minutes later with a to-go coffee for herself and a sprinkle-covered cake pop for him. She proffered the stick, and he took the gooey treat.

"Thanks, I guess."

"It's birthday cake flavor," she told him.

"Birthday cake isn't a flavor."

"Beggars, choosers."

They jay-walked across the traffic circle, out of view of the traffic control police and cut across a parking lot on a diagonal, headed for the alley behind Landon's office.

"Bet those shoes are easier to walk in," Leo observed,

pointing at the reasonable heels she was wearing in lieu of her usual four-inch spikes.

She pulled a face and didn't respond. After a beat, she said, "Is there something wrong with us?"

"Such as?"

"Such as, are we dead inside? We're on our way to an active crime scene, which is almost certainly going to be the suicide of a person we both interacted with just hours ago. And I'm drinking this frankly terrible over-priced coffee and you're critiquing your cake pop. Are we broken?"

He turned to face her. He'd planned to say of course not, but what came out was, "I hope not."

"Very comforting, Connelly. I hope not, too."

He scrubbed his hand over his chin, the stubble from his five o'clock shadow tickling his palm. "What I mean is, I think we're coping in the healthiest way we can with what is inarguably a life full of darkness and evil."

"Oh yeah, that's better. Much better. You should stop talking," she told him.

He flung out his arm to stop her from walking forward and pressed his lips to her ear, "We both should." He pointed ahead and then to the right.

She nodded. She saw them, too. Four police officers forming a cordon as they lounged against sawhorses set up in the alley. She chugged what was left of her coffee, then chucked the empty cup into a recycling bin as they hurried past the roadblock.

They crept low and ran to the right to circle behind the warehouse that had housed Landon's shop of horrors. They pressed themselves against the side of the building and shimmied forward until they reached the front. Leo craned his neck around the corner of the warehouse and scanned the parking lot in front of the warehouse. The wide gates had been opened, and a police officer stood beside them, her patrol car parked off to the side.

"It looks like they're going to use this lot as a staging area," he whispered.

Her eyes were luminous in the fading light. She searched his face. "What's the plan here?"

"I'm thinking we go with the truth."

"The truth?"

"Not the whole truth, obviously. Just follow my lead." Even as he said the words, he wondered if she was constitutionally capable of doing such a thing.

She nodded. "Okay, let's do it."

He grabbed her hand and stepped out from the shadows. They strode across the lot, straight toward the police officer guarding the gate.

"Officer," Leo called while they were still a good distance away.

She turned and surveyed the parking lot. When she spotted them, she clicked on her flashlight.

"Stop and turn back now. This is an active crime scene."

Leo stopped walking, and Sasha followed his lead for once, stopping alongside him. He estimated they were fifty feet away from the officer.

He called back to the officer. "I'm a federal agent. I'm going to reach inside my pocket for my identification, okay?"

"Slowly," she instructed him.

He used a slow, exaggerated movement to remove his wallet from the pocket of his linen pants. He flipped to the card holder, which displayed a photo ID listing him as a member of the HRS Strike Unit. It was a real government identification card for a wholly fictional entity. There was no HRS Strike Unit. He and his boss, Hank Richardson, had fabricated it for those awkward situations in which a federal agent working for a secret shadow agency didn't feel like going round and round with local law enforcement.

Sasha stood on her tiptoes and peeked at the card.

"Did you get that in a cereal box?" she whispered.

He hid his smile and stretched out his arm toward the police officer. "I'm Agent Leo Connelly, with the HRS Strike Unit. Okay to approach?"

She shifted her gaze to Sasha. He watched the beat cop assess his wife: not quite five feet tall, wearing a tailored dress and a light pink sweater, her hair twisted up in some elaborate knot. Then he watched her dramatically miscalculate as she dismissed Sasha as harmless.

"Who's your friend?"

"This is my wife, Sasha. We were just out for a walk and saw the commotion. I have a contact who works in this building. Thought I'd stop and make sure he's okay."

She waved for them to move forward. He gripped Sasha's hand in his and held the ID out in the other as they closed the distance between them and the officer. When they drew close enough, she held her hand out and he gave her the wallet. She trained her flashlight on the ID card, studied it for a few seconds, then passed it back to him.

"Well, Agent Connelly, this appears to be a suicide." She jerked her thumb over her shoulder and aimed it at the alleyway. "A jumper. It's messy."

His stomach tightened. Beside him, Sasha drew in a sharp breath.

"My contact who has an office here was involved in an investigation with DHS and DOJ not too long ago," he told the police officer. The statement had the benefit of being true. "Any identification on the body?"

"No, but the window he jumped from is in the offices of something called The Joshua Group. Maybe his name's Joshua. We're trying to get in touch with the landlord now."

"Joshua was his son's name," Sasha said in a quiet voice.

"Could you repeat that?" The officer leaned forward to hear her.

"The Joshua Group is a single-party LLC owned by Landon Lewis. It was named for his son."

The cop took another, longer look at Sasha. "And you know this how?"

"I'm a lawyer. Mr. Lewis is—or was—a witness in a civil rights case pending in federal court."

Leo watched the police officer's posture stiffen and her face harden.

"That's quite a coincidence, you two each knowing someone in the building and just happening to stroll by."

"Pittsburgh. You know how it is. Everybody knows everybody." Leo flashed an easy smile.

"Huh." The officer seemed to be torn between telling them to beat it and using them to make her job easier.

Leo figured he'd give her a nudge. "I could probably ID the body if you'll let me see it. Or at least tell you if it's not Mr. Lewis. Save you some time."

"You know him well enough to do that?"

"Yes, ma'am."

She could either take the gift that fell in her lap or spend a long, hot night guarding an alley. After a beat, she gave a brisk nod. "Okay." She pointed at Sasha. "You stay right here. Trust me, you don't want to see what's left of this guy, and I don't want you wandering around an active scene. Got it?"

"Yes, officer," Sasha said dutifully.

A bit too dutifully for Leo's liking, but he couldn't say much in front of the patrolwoman. So he leveled Sasha with a gaze and thought it. *Seriously, just stay put.* She gave him a reassuring smile, which did nothing to reassure him.

He followed the cop through the open gate and down the alley. Large flood lights had been set up on both sides of the alley. They cast bright light on the ground and long shadows that danced on the walls of the buildings lining the narrow passage.

The alley was a hive of activity. They wove through the sea of people, and she stepped over a ribbon of crime scene tape that was attached to two sawhorses. He did the same. A cluster of men wearing blue law enforcement windbreakers despite the heat stared down at the ground.

"Coming through," the officer announced.

Two men in the circle lifted their heads and looked at her. She addressed the older one. "Bass, this is Agent Leo Connelly with the HRS Strike Unit. Says he might be able to ID the body."

Bass eyed Leo. "That so?"

"If it's who I think it is."

Bass gestured for the men to move aside. The circle parted, and Leo took a step forward.

He stared down at Landon Lewis' broken body and his chest tightened. It hadn't been five hours since Leo had asked him if he was sure he was okay. Now he was very much not okay.

He nodded to Bass. "That's Landon Lewis. He owned a business—the Joshua Group—that he operated from up there." He pointed up at the open window.

"What's your relationship to Mr. Lewis?"

"He was a player in an investigation a few years back."

"Do you happen to know how to reach his next of kin?"

Leo thought for a moment. "He was divorced. His only child predeceased him. I'm not sure who you'd contact. The ex-wife?"

"If she's all we have, then yeah. Do you have her contact info?"

Leo shook his head no.

"Maybe you can get it from, what's it called, Strike Force?"

"HRS Strike Unit. No, but my wife might at least have a name for her."

"Your wife?" Bass asked.

The patrol officer piped up. "She's a lawyer. She was working on a case with the dead guy."

"Go get her, Evans."

The officer hesitated. "Maybe we don't bring a civilian over here, sarge?"

"Fair point. See if she has a name."

Leo looked up at the open window again, then down at the man splattered all over the alley. "He landed like that, on his back?"

"We sure as heck didn't move him," Bass told him.

Leo nodded.

"Sir, you want to come with me to tell your wife?" Officer Evans asked.

"Okay, sure." He glanced up one last time and had to stifle a groan.

The profile of a small woman passed by the window in Landon's office. Her hair was twisted into an updo, and Leo would have bet his pension that she was wearing a light pink sweater and a pair of tiny heels.

"Sir?"

He turned away from the sight of his wife breaking into a crime scene. "Right, sorry."

He shook Sergeant Bass' outstretched hand, then joined the officer for the short walk back to the spot where they'd left Sasha with clear instructions to stay put, already shaking his head.

26

S asha spotted Connelly and the police officer leaving the group of people huddled around Landon's dead body and her heart rate ticked up a notch. They crossed the alley and headed back to the parking lot where they'd left her.

Crud. Couldn't he have bought her more time?

She circled the tidy office, snapping cell phone pictures as she went. She paused and looked down at the handwritten note on Landon's desk and took a closeup of the message. Then she used Landon's pewter letter opener to flip it over, photographed the back of it, then carefully returned it to its original position with the letter opener.

She slipped the slim knife-shaped opener into her dress pocket and hurried out of the office. She clattered down the steps, raced through the propped-open fire door, and ran across the alley with her head lowered. On her way into the building, she'd spotted the patrolman who'd told her and Leo to move along in front of the church. He hadn't noticed her, and she wanted to keep it that way.

She sprinted through the gate and toward Connelly and the police officer.

"I'm over here," she called.

Connelly turned and gave her a knowing look.

"Ma'am, I told you to stay put," the officer growled as Sasha came to a stop beside them.

"Sorry. I had to pee." She smiled sheepishly.

"Did one of those boneheads actually let you go into the building?"

"Oh, no. I used the bathroom in a bar across the street. So? Was it Landon?"

Connelly pursed his lips, then said, "I'm afraid so. Officer Evans was wondering if you knew his ex-wife's name."

She rolled her neck while she called up what little she knew about Landon Lewis' personal life. "I think her first name is Deanne, and she lives somewhere on the West Coast. Sorry I can't be more helpful."

Evans jotted it down in her small black notebook. "Did he have an assistant or any employees?"

"Uh, not that I know of. He shut down most of his active operations at the end of 2019." She flashed back to Landon's sparse office. "Maybe you can get his contacts from his cell phone? Oh, unless he had it on him when he … you know. In that case, it's probably smashed to pieces."

"There was no phone on his person," Evans replied.

"Maybe it's in his office," Connelly suggested.

Evans snapped her notebook closed and stowed it in

her shirt pocket. "I think that's all we need for now. Do either of you have a business card on you so Sergeant Bass can get in touch if we need to follow-up."

Connelly raised an eyebrow. Officer Evans' sergeant wouldn't get very far trying to call him at his nonexistent office.

Sasha reached into her purse and dug out a card. "Here. You can reach me at this number, and, of course, I can put you in touch with Leo if you need to speak with him."

The police officer tucked the card into her pocket. "Thanks. You folks go on and clear out now."

Sasha and Connelly walked in silence through the dark parking lot.

After they emerged from the bushes behind the empty warehouse and fell into step on the sidewalk, Connelly said, "Please tell me you didn't touch anything during your little breaking and entering adventure."

So he had seen her. She'd wondered.

"Only Landon's letter opener," she told him.

Connelly stopped short. "Sasha, you can't—"

"Relax." She pulled the thing out of her pocket. "I brought it with me."

"You stole that from a crime scene."

"Okay, first of all, is a suicide really a crime scene? Second of all, if I hadn't taken it, you'd be lecturing me right now about leaving fingerprints. So what did you want me to do?"

She knew as soon as she said the words that she'd regret them.

"I don't know, maybe stay put like Officer Evans instructed?"

She waved her hand, dismissing that idea. "Come on. They left the fire door propped open. They were basically *inviting* me to go inside."

He shook his head. "Please tell me the office door was also open."

"It was."

He narrowed his eyes and stared at her.

"It *was*. Scout's honor."

"We've established that you were never a Girl Scout, remember?" he asked as they resumed walking.

"It's a saying. I'm being truthful. There was an officer posted at the end of the hallway, but he was playing backgammon on his phone. He didn't see me. And I was only in there for a few minutes."

"Did you see anything out of the ordinary?"

"I don't know what Landon's office usually looks like, but nothing jumped out at me. It was very tidy, minimalist. His desk doesn't even have drawers to shove stuff into. There was a wireless cell phone charger on the desk, but no phone."

He frowned. "Evans said he didn't have it on him."

She shrugged. "I don't know. I guess it'll turn up." After a beat, she said, "There was one thing."

"What?"

She hesitated. "A note."

"A suicide note?"

"Kind of. I took pictures of it, front and back. That's why I needed the letter opener—to flip it over."

"Let me see the pictures."

"Not out here on the street. How about when we get home?"

"How about when we get to the car?"

She sighed. "Only if you promise you aren't going to blame yourself."

"Why would I blame myself?"

This time, she was the one who stopped walking. She reached for his arm. "Because I know you. You saw him just hours ago, and he was distraught and frantic. Remember, I talked to him thirty minutes before you ran into him. I thought he was lying and nervous, but I didn't think he was suicidal."

"I can't say I won't always wonder if I should have done something differently. But I made what I thought was the best decision at the time. Why? What does the note say?"

"In the car. I promise."

They trudged across the street, jaywalking with impunity because the block was still closed to traffic, and ducked into the parking garage. Once they reached the SUV, he popped the locks and held the passenger door open for her. He settled into the driver's seat and turned to her with an expectant expression. She pulled up her camera roll and found the two photos.

"This one. Then swipe left for the back." She put the phone in his palm and watched his face while he read Landon Lewis' final words, written in beautiful cursive on a thick linen notecard:

I have made mistakes in my life. Lord knows I have. But I have always tried to do the right thing. I didn't always succeed, but I tried. That's why I have to find a way to make amends for my recent errors of judgment.

It may be too late, but all I can do is try. It's better than being haunted by the unknown, better than always wondering if there was more I could have done.

Everything I did, I did in Josh's memory, as an effort to honor him. Please bear that in mind when you judge me.

He looked up. "It's sort of strange, isn't it? It's not addressed to anyone. It's not signed. It's pretty … nonspecific."

"Landon was a strange guy. I mean, I don't have a lot of experience in this area. Is there a convention these notes follow?"

"I don't know," he conceded. "But the tone of this note doesn't match the panic he exhibited this afternoon."

"Maybe once he'd decided what he was going to do, he felt … calmer."

"Maybe." He handed her phone back to her. "There was nothing else unusual in the office?"

She gave it right back. "Here, look for yourself. I took pictures of everything."

He scrolled through the photos once, then again, shaking his head. He stopped on the picture of the open window and pinched the screen to enlarge it.

"What? Do you see something?"

"How did he get that window open?"

She leaned over. "It looks like they're casement windows. The kind that swing in when you turn the little crank."

"In, not out, right?"

"Right." She wrinkled her brow. "Why?"

"It's just weird. He decides to jump. He writes this note, walks over to the window, cranks it open, then— what? He sits on the sill and pitches himself out backward?"

She blinked, surprised. "He was on his back?"

"Right."

"I'd have thought—" She cut herself off. "I don't know what he was thinking and neither do you."

"You're right." He nodded and placed her phone in the center console. "I know what I'm thinking."

"What's that?"

"I could use a drink."

She buckled her seatbelt. "Amen to that. And by the way? Yeah, definitely the worst date night ever."

27

Thursday morning

Cinco ran a finger along the railing as he descended the wide, curving marble staircase from the top floor of the building. He lifted his finger and discreetly checked for dust. None. Excellent. He usually used the elevators, but every so often he took great pleasure in standing at the top of the stairs and surveying his kingdom. And Cinco was feeling particularly powerful and regal on this fine morning.

He strolled along the hallway, stopped to greet Lettie, then knocked on Ellie's door.

"Come in," came her muffled reply.

He opened the door. "Good morning, Eleanor."

She glanced up blearily from a mound of papers that covered her desk and threatened to skitter off in all directions. She looked sallow and exhausted. A long blue smear crossed her chin and curved up her right cheek.

"Is that ink?" He gestured toward the line.

She yawned. "Probably. I put my head down a few times to rest. I'm sure I encountered a pen or two."

"Were you here all night?"

"Yes. Researching the modern judiciary's views of third-party litigation financing." She gestured to her printouts and a stack of treatises from the firm library.

"Forget about that for now. There's been a positive development in the case." He lifted a pile of notebooks from her guest chair and deposited them on the corner of her desk, then sat.

She blinked, waking up. "Are plaintiffs going to settle?"

"I haven't heard from Sasha yet, but I am certain I will."

"Why? What happened?"

"Her star witness is dead." He didn't attempt to hide his glee.

"Dad!" Ellie rebuked him, scandalized.

"What? It's not as if I personally killed the man, Eleanor. He committed suicide last night. Jumped right out his office window."

"That's horrible."

He rearranged his face, trying to achieve a more somber expression. "Indeed. But, Mr. Lewis' tragic demise might force Sasha's hand. They ought to accept the offer now."

"Mr. Lewis is dead? Landon Lewis?"

"Yes, I believe that's his name. Was he the gentleman who ran the short-lived Predictive and Preventive Crime pilot program with the Milltown Police?"

"That's him," she confirmed. "How did you hear about his suicide? Did it make the morning news?"

"I couldn't say. I didn't watch."

"Then how—?"

"Leith called to let me know." Cinco knew he sounded a bit like a schoolboy whose crush had finally noticed he was alive, but he didn't care. One of the most powerful people on the planet called to give him an update. He was the lord of this manor.

Ellie wrinkled her forehead. "How did he find out so fast? Isn't he in Switzerland or something?"

"Currently, he's in Argentina. And I don't know how he learned. I presume he has sources everywhere." He threw his arms wide and gestured.

"I guess." She stifled another yawn. "Does his death really change anything? The plaintiffs have his deposition testimony if they want to use it at trial."

"Of course it changes things," he snapped. "Reading a deposition transcript into the record is deathly dull and boring. Even at a bench trial, it lacks pizzazz. But in a jury trial, trust me, Sasha's going to want to have a warm body in the witness chair."

"Oh, okay. Then, uh, congrats. I guess."

"Indeed, congratulations are in order. You should go home and get some rest. You look awful."

She nodded sleepily. "Maybe I'll do that."

He stood to leave. "You'll see, Eleanor. Sasha McCandless-Connelly will have no choice but to advise her clients to settle."

∽

SASHA WAITED until Connelly left to retrieve the twins from their sleepover with grandma. Then she took a mug of fresh coffee and her laptop out to the back deck. She curled up in one of the freshly re-oiled Adirondack chairs and fired up her videoconferencing app. Three little boxes appeared on her screen. Soon the boxes were populated with images. First, she saw the mirror image of herself, sitting on her deck under the shade of a blooming magnolia tree. Next, Max materialized in his living room. She noted the lace doilies and needle-point throw pillows and surmised that he still hadn't gotten around to redecorating. Or perhaps, she allowed, he liked his late grandmother's style. Finally, Charlie and Sam appeared shoulder to shoulder at Charlie's kitchen table.

"The gang's all here," Max announced. "So, we can get started."

"Thanks for agreeing to this early morning video call. I wanted you to learn this from me before you hear it on the news."

"Oh, no. Now what?" Charlie asked, signing as he spoke.

"Landon Lewis died last night."

There was a long silence. Then, "Was he sick? Sam wants to know," Charlie added.

"I don't think he was ill, but I don't know for sure. He killed himself."

"Lewis?" Max exclaimed. "Nah."

"I saw his body myself. He jumped out his office window."

"God rest his soul," Max murmured.

Charlie shook his head. "Why would he do something like that? He was coming out of all this with a redemption arc—from villain to … not a villain. I mean, he wasn't exactly a hero, but he *was* helping us."

"He was," she agreed. "He left a note. It seems he was struggling with the mistakes he's made. I think he realized how much harm Cesare had done—and could have done if he'd continued on with the program."

They fell silent again. She sipped her coffee and gave them a moment to absorb the news. Then, "His death does change our case somewhat. We have his testimony preserved through deposition transcripts, but …"

"But he's not going to be testifying at trial unless we have a seance," Max said bluntly.

"Right. So, Landon's unavailability to testify is another piece of information you should take into consideration when you think about the settlement offer." She paused. "I don't want to pressure you. I know it's a big decision. But are you any closer to coming to a decision?"

Sam signed a response. Charlie nodded. "He said we all agree that twelve million dollars makes this feel like it should be a no-brainer, but—"

Max broke in, "We all feel like someone's trying to buy our silence. This big pile of money, it doesn't come with any kind of admission, right? Ron Botta doesn't have to say what they did?"

"That's right. The agreement explicitly states that the district attorney's office isn't admitting anything. And there's a clause that forbids any of you from giving any interviews or talking at all about the settlement terms."

"So they are trying to buy our silence," Charlie said.

Sasha lifted her shoulders. "That's one way of looking at it."

"Does Mr. Lewis' death really change anything, though? I mean, we all know if we go ahead with the trial, we're not ever winning twelve million dollars. But if we win at trial, we can say whatever we want about that trash prosecutor, right?" Max asked.

She laughed. "Well, not *anything*. You can't slander him. But, you're right, you wouldn't be constrained by a nondisclosure clause."

There was a meaningful pause. Then Charlie said, "I think we're close to deciding. We'll get back to you later today, okay?"

"Great. If any last-minute questions come up, let me know. Don't feel rushed."

"Understood."

Max signed off first, and Charlie hurriedly said, "You're coming tonight, right?"

"Wouldn't miss it," she promised.

She ended the video meeting and leaned back in the deck chair, listening to the birds and watching the bees pollinate her garden while she finished her coffee. After the events of last night, she needed a slow and peaceful start to her day.

28

Ellie didn't take her father's suggestion that she go home. But she did catch a catnap and a shower in the firm's gym. She returned to her desk with a fresh mug of tea and a brighter complexion. But she was still out of sorts.

She opened her burner email account. She didn't expect an immediate response, but her father's ghoulish glee over a man's death—by suicide, no less—made her so uneasy that she thought she'd check the account anyway. If only to distract her from her dad's macabre joy.

To her extreme surprise, there was one unread message in the inbox. She held her breath as she clicked on the response. She skimmed it quickly first, then read it a second time more slowly.

Summer hadn't responded. Maisy Farley had. That was an unexpected development. Summer Reed was nobody. Maisy Farley was a Pittsburgh institution. Ellie had grown up watching her on the news. And now Maisy wanted to meet to get more details and some sort of proof that she knew who was funding the multimillion-dollar settlement.

"Now what, genius?" she said aloud.

She'd known this was a mistake. As soon as she'd hit 'send' on the message, her stomach had flipped over. She shouldn't have done it. But, she couldn't exactly undo it.

It wasn't as if she'd done anything *illegal*. Improper, maybe. Was this the sort of thing that could get a lawyer a bar suspension?

She wasn't actually sure. They didn't teach this stuff in law school. If she had even one coworker whom she could count as a friend, she'd bounce the scenario off them. Problem was, she didn't. She was friendless in the office—friendless except for Lettie. For a moment she entertained the possibility of talking to Lettie, but that was unfair. She couldn't drag Lettie into her mess.

She tapped her finger on her lip and thought. She could call the ethics hotline, ask the faceless nameless lawyer on the other end of the line what she should do —what she could do. She could get anonymous legal advice. The idea was comforting and rebellious at the same time.

She inhaled deeply and reached for the phone. Before she could punch in the hotline number, there was a rap on her door. She dropped the phone back into its cradle.

"Come in," she called.

The door swung open. Lettie stood in the doorway. Her eyes were wide and her hair was disheveled. She seemed to be out of breath, panting slightly.

Ellie jumped up from her seat. "Lettie, what's wrong?"

"I filed the appearances for you and Mr. Prescott in the Botta matter yesterday."

"I know, thanks." She gave Lettie a confused look. "Was there something wrong with them?"

Lord, she hoped not. Her dad would chew her out mercilessly if the first papers they submitted to Judge Cook had contained a mistake.

"No, nothing like that. But Judge Cook's assistant Diane just called. The judge wants to see you and your dad in chambers in twenty minutes."

"Why?"

"Diane didn't know."

"Great. Just great," Ellie groaned.

"You haven't heard the worst part yet. Your dad's not here."

Ellie stared at her. "What do you mean he's not here? Of course he is. I saw him myself this morning."

Lettie shook her head. "Diane called his number first. Darcy explained that he was unavailable and Diane asked to be transferred to me."

"Where is he?"

"Your guess is as good as mine. Darcy said he came back from your office earlier today, packed up his stuff, and said he had to leave for the rest of the day. And he's not answering his cell phone."

Ellie sighed. "He probably went to the art museum. He does that sometimes. He never takes his phone inside a museum."

"Which museum? I'll send a runner to get him."

She pursed her lips. "Start at the Carnegie. If he's not there, try the Warhol. But, Lettie, that's going to take way more than twenty minutes."

"I know. You're going to have to go over to the courthouse alone."

"Me?" Ellie squeaked.

Lettie gave her an encouraging look. "Yes, you."

"But—"

"You dad was very clear with the Management Committee that nobody else is authorized to work on this matter. So you can't tap Kevin or Marcus to step in. And, frankly, it would just upset the judge. You're one of the two attorneys of record. You can do this, Ellie. Trust yourself."

Ellie bowed her head, placed her palms on her desk and took a very long, very deep breath to gather herself. Then she raised her eyes and met Lettie's gaze. "You're right. I can do this," she said in a strong voice.

Lettie smiled. "That's the spirit. Now get moving."

Sasha stared at Caroline in disbelief. "In twenty minutes?"

"That's what Diane said." Caroline raised her shoulders in a shrug.

"You reminded her that our offices are in Shadyside, right?"

"I did. But she seemed … unmoved."

"Of course she did. And Judge Cook didn't say what this is about? Not even a hint?"

"Not even a hint."

"Fan-freaking-tastic," Sasha muttered.

Caroline gave her a pained smile. "Maybe it's good news?"

Sasha pinned her with a look. "I appreciate the effort, but let's be real. It is *never* good news to be summoned by a federal court judge with no warning."

"I tried."

Sasha nodded. "I need to get going. Do me a favor, if any of the plaintiffs from the Botta case call, put them through to Naya or Will. If they aren't around, get Jordana on the phone. Just make sure they get to speak to a person, not voicemail."

Caroline nodded her understanding. "I imagine Mr. Lewis' death threw them for a loop."

"Not as much as you might think. They're a pretty stoic group."

Caroline's eyes shifted to her computer monitor and then back to Sasha. "So is this a good time or a bad time to tell you that there's an eight-minute construction delay on Bigelow Boulevard?"

"Tell me you're kidding."

In answer, Caroline swiveled her monitor around so Sasha could see the solid orange line snaking across the route map for herself.

"This day just keeps getting better."

She took the last swig of her coffee, abandoned her mug on the cart outside the kitchen, and ran through the office as fast as her kitten heels could carry her.

29

Sasha careened into a spot in the parking garage with six minutes to spare and raced to the courthouse's main entrance, taking the wide stairs two at a time. She pushed through the doors and skidded to a halt. A long line of people waiting to go through the metal detectors snaked across the lobby. She bobbed up and down on her toes to scan the crowd, looking for a friendly face, an attorney who owed her a favor, a kindly court watcher who would let her cut in line. She didn't see a likely candidate.

She did see one other person who appeared to be as desperate as she was. Tall, with blonde hair cut into layers, the woman was out of breath and wild-eyed, surveying the crowd in a panic. Judging by the conservative cut of her skirt and suit jacket she worked for one of the big firms. She was also very young.

The clock on the marble wall ticked off another minute. Five minutes left.

Sasha decided to take a flier. She darted out of the

line and hurried toward the armed marshal guarding the stairwell. As she rushed past the young attorney, she took her second gamble.

"Ellie? Eleanor Prescott?" she asked.

The woman whipped her head in Sasha's direction. "Sasha?"

"In the flesh. Is your dad already upstairs?"

"No. He's ... unavailable." Her voice shook.

Some things never changed. Back when Sasha'd worked at Prescott, Cinco had been famous for vanishing without explanation. But leaving a first year —not to mention his own daughter—to fend for herself with a pissed-off federal judge was next level, even for Cinco.

"Come with me," she ordered.

She took off toward the stairwell again without checking to see if Ellie was following her. She ran straight up to the large, serious-looking marshal.

"Ma'am, you two need to get back in line," he intoned without expression.

Ellie stopped short behind her, breathing hard.

Sasha smiled up at the marshal. "We have a problem, and we could really use your help."

His expression remained stony, but his eyes flicked from Sasha to Ellie and back. She could see him calculating and deciding they looked harmless enough. He raised an eyebrow.

Sasha took it as an invitation. "We're attorneys. Judge Cook has summoned us to his chambers with only twenty minutes notice. We got here as quickly as we could, but if we have to wait in the security line, we're going to be very late, and Judge Cook is going to be *very* angry."

"That sounds like your problem. Not mine," he told her flatly.

"It is our problem, definitely. But you could help us. You could pat us down and let us take the stairs. Please?"

She really didn't want to have to use Connelly's name. She would if she had to. But surely she could sweet talk this guy into letting them through.

"Sorry. No can do."

She sighed. Before she could play the Connelly card, Ellie piped up.

"Please. This is my first federal appearance. I don't want to start off on a bad foot with the judge." Her big eyes pleaded and her voice quavered.

The marshal scanned the lobby. Then he shook his head as if he couldn't believe what he was doing. "Okay. Fine. Open your bags."

Sasha glanced at Ellie in amazement for a beat, then yanked her bag open and held it up for the marshal to inspect. He glanced inside at the jumble of folders, goldfish crackers, and receipts she'd been meaning to file, then looked at her. "Do you have a cell phone on you?"

She pulled it from her dress pocket and held it out. "Do you need to take it?"

"No, just make sure you turn it off. Judge Cook will explode if it rings in his chambers."

She smiled. "Thanks for the tip."

He motioned for her to step forward and repeated the bag inspection and cell phone warning with Ellie.

Sasha kept her eyes locked on the clock. Two minutes to get up the stairs and into chambers.

He waved Ellie through.

"Thank you so much," she enthused.

"You're welcome. Good luck in your first appearance," he told her, cracking the faintest of smiles.

She beamed back at him.

He pushed the door open and they ran through the doorway into the stairwell.

"And Ma'am? Ms. McCandless-Connelly?"

Sasha wheeled around in surprise.

He laughed. "Yeah, I recognized you. Tell Leo that Lin Toland said hi."

"I will," she promised.

Then she and Ellie pounded up the stairs and burst out into the hallway outside Judge Cook's chambers. Sasha thought her heart might explode as she leaned on the buzzer and panted, "Sasha McCandless-Connelly and Eleanor Prescott are here."

They leaned against the wall, their chests heaving. A moment later, the door clicked open and Judge Cook's deputy clerk poked his head out into the hall.

"You're two minutes late."

Ellie gave Sasha an uncertain look. Sasha lowered her chin and stared at the deputy. "Brett, you've got to be kidding. We only got the call to get here twenty-two minutes ago. My office is in *Shadyside*."

Brett winked. "Just messing with ya. Come on in."

Sasha muttered under her breath as she passed by the deputy clerk with Eleanor on her heels.

"Touchy, touchy," Brett told her as they settled themselves on an overstuffed couch.

"It's been a long day," she explained.

"It's only two-thirty."

"I said what I said. Do you have any idea what this conference is about?"

Brett leaned over and whispered conspiratorially, "I haven't the foggiest. We'll all find out together, I guess."

"Oh, yay," Sasha deadpanned.

Ellie looked faintly green.

"Is she gonna be okay?" Brett asked Sasha, nodding toward the young attorney.

"First-time nerves."

"Where's her dad?"

"At one of the art museums, if I had to guess."

Ellie blinked in surprise.

Sasha laughed. "Yeah, he's been pulling that disappearing act since I was a first year."

"When dinosaurs roamed the earth," Brett chimed in.

Sasha was about to object to the characterization. But she saw the hint of a smile creasing Ellie's lips and let Brett's jab stand. It would be better for both of them if Ellie could get a handle on her nerves before they went into the judge's chambers. If pot-shots at Sasha helped the cause, then so be it.

Ellie turned to Sasha. "It's unusual for a meeting to just pop up like this, right? The judge will understand why my ... Mr. Prescott isn't here. Right?"

"He should understand. Federal judges never—ha,

never say never. Federal judges *rarely* schedule same-day conferences."

"I can't remember him ever doing something like this. Short of an emergency restraining order or something like that," Brett mused.

Ellie blanched.

Not helping, Sasha thought. It was clear the baby lawyer was quaking inside. For her part, she just wanted to get this over with so she could get back to the office and finish up for the day.

Diane emerged from the judge's inner chamber. "He's ready for them."

ELLIE TRAILED Sasha like a duckling across the reception area and through the ornately carved oak door that led to Judge Cook's private conference room. She gazed around the inner sanctum, taking in the highly polished conference table that dominated the book-lined room, the thick carpet that muffled their footsteps, and the clusters of silver-framed photographs that were crammed together on every side table, shelf, and other available horizontal surface. She noted with interest that while the Honorable Cliff Cook displayed loads of vacation photos, landscapes, family portraits, and a series of closeups of a droopy-eared basset hound, there were no stiffly posed photos of him with politicians, celebrities, or titans of industry. It was a striking contrast to the offices of most lawyers, and she hoped it said something about the jurist's temperament. Something comforting and warm, perhaps.

Judge Cook greeted Sasha, then eyed Ellie with curiosity.

"And you must be Ms. Prescott."

She suppressed the urge to curtsey and reminded herself that he wasn't royalty. "Yes, Your Honor."

Judge Cook looked at her expectantly. "Is Mr. Prescott planning to grace us with his presence?"

"Um, he was out of the office when your chambers called. If he's able to join us, I'm sure he will."

The judge held her gaze for an uncomfortably long moment. "Then I suppose we should get started. Take a seat, both of you." He turned to Brett. "Will you let the court reporter know we're ready for her?"

"You got it, Boss."

Brett slipped through a second door that Ellie hadn't noticed and returned with the court reporter in tow. The woman set up her equipment at the end of the table in an efficient, practiced motion. Sasha slid a business card along the gleaming table to the court reporter, so Ellie dug out a card of her own and sent it down the table.

The judge rested his forearms on the table and seemed to gather his thoughts before speaking. He looked first at Sasha, and then at Ellie, who had taken the seat next to her. She realized belatedly that she probably should've sat across from opposing counsel, rather than beside her. Her cheeks burned, but moving now would do nothing but draw attention to her glaringly obvious lack of experience.

"Counselors, thank you both for accommodating the court on short notice. I thought it important that we meet right away given the latest development in this case."

Sasha cleared her throat. "Your Honor, just so my understanding is clear, are you referencing Prescott & Talbott's substitution as counsel in place of Mr. Botta?"

"Ah, good point. I suppose the change in defense counsel is the most recent activity in the case, but I actually mean the untimely death of Landon Lewis."

Sasha blinked. "Oh, I see."

"His death does affect plaintiffs' case, doesn't it, Ms. McCandless-Connelly?" the judge pressed Sasha.

"To some extent, yes. As the court and defense counsel know, Mr. Lewis is—was—on our witness list. He planned to testify as to his understanding of the district attorney's use of the inevitable discovery exception and the circumstances in which he came to that understanding. While death is perhaps the ultimate unavailability, we do have his deposition testimony. So, if this case proceeds to trial, plaintiffs will rely on the transcript."

Ellie could see Sasha calculating and she suspected she knew what Sasha was thinking, because Ellie was thinking it, too: surely the judge hadn't hauled them in to ask one question that wasn't even time-sensitive.

The judge nodded. "And I presume Ms. Prescott doesn't intend to object to the use of the deposition transcript."

Ellie stared at him, her mind a complete blank.

Should she object? *Could* she? On what grounds? As she was formulating a response, Sasha spoke.

"Your Honor, if I may? While Prescott & Talbott was obviously not present at Mr. Lewis' deposition, original counsel in this matter did attend. And if memory serves, Mr. Botta was not shy about voicing objections at that time. Once Ms. Prescott has a chance to read the transcript, I'd be happy to hear any objections she may also have."

Judge Cook turned to Ellie and raised one silver eyebrow. "Ms. Prescott?"

"That sounds fine to me, Your Honor."

He steepled his fingers. "Very well. I note that plaintiffs' counsel said *if* this case proceeds to trial. I take it you intend to file a motion for summary judgment, Ms. McCandless-Connelly?"

Ellie wondered why she hadn't already done so.

"No, Your Honor. We have no current plans to request summary judgment."

"Why on earth not?"

The judge seemed as surprised by his question as Sasha and Ellie were. He glanced at the court reporter at the end of the table, and she gave a brisk nod. Ellie knew with sudden certainty that when she requested a copy of the transcript, neither the judge's question nor Sasha's answer would appear on the record.

As Sasha opened her mouth to respond, there was a knock on the door. Judge Cook looked at Brett, who loped across the room in two long-legged strides and opened the door a crack. After a moment of muffled conversation with whomever was on the other side, he turned back to the judge.

"Mr. Prescott's in the reception room. Should Diane send him in?"

The judge nodded and motioned with his hand.

Ellie expected to feel relief. Now that her dad was here, she was off the hook. She could observe and learn instead of struggling to keep her head above water. To her surprise, her relief was tinged with disappointment.

30

Cinco ducked under the deputy clerk's outstretched arm and hurried through the doorway. "My apologies for being tardy, Judge Cook. I was out of the office at an important meeting when your chambers called." He straightened his suit jacket and caught his breath.

Judge Cook eyed him coolly. "I trust you're not implying that this meeting is unimportant, counselor?"

Cinco pressed his lips together to trap the words that wanted to come out. He didn't need to start off this … whatever it was … on the wrong foot with the judge. He exhaled through his nose, then forced a smile. "Of course not, Your Honor."

"Good. Find a seat. Your colleague did a fine job in your absence. I'd expect nothing less from a Prescott & Talbott lawyer."

Cinco smiled at Ellie as he took the seat across the table from Sasha. "That's gratifying to hear, though not surprising. Why don't you come sit over here, Eleanor?"

Sasha examined her fingernails with great interest while Ellie gathered up her things and scurried to the other side of the table to sit next to him. Once she was situated, Cinco said, "Oh, hello, Sasha," as if he'd just noticed her.

Sasha took her time looking up from her cuticles. "Charles." Her tone was utterly neutral.

Judge Cook said, "To bring you up to speed, Mr. Prescott, I called this meeting on short notice in light of Mr. Lewis' unfortunate passing."

"Yes, it's tragic," Cinco murmured.

The judge went on as if he hadn't been interrupted. "Ms. McCandless-Connelly informs the court that his death does not change plaintiffs' litigation strategy. If this case goes to trial, plaintiffs will read in those portions of Mr. Lewis' deposition testimony that they find relevant. Ms. Prescott agrees that defense counsel will be prepared to file any objections to deposition excerpts at that time."

Cinco gave Ellie a side-long glance. It was a perfectly fine decision to make, but she shouldn't have been making the decision. She ought to have simply delayed until Lettie reached him. He realized the judge was waiting for a response.

"Very good, Your Honor."

"Now then, I'd just asked Ms. McCandless-Connelly whether plaintiffs intend to file a summary judgment motion, and she indicated that they do not. I inquired as to her reasoning, and she was about to share that with us when you arrived. Ms. McCandless-Connelly?"

"Yes, Your Honor. Plaintiffs' decision not to seek

summary judgment has two bases. One, we believe the district attorneys' office should be held to account for its egregious behavior in a public forum. While motions are, technically speaking, public documents, it's highly unlikely that the good taxpayers of Milltown will have the knowledge, inclination, or time to request and absorb the cost of obtaining copies of documents from the docket. In particular, summary judgment briefs, which, as the court knows better than anyone, can be voluminous given all the exhibits that might be attached."

Cinco couldn't hold his tongue. "Are you actually admitting you're pushing this case to trial for the publicity?"

Sasha's green eyes turned icy as she stared at him. She paused to put some space between her anger and her response.

"No, not in the least. Plaintiffs believe a public trial —a jury trial—is necessary because the district attorney is a public official. His behavior, and that of his assistant prosecutors, impacts every resident of Milltown. It's important that the DA's dirty laundry, for lack of a better description, be aired publicly."

She turned her attention back to Judge Cook. "The second reason plaintiffs made the strategic decision not to seek summary judgment arises from the pattern and practice at issue in this case. Mr. Botta's office made a point of tailoring the evidence to fit the crime, as it were. Plaintiffs are concerned that if the defendant is given a road map of the plaintiffs' trial strategy, well, the prosecutors in the district attorney's office will simply gin up evidence to counter it."

Cinco sputtered. "That's absurd, not to mention insulting. What eleventh-hour evidence could the DA 'gin up' and sneak into evidence. Does Ms. McCandless-Connelly think this court is an idiot?" Judge Cook's glower seemed to be directed at Cinco rather than Sasha, so he hurried to add, "And I take exception to the suggestion that I, Ms. Prescott, or anyone working at our firm would be party to such misconduct. As you know, Prescott & Talbott is one of Pittsburgh's oldest, largest—"

The judge raised a hand, cutting him off. "No need to go on the record with a history of Prescott & Talbott, Mr. Prescott. I'm certain everyone in the room has read the tome, *P&T: The First Two Hundred Years.*"

Sasha made a choking noise that sounded to Cinco suspiciously like strangled laughter.

"Brett, please get Ms. McCandless-Connelly a glass of water," the judge requested.

"You got it, judge. Anybody else?"

The others shook their heads. As the deputy clerk vanished to fulfill the request, Judge Cook took control of the discussion. "Mr. Prescott, I am confident Ms. McCandless wasn't accusing you or your colleagues of shenanigans. It seems her caution about Mr. Botta's office is merited based on the undisputed evidence that this court has seen to date."

The clerk returned with a glass of water and a coaster and placed both in front of Sasha. She took a long drink. "Thanks, Brett. Your Honor, if I may?"

The judge nodded.

"Of course I'm not accusing Mr. Prescott or anyone else at his firm of misconduct. As everyone at this table is aware, I started my career at Prescott & Talbott. I know firsthand that P&T attorneys are trained to be strategic and hard-charging. But that's a far cry from the court of misconduct that ran rampant at the district attorney's office."

"Allegedly," Cinco mumbled.

"Allegedly ran rampant at the district attorney's office," she amended.

The judge gave Sasha a thoughtful look. "Given plaintiffs' not-unreasonable hesitancy to file for summary judgment, the court does have to wonder what you meant when you said 'if' as in, *if* this case proceeds to trial. It's my understanding that settlement is out of the question in this case. Mr. Botta's made that abundantly clear."

Sasha turned to Cinco. "Would you like to clarify, or should I?"

"I will. Your Honor, there's been a recent change of strategy on the defendant's part."

"I surmised as much when I saw your substitution of counsel papers."

"Yes, one prong of that new strategy was to bring Prescott & Talbott on as counsel. And the other is to pursue settlement. For a host of reasons, the district attorney's office would like to put the distraction and expense of this case behind it so that the prosecutors can focus on their mission and serve the people of Milltown to the best of their ability."

"I see." The judge sounded intrigued. "Did this strategy change arise after I issued my order denying summary judgment?"

"No, Your Honor," Sasha explained. "Mr. Botta sent a settlement offer over to me the night before the court issued its order. In fact, the order came down while the plaintiffs were in my office discussing the original offer."

"The original offer," the judge mused.

Cinco, spoke up. "Yes, although the decision to try to settle the case preceded the summary judgment decision, if only briefly, once your decision came out, the defendant's interest in settlement increased. Accordingly, so did its offer."

"Interesting. So, tell me, Ms. McCandless-Connelly, are plaintiffs inclined to settle?"

"They're discussing it. Because the offer is structured as an all-or-nothing offer, all three plaintiffs need to be in agreement."

"I see. Would it be helpful to the parties if I were to mediate? I'd be happy to bring everyone to the table if that would make the process easier."

Sasha eyed Cinco, then said, "Possibly. There are some aspects of the settlement offer that make plaintiffs uneasy."

"Oh? Such as?"

"Well, Your Honor, the size of the offer, for one thing."

Judge Cook laughed. "Counselor, no offer's ever substantial enough to match the plaintiffs' fantasy. It's your job to bring them around to reality."

"In this case, the concern isn't that the offer is low. It's too generous."

"Come on," Cinco scoffed.

The judge turned slowly toward Cinco and gave him a steely warning look. "Don't forget yourself, Mr. Prescott."

"Apologies, Your Honor. But, honestly, she's complaining that the offer's too high? Maybe WACB's reporting is right. She does seem to be gumming up the works for her own purposes."

"WACB?" Judge Cook caught his deputy's eye. "What is he talking about?"

Brett shook his head slowly and raised his hands in a 'beats me' gesture.

Sasha explained, "Tuesday was a busy day. You issued your opinion. Mr. Botta, who at that time was still counsel of record, called with the new and improved, higher settlement offer. And then, a field reporter for WACB attempted to ambush me live on the evening newscast. I didn't talk to her, but she evidently said, without revealing a source, that there was speculation that I was trying to torpedo a settlement in this case." She paused to let that sink in, then added, "I can't say whether that rumor hit the airwaves before or after Prescott & Talbott were retained, but we got the substitution of counsel papers very early the next morning."

Judge Cook's face took on a dusky red hue. He spoke loudly and slowly. "Let me be very clear. I will not have this case tried in the press. Counsel and the parties are forbidden to talk to the press about settlement negotiations. Is that understood?"

Sasha and Cinco both hurried to say, "Yes, Your Honor."

"Ms. Prescott?" the judge asked.

Ellie looked stricken. She swallowed hard and stared wide-eyed at the judge. "Y-y-yes, Your Honor."

Cinco began to wonder what she found so upsetting, but Sasha's next words made him forget all about his daughter's apparent distress.

"There's something else about the offer that the court should know," Sasha added.

"Yes?"

"The offer exceeds Milltown's contributions to the state insurance consortium. Substantially. It's a multiple of what Milltown has paid into the fund. So, my clients are understandably concerned about the source of these funds and if this offer has even been made in goodwill."

Judge Cook drew his eyebrows together. "Just how substantial is this offer?"

Sasha gestured for Cinco to respond. He coughed. "The current offer is four million dollars per plaintiff. Twelve million total."

Cinco had rarely seen Cliff Cook at a loss for words, but it took the jurist a long moment to formulate a response. "I see. That is unusually large. Tell me, Mr. Prescott, does the district attorney's office actually have access to that kind of money?"

Cinco chose his words with care. "Not ordinarily. As Ms. McCandless-Connelly noted, the amount exceeds their contribution to the insurance fund, not to mention the annual budget for the office. However, a concerned private citizen has offered to fund the settlement."

"A concerned private citizen," the judge repeated.

"Yes, Your Honor."

Sasha spoke up. "Your Honor, if I may?"

The judge nodded.

"Mr. Prescott's revelation that a 'concerned citizen' is funding this settlement offer raises more questions than it answers. Given the extraordinary amount being offered and the shenanigans with the press, I have serious concerns about this mysterious third party who's trying to buy off my clients."

"As do I, Ms. McCandless-Connelly. As do I." The judge fixed Cinco with a stern look. "A proffer as to this party's identity would go a long way to easing some of my qualms."

Sweat beaded along Cinco's brow. "I'd prefer to make sure a proffer to the court *in camera*, out of the presence of plaintiffs' counsel."

"That won't alleviate plaintiffs' concerns. We'd like discovery as to this agreement between the defendant and this so-called concerned citizen," Sasha protested.

Ellie cleared her throat. "It's not clear that plaintiffs are entitled to discovery regarding the funding source. Um, under Pennsylvania law, I mean."

Cinco had forgotten she was there. Apparently, so had everyone else. They all turned to stare at her.

"Do you have a citation, young lady?" Judge Cook leaned forward, interested by the prospect of actually discussing the law for a change of pace.

"There are several recent cases out of the Eastern District of Pennsylvania—"

"—Bah, Philadelphia. What about this district?"

Ellie thought for a moment. "Well, in a 2018 decision, a court here in the Western District refused to compel discovery of a funding agreement."

"Ah, *Lambeth*, correct?"

"Yes, Your Honor."

"Ms. McCandless-Connelly?"

"I'm not familiar with that case. However, there is a 2020 case, *Midwest Athletics & Sports Alliance*—and I'm sorry to say it's out of the Eastern District—where the court indicated that litigation funding document would *not* be protected as work product."

"It sounds as if briefs might be in order," the judge observed with something approaching joy.

Cinco stifled a yawn.

Sasha said, "Your Honor? While plaintiffs are happy to brief the issue, I do want to note that these modern cases all seem to involve, for lack of a better word, corporate litigation funding companies. That is, financial corporations that exist to provide this capital. Whether this trend is a positive development is an open question, but it doesn't appear to be the situation that we have here."

"Hmm. It is true that typically, the funding arrangements operate similar to a contingent fee arrangement. That is, the funder provides money up front in exchange for a portion of any award."

"Exactly, here we have the inverse, almost. This mystery funder isn't seeking a portion of an award.

They are effectively donating twelve million dollars to settle a case that they aren't involved in or otherwise at risk of liability. 'Why?' seems like a reasonable question to ask." Sasha spread her hands wide.

"I tend to agree with you. I doubt very highly that we'll find a case that squares with this one on the facts. Most philanthropists choose causes other than settling litigation."

"I also looked at historical cases to see if there might be an analogue at common law," Sasha offered.

"And?"

"I reviewed case law addressing champerty, maintenance, and barratry."

Cinco narrowed his eyes. He'd never heard of any of these supposed causes of action, if that's even what they were. For all he knew, Sasha was making them up.

"You have the same problem with those cases," Ellie said. "All three involve prosecuting a suit, not settling one. Assuming those defenses are still good law."

"Oh, I know this one," the judge interjected cheerfully. "In 2015, the wise souls on the Third Circuit, in affirming the lower court's decision, held that champerty is still a valid defense under Pennsylvania law, even though it's *rarely invoked in modern times.*' That was in *Dougherty v. Carlisle Transportation Products*," the judge added. He sat back with a satisfied smile.

Cinco couldn't believe Lettie had dragged him away from an exhibition of Japanese *ukiyo-e* art for this. These three would have loved it, the woodblock prints the artists created dated as far back as the 1600s—just like their musty caselaw.

The judge glanced at the clock on the wall, then rose without warning, and everyone else in the room popped to their feet in a hurry. He growled as he reached for the black robes hanging on the hook on the back of the door. "I've got a hearing that was supposed to start twenty minutes ago. See if you three can't put your heads together and make this settlement happen."

Judge Cook swept through the door and the court reporter and deputy clerk raced after him. Once the door closed behind them, Cinco cleared his throat. "What do we have to do to make this happen, Sasha?"

"One thing that would help is a public statement from Ron Botta acknowledging that the office's past conduct was wrongful and a public commitment to clean up the office going forward. He needs to stand up and do something like the chief prosecutor in New Orleans did."

Cinco stared at her blankly.

"The fake subpoenas case?" Ellie asked.

"Right. The plaintiffs in that case settled their federal civil rights claims and the prosecutor agreed to allow a court-appointed monitor to supervise and oversee the prosecutor's office for a period of several years—in addition to a monetary settlement."

"I doubt they got twelve million," Cinco scoffed.

"Cinco, I don't know how to use smaller words to say this: They. Don't. Care. About. The. Money."

"Sasha, everybody cares about the money."

She shook her head and addressed Ellie. "See if you can get Mr. Botta to agree to court oversight. I can try to sell that, but without knowing who the mystery funder is, it'll be a hard sell."

"I'll see what I can do," Ellie said.

"Great. I'm supposed to talk to my clients later today, and I'm going to see them tonight at a surprise birthday party for Mr. Barefoot. So even if it's late in the day, call me. I'll be in Milltown from seven until nine or so."

"Uh, do I have your mobile number?"

"I forward my office line, but here, take this, too." Sasha handed her a business card and hurried out of the room.

31

Ellie's first status conference left her feeling elated and excited—for a brief time. She'd enjoyed matching wits with Sasha and discussing esoteric legal principles with a federal judge. She'd floated out of the courthouse, her feet barely touching the hot pavement underfoot.

Trust her father to bring her down to earth. As soon as they stepped out onto Grant Street, he pitched his voice high and mimicked her, "'You'll see what you can do?' Perhaps you've forgotten your place in the pecking order."

She looked at him dumbfounded. "Opposing counsel asked me to contact Mr. Botta. What should I have said? You're the one who says we have to settle at all costs. I think we can get it done if he agrees to a court monitor. I'd have thought you'd be thrilled."

He snapped, "Nobody cares what you think. Or what Ron Botta thinks. Or if I'm thrilled. What matters—the *only* thing that matters is ramming this settlement down the plaintiffs' throats. The only opinion that matters is Leith Delone's." He dropped his voice to a harsh whisper when he said the billionaire's name. As if any of the late afternoon shoppers scurrying along the street or hiding from the sun in bus shelters cared.

"And if plaintiffs will settle so long as there's a court monitor, it's no skin off Mr. Delone's nose. Am I missing something?"

He rubbed his forehead as if she were giving him a headache. "Eleanor, you acquitted yourself well in the conference. You were prepared and well-spoken. But, I'm afraid you're a touch idealistic. Sasha McCandless-Connelly isn't the reasonable person you think she is. She's just trying to make us dance. First it'll be a court-appointed monitor. Then it'll be a public apology. Or a donation to the ACLU or Project Innocence or something. You don't know her the way I do."

"But, even if she did make those demands, Leith Delone—" He glared at her, and she dropped her voice to a whisper. "Sorry, Leith Delone shouldn't care, right? If it doesn't expose him personally, and it gets the case settled, he should be all for it. Isn't Mr. Botta going to be the tough sell? After all, he's the defendant."

Her dad laughed. "Oh, Ellie, really. If Leith Delone tells Attorney General Nolan to jump, Ron Botta asks, 'how high?' Botta's a puppet. Delone decides."

"But that's not how it's supposed ..." she trailed off.

"You're proving my point. You still have an idealized vision of how the law is *supposed* to work. It's not unique to you. Most first-year associates are ill-prepared for the unpleasant reality of civil litigation."

His assessment stung. What she wanted to say was *if you have so much disdain for the law, why are you still practicing? Retire already.* But no other first year at Prescott & Talbott would dare to speak to Cinco Prescott in such a way, so she bit back the words.

Instead, she asked in a mild voice, "So do you want me to call Mr. Botta or no?"

"I'll call him myself."

Apparently, he meant right now. So, after admonishing her for speaking the name of Leith Delone on a public street, her father pulled out his cell phone and proceeded to conduct attorney-client privileged business in the middle of Pittsburgh's legal district. At full volume.

She trotted along beside him, keeping her eyes down and listening to her father's end of the conversation. It could hardly be considered eavesdropping, considering the circumstances.

"Is Ron there? Tell him it's Cinco Prescott."

A brief pause, then, "Yes, hi, Ron. No, they haven't accepted the offer yet. Ellie and I just left a conference with Sasha and Judge Cook. He called it on short notice after he heard about Landon Lewis' death."

A longer pause.

"No, I don't think so, Ron. I heard it was a suicide. Yes, I'm sure losing a child changes a person, no matter how long it's been."

They reached the intersection, and Ellie had to throw out her arm to keep her distracted father from stepping out into oncoming traffic. He mouthed 'thank you,' while Ron rambled on about something.

The light changed and they crossed the street. "So, here's the thing, Sasha's proposed that you agree to a court-appointed monitor as part of the settlement. Right, like in New Orleans."

Mr. Botta's voice grew sufficiently loud and agitated that Ellie could hear it through her father's handset. She didn't need to make out every word to get the gist of his reaction.

Her father tried to interrupt his tirade. "Ron, Ron ... Ron! Of course, I haven't mentioned this to our mutual friend yet. I called you first. But I imagine it'd be no skin off his nose if you were to agree."

Ellie couldn't help but note how her father casually used her words as his own assessment.

He fell silent for a long moment, then said, "I'll tell you what, Ron. I'll do that—I'll hold off calling our friend and when I do I will recommend against agreeing to that term if you'll do a favor for me. Excellent. Sasha mentioned that she'd be in Milltown this evening. I don't know, a birthday party for one of those plaintiffs. Barefoot, maybe? Right, the ex-felon. She'll be leaving his house at around nine p.m."

Ellie shot a sidelong glance at her father. What was he doing?

"If you could arrange for one of the boys in blue to stop her while she's in their jurisdiction and ... no, just scare her. Nothing like that. Just enough to shake her up. Right. Great. Give Julie my best."

He ended the call and stowed the phone in his

pocket with an air of triumph. His walk became more of a swagger.

Ellie gaped at him. "What did you just do?"

"Eleanor, if you don't want to know how the sausage is made, you shouldn't have become a butcher."

He strode ahead of her into the office building and took his private elevator to the top floor.

She raced up the stairs to her floor and into her office on wobbling legs. She slammed her door shut, flung herself into her desk chair, and tried to catch her breath. She would not cry. She *could not* cry.

Think, Ellie. Think.

She took a shaky breath and raised her chin. Then she logged into her burner email account and typed out a response to Maisy Farley's message. Her fingers flew over the keys:

```
I can't meet with you or go on
the record at this point. But I
promise, I'm legit. The attached
document was used to set up the
trust that will disperse the
money for the settlement.
There's a series of strawman
transactions, but I'm sure a
reporter of your caliber will be
able to trace it. Follow the
money.
```

Before she could second-guess herself, she took out her phone, snapped a picture of the trust documents, and uploaded it to the cloud. Then she attached the photo to the email and hit 'send.' Then, and only then, did Eleanor Anderson Prescott allow herself to cry.

32

M aisy managed to shake her lunch date before he could suggest they check out the gelato shop around the corner. Pete was a perfectly nice guy, but there was no spark there. She might hit the gelato shop herself, later, to soothe the pain of another lackluster date with something in the salted caramel family.

On the whole, though, Maisy was happy with her switch to a lunches-only policy for first dates. For one thing, she didn't have many evenings to herself, what with all the social engagements she attended on behalf of WACB. She should mention that to Naya. Was she contractually obligated to go to every silent auction and high school sports team fundraiser in Pennsylvania? The other reason Maisy preferred the lunch dates was there was less danger of making a cocktail-fueled bad choice at one o'clock on a weekday afternoon than there was on a Saturday at one in the morning. She got better sleep, kept her evenings open for her friends, and had fewer morning-after regrets this way.

She ducked into Jake's for a dirty London fog before heading into the station. While she waited in line at the coffee shop, she checked her email on her phone. She scrolled through a dozen emails from Preston to the entire news team forwarding edicts from the new management. Couldn't he just put them in one memo? Or maybe revise the employee manual? She supposed she should count herself lucky that he'd emailed. Last year, his assistant had a habit of disseminating all important information through the Water Kooler messaging channel only. Only after Maisy had missed four meetings in a row, she realized she'd never joined the proper channel.

Scroll, scroll, scroll. Maisy's finger stopped moving. Seissez had responded to her email. She'd told herself not to count on a response. Lots of people thought they wanted to be a whistleblower or an informant. A few even dipped a toe, like this person had done. But it was rare for someone to follow through; and, if they did, odds were they had the inside scoop on the love child of Elvis and an alien. Maisy warned herself not to expect too much. But, still, her heart ticked up.

She felt a frisson of disappointment when she read that her source didn't want to meet. But the attached document might make up for that setback. She held her breath as she clicked on the attachment. She was squinting at it when Jake himself called her name.

She glanced up. "What are you doin' behind the counter, sugar?"

"Oh, the pitfalls of hiring college students. They all want to go to the beach at the same time."

"Oh, to be young again, huh?"

"Nah." Jake flipped a microfiber towel over his shoulder with a snap. "Waking up hungover, dehydrated, and sunburnt wasn't all that great twenty years ago. I'd hate to do it now."

"Amen to that."

"So what it'll be for Pittsburgh's brightest shining star?" he teased.

"I want that dirty London fog you make. I've tried making it at home, but it's just not the same."

"Must not be dirty enough," Jake said as he turned to make the Earl Gray tea with a shot of espresso.

It took Maisy a second. Was Jake *flirting* with her? Oh, but what if he wasn't? She'd hate to have to find another coffee shop. Jake's was great. Plus it was so convenient. Halfway between home and the office *and* in the lobby of Sasha and Naya's building. No, better not to even go down that road.

Jake returned with the drink in a ceramic mug, not a takeout cup.

"Oh."

"Oh, you weren't headed up to McCandless, Volmer & Andrews? I just assumed—"

"No, it's okay. Actually, I need to talk to Naya anyway, so this is perfect." She smiled brightly. It was a great excuse to pick Naya's brain about the document Seissez had sent her. Maisy doubted she'd be able to make heads or tails of it, no matter how much she magnified the thing.

"Are you sure? I can remake it. It's no problem. Especially for you—"

"Jake, it's fine. Honestly. I'm going upstairs. I'll be sure to bring your mug back when I leave."

He gave her a mock serious look. "See that you do."

She laughed. Then she waited. And she waited. But he wasn't ringing her up. Maybe it had been so long since he'd worked the register, that he'd forgotten about this part.

"So, um, what do I owe you?"

"Oh, nothing. I mean … it's on the house. You know … the law firm arrangement."

"But, I'm not—"

"You're going up there, though."

"Oh. Okay. Well, thanks."

"Don't mention it. But, uh, don't forget to bring the mug back." He winked.

He turned and busied himself with cleaning the espresso machine. Maisy took her coffee and headed for the stairs. Jake was *definitely* flirting with her.

SASHA TRUDGED up the stairs to the law firm. She was mentally exhausted from the verbal jousting with Cinco and physically drained from the adrenaline-fueled mad dash to the courthouse. She wanted nothing more than to call it a day, go home, and cuddle on the couch with the twins until bedtime.

She sighed. But it was not to be.

She waved hello to Caroline, who was taking a

phone call at the reception desk, and plodded down the hallway to her office. Halfway there, the unmistakable aroma of Jake's espresso wafted toward her. She made a U-turn and headed for Naya's office.

"Fee fie foe fum," she said as she popped her head in.

Maisy and Naya looked up from Naya's monitor.

"Uh, hi," Maisy said with a bewildered expression.

"She smelled the coffee," Naya told her. "Sorry, Mac. Yes, it's espresso, but Maisy ruined it by having Jake put it in tea."

Sasha and Naya wrinkled their noses in unison. Sasha craned her neck to look in Maisy's mug. "What is that? A dirty chai?"

"Dirty London fog," Naya answered.

"Come on, Maisy, have some self-respect." Sasha bumped the back of her head against Naya's door. "I could really use a cup of strong coffee. Why didn't I stop at Jake's on my way in?"

"Why, indeed?" Naya countered.

"Probably because I was distracted by my encounter with Cinco and Seis."

Maisy went wide-eyed. "Who?"

"Oh, you know Cinco Prescott? His daughter's a lawyer now. Eleanor. She's a first year at P&T. Apparently everyone calls her Six behind her back. I was just making a joke. You know, six is *seis* in Spanish," Sasha explained. Then she turned to Naya. "You know, she's sharp. She's gonna be a good attorney. Smart, principled."

"Sasha 2.0," Naya responded.

Sasha shook her head. "Anyway, what are you doing

here, Maisy? Contract stuff? Don't you need to get to the station soon?"

Maisy checked the time and gasped.

"I think that's a yes," Naya said. "And no, we weren't doing contract stuff. Maisy has a mystery on her hands. And it involves you."

"Me?"

Maisy groaned. "I can't be late. Especially not if I'm going to tell Preston I want the leeway to run with this lead."

"Don't do that," Sasha said.

"What?" Maisy and Naya both turned to her.

"I have no idea what's going on—obviously. But Noah Peterson taught me this when I was a baby lawyer, not much more experienced than Ellie Prescott: ask forgiveness, not permission. Do whatever it is you're going to do to run down your story. If it blows up in your face, then you apologize, beg forgiveness. Better that than asking if you can do it and getting shot down."

Maisy bobbed her head from side to side as if she was weighing Sasha's counsel.

"She's not wrong," Naya said. "Plus that's some solid seven-hundred-and-fifty-dollar an hour legal advice, and you just scored it for free."

Maisy's hand went to her throat. "My word. Is that what you charge, too, Naya? I don't think mani/pedis is going to cover your time."

"Don't worry," Naya assured her. "I only bill out at five hundred an hour."

Maisy looked like she was about to faint.

"You okay?" Sasha asked with some concern.

"Honestly, you two. At those rates, you can afford to pay for your coffee! Poor Jake's trying to run a business."

"So are we," Naya told her. "Have you *seen* how much coffee Mac drinks? We'd be underwater in a month without the free coffee arrangement."

"People, focus. This is about me. How am I involved in Maisy's mystery?" Sasha demanded.

"That's our Sasha. Always the main character in the drama of the day," Maisy said fondly. "I really do have to scoot. Naya can fill you in."

Maisy and her dirty London fog swept out of Naya's office in a blur of blonde curls and subtle citrusy perfume.

"What was that all about?" Sasha asked.

"I think she might have a thing for Jake. Who knows? Anyway, Maisy has a tipster who claims to know who's funding the settlement in your Botta case."

"Really?" Sasha's belly registered the first flutters of excitement.

"Apparently. I don't know all the details, but come look at this."

Sasha hurried around Naya's desk to peer over her shoulder at the computer monitor. Some arcane trust agreement filled the screen.

"What am I looking at?"

"Maisy's tipster sent it, along with an email that claimed this trust—" Maisy paused to tap the screen, "— was created to fund the settlement through a series of

strawman transactions designed to obfuscate the identity of the funder."

"Huh. And Maisy brought this to you because …?"

"Honestly? I think she came up here because Jake
gave her a ceramic mug and she didn't want to offend
him by asking for a to-go cup."

"Offend him?"

"Like I said, I think there's something between the
two of them. A spark. Anyway, she played the whole
thing close to her vest, which I can respect. She
wouldn't show me the emails, but she forwarded me
this document."

"You're going to dig into the transactions for her?"
Would Naya share the results with her? Was it fair
to ask?

"Nah, you know the saying, give an investigative
journalist the answer, and you feed her for a day."

"You taught her to fish?"

"Yep." Naya deleted the document, then dragged it to
the trash and emptied the bin. The document vanished
into the cyber landfill where old documents went to die.
She met Sasha's eyes. "So neither of us is tempted."

"Smart." She settled into Naya's guest chair. "I don't
suppose you fielded a call from my clients in the Botta
case."

"Oh, right." She snapped her fingers. "Charlie called.
He said they have a counter-proposal and they'll give it
to you tonight. What's tonight?"

"Charlie has organized the world's most poorly kept
surprise birthday party for Max."

"Max knows?"

"A hundred percent."

"You're going out to Milltown? That's three nights this week of you not putting your kids to bed."

Naya knew her well enough to know that fact would be weighing on her. "It is. But I have a feeling this case is going to wrap up one way or the other very soon."

"A feeling?"

Sasha smiled enigmatically.

"Be that way. I have work to do anyway. You look beat. You should get yourself down to Jake's and get a double shot of espresso."

"I considered it. I think I'm going to get myself over to Daniel's and get myself punched in the face instead. He's holding space open for me this afternoon for a private sparring session. And I've missed so much training lately, it'll probably be better for me than all the coffee in the world."

"Well, kick him in the groin for me or however you say hi to a Krav Maga instructor."

"Uh, usually, just by saying hi. But I'll give him your regards."

She left Naya's office and stopped by her own to gather a few things before heading to Daniel's studio. She did need to refresh her self-defense skills, just in case the seed she'd planted came to fruition tonight.

33

The last of the partygoers had straggled from Max Barefoot's house. Sasha surveyed the wilting helium balloons, the streamers, and the paper plates left behind in the kitchen and began cleaning up the detritus. Max wandered in with an armload of bottles and dumped them into his recycling bin with a clatter.

"You don't have to clean up."

She waved a hand. "Happy to help. I think Sam went looking for your vacuum to take care of the confetti all over the living room."

Max chuckled and shook his head in wonder. "Confetti."

"It's only fair," she told him. "The confetti cannon was Sam's idea. Did you enjoy the party? I know you weren't surprised."

He jerked his head to her. "Charlie doesn't know, does he?"

She shook her head. "I won't tell him if you don't."

He smiled. "I didn't want to ruin his plan. You know I haven't had a birthday like this since ... maybe forever."

"Really?"

"My old crowd wasn't really the cake and ice cream kind."

They fell silent. Max rarely talked about the old crowd. Understandable given that they were a well-organized and brutally efficient gang of car thieves.

"Well, I hope this birthday was a happy one."

"It was," he said in a soft voice. Then he cleared his throat, "Where's Charlie?"

"He walked his partner and her sister out to their car. He'll be back in a minute."

As she spoke the front door opened and then closed with a loud bang. She heard the *snick* of the deadbolt against the door. She and Max headed for the front of the house. By the time they got there, Charlie was peering through Max's grandmother's lace curtain out at the dark street. Sam hovered over his shoulder.

"What's up?" Max asked.

Charlie turned from the window with a stricken expression. "There's a black and white parked down the block, he's watching the house. Not even being subtle about it. I walked past him with Raquel and her sister, and Raquel said he was there when they arrived. So he's been out there for two hours."

Max's jaw tightened, and the muscles in his neck

bulged out. Sam, who'd been reading Charlie's lips, closed his eyes and shook his head in a slow, defeated motion.

Sasha clapped her hands to get Max and Charlie's undivided attention. "Hey, hey, party people. Snap out of it. He's here for me. Charlie, tell Sam."

Charlie nudged Sam.

"What do you mean, he's here for you?" Max asked.

She evaded the question. "Are we set? You want to counter the settlement offer on the terms we talked about in the kitchen?"

The three men nodded.

"Okay. Well, let's just say I've put an insurance policy in place to make sure our counteroffer is accepted."

"I don't think I like this," Charlie said.

She looked at each of them in turn, holding their gaze for several seconds each. "Trust me, okay? Have I led you guys astray yet?"

After a long moment, Charlie sighed. "Okay."

"Sorry to bail on the rest of the cleanup, but I do have to run."

"Sure," Charlie said absently. Then, "Sam says to tell Leo and the kids we say hi."

She smiled at Sam. "I will."

"I'll walk you to the door," Max said.

She grabbed her purse from the table and walked with Max through the narrow hallway. At the door, she turned to him. "Happy birthday, Max."

"Yeah."

She reached for the door and he put his hand out to

hold it shut. Then he bent his head and said in a low voice. "Are you sure you know what you're doing?"

"I'm sure."

He gave her a hard look. "You've had a certain kind of interaction with the police up until now. A white lady kind of interaction. But that guy out there? He's gonna judge you by the company you keep. So you should expect a different kind of interaction. You understand what I'm saying."

"I understand, Max." She flashed a smile even as her heart rate ticked. "That's what I'm counting on."

She ducked under his arm, and he pulled the door open with a heavy sigh.

"Be careful," he said to her back.

She waved over her shoulder. "Talk to you tomorrow."

She ignored the tremble in her hands as she reached for her car keys and strode purposefully toward her station wagon. She clocked the patrol car parked across the street, just past the streetlight. She popped the locks with her key fob and heard the police car's engine spring to life and begin to idle. She took the deepest breath she'd taken all day, paused when it expanded her lungs, and then exhaled slowly. She got into her car in a quick motion and fumbled with her phone for a moment, unlocking it and waking it up, before clicking it into the mount on the dashboard.

She started the engine, turned on her headlights, and eased the car out into the street. "Here goes nothing."

~

THE POLICE OFFICER following her hit his lights as she was rounding the bend in the road where Vaughn Tabor had been shot and killed by a rookie policewoman with an itchy trigger finger. The same isolated stretch of road where Landon Lewis had arranged her abduction. As she pulled over to the shoulder next to the dark woods, her breath caught in her throat.

She doubted there was any intentional symbolism in the spot. It was just a convenient spot to pull someone over if you didn't want to be seen. She hit the button on her phone, put the car in park, buzzed down her window, placed her hands on the steering wheel, and waited.

Time seemed to slow down and stretch out. Finally, she heard the crunch of gravel under his boots as he approached the driver's side of the car. She swallowed hard. He clicked on his flashlight and aimed it through her open window. She closed her eyes against the burst of light, then blinked them open.

She turned toward him. "Evening, officer. Is there a problem?" She smiled.

He didn't. "Ma'am, turn off the engine and step out of the car."

"What did I do? Did I miss a stop sign?"

"Ma'am, step out of the car."

"Do you need my license or—?"

"Step out of the car. Now." His hand shifted to the butt of the gun holstered at his hip.

She killed the ignition. "Okay, I'm going to open the door now."

He stepped back a pace.

She emerged from the car with slow, exaggerated movements. The officer was tall, taller than average, because she wasn't even at armpit level. The badge affixed to his uniform was at exact eye level. She took a long look at it, memorizing his badge number.

He stared down at her.

"So, um, what's this about, officer?"

"Have you been drinking?"

"No."

"You did just leave a house party in Milltown, didn't you?"

"Yes. It was a birthday party. You know, cake, ice cream. There was some beer, but I had coffee instead."

"Coffee at nine p.m.?"

"I have to do some work when I get home." She shook out her hands and let them hang loosely at her sides.

"You're claiming Max Barefoot, a convicted felon, had a cake and ice cream birthday party."

"Yes," she confirmed. She shifted her footing to assume a wide defensive stance.

"Stop shuffling around." His hand tightened on his gun.

"Sorry. I'm nervous. I don't understand why you pulled me over and made me get out of the car."

He took a step toward her and leaned down to peer into her face. She could feel his hot breath against her forehead as he said, "I have a message to deliver."

"A message?" she repeated loudly. She backed up several steps.

He strode forward, closing the gap she'd created. "If

you know what's good for you, you'll stop poking into the source of the settlement money."

She blinked up at him.

"Did you get that?"

"I'm confused. What?"

He leaned in closer and bit off the words in a slow, clear voice. "Stop asking where the money for the settlement is coming from."

"The Botta settlement, you mean? The case where Max Barefoot and the others are suing for misconduct? That settlement?" She kept her voice innocent as she baited him.

He raised his fist and punched into the side of the car, inches from her head. She shrank back further.

"That's the one," he said low in his throat. "Do you understand the message or do you need more ... explanation?" He leaned into her, pressing her back into the window. The metal trim dug into her back.

For an instant, she considered her options. Knee him in the groin, smash an elbow into his ribs with a satisfying crack, reach up and twist his wrist until it snapped. She had the ability to do any or all of them. Wasn't that the point of all her training?

Daniel's words rang in her ears. *The purpose, the ultimate goal, is to walk in peace. You have the training to handle the most violent confrontation. You must also have the self-discipline to avoid physical contact whenever possible. De-escalate and walk away.*

Still, she'd gotten the jump on more well-trained law enforcement agents than this bully. She was pretty sure she could take him, and it was awfully tempting to find out. She flashed to Naya deleting Maisy's document so they could avoid temptation. That's what she should do. She had everything she needed.

"I understand," she said, widening her eyes and sending her voice up an octave.

He laughed, spittle hitting her face, and eased his body off of hers.

"Am I free to go?"

Still laughing, he waved a hand for her to get back in the car. She didn't waste any time. As she turned the key in the ignition, he leaned in through the open window. "You're not the ballbuster they said you are. You're just a scared little girl."

"Who said that?"

He ignored the question. "A word of advice? Keep better company."

He hit the side of the car with his hand. She jumped at the thud.

He laughed again as he walked back to his squad car. She waited until he was behind the wheel to reach up and turn off the recording app on her phone. Then she exhaled a long, ragged breath and let loose a string of profanity that would have given Fiona material for years.

34

10:00 PM

Maisy's head was bent over the documents she'd spread out all over her desk. If she was reading these right, and who knew if she was, the trust created to fund the settlement in Sasha's case had been set up through a series of intermediaries by ... Leith Delone? The billionaire who owned the moons.

She shot upright. The billionaire who owned the moons had just bought the station, too. Coincidence? Not a chance. No doubt he was behind that attempt to air an unsourced story about Sasha 'gumming up' the settlement. He certainly had the money to fund the settlement—probably with loose change he found between his couch cushions. But why?

She shook her head. She didn't need a reason. Not yet. What she needed right now was a way to confirm what these documents were telling her. But how?

Two light knocks sounded on her door. She flipped the printouts over and grabbed the closest thing at hand to cover them.

"Come in," she trilled.

The door opened, and a weary Preston stood in the doorway. His tie was askew and one shirttail hung out from his pants.

"Burning the midnight oil?"

"Something like that. Following a lead."

"A lead? Is Elvis rotating tires at that auto shop after all?" He leaned forward to get a peek at her desk, and she congratulated herself for hiding her work. Then he smirked.

She followed his eyes. She'd covered up the papers with a full-color spread that the local paper had run after she'd won the award. "Celebrating Miss Maisy!" was splashed across the top of the page, and an old file photo of that had been taken at a benefit gala was centered in the page. There she was, decked out in a stunning red gown, posing like a game show hostess next to the Stanley Cup. The Penguins then-current goalie stood beside her with one arm looped over her bare shoulder.

"Um ..."

"Didn't you used to date him?" He nodded at the photo.

"For a while. You look like you've been through the wringer. What are you doing here so late, anyway?"

"Not looking at pictures of myself."

She let that pass without comment.

He lowered himself into a chair with a sigh.

Great. She suppressed a sigh of her own.

"The reason I look like I've been through the wringer is I was just put through the wringer."

She gave him a blank look.

"Meeting with the new management, Maisy."

"About me?"

"About a lot of things. But, yes, your name came up."

"And?"

Another sigh. "And I told them you want to talk about your contract. They seemed to think that's a good idea."

She clapped her hands. "Well, good."

"Not good." He shook his head. "The suggestion is that, um, how do I say this? … Maybe you're getting a little long in the tooth to be anchoring the evening news."

Long in the tooth? She blinked at him. "Wait, they said I'm too *old* to anchor? That's age discrimination! And Chet's twelve years older than me."

Preston lowered his chin and looked at her. "Come on, Maisy. You know it's different."

She put a finger to her lips and pretended to ponder his words. "Different. Different. Hmm, what could the difference be? Preston, now it's age *and* sex discrimination. Does this new outfit not have a Human Resources department?"

He dragged his fingers through his hair and left it sticking up in spikes. "Maisy, we don't have to do this the hard way, do we? They just want you to consider a proposal."

She gave him the stink eye while she waited to hear this proposal.

He cleared his throat. "So, what if we moved you to the morning talk show? You'd have a lot of leeway and artistic freedom. The segments are longer. They'd keep your pay the same."

"You want me to give up the anchor desk to do entertainment news on 'Sunrise Pittsburgh' with a call time of four am."

"Not me. Them. *They* want you to consider it."

"I'll bet they do."

Preston's already-pained expression worsened. He looked for all the world as if he were having a gall-bladder attack while being sprayed by a polecat. "There's one more thing. They'd like you to consider taking a little sabbatical before you start the new position—if you decide to take the offer, of course."

"A sabbatical," she repeated.

"A little rest and relaxation. On their dime, of course. A spa retreat—maybe get a facial. Some Botox, fillers, whatever you want."

"Preston, are you telling me that I'm being told to get some work done if I want to stay employed?"

"I didn't ... it's not ..."

"Out."

"Maisy, listen to me. We've worked together for a long time."

"Yes, we have. And you know I'm a good—no, great—reporter."

"You are. But sometimes we have to go along to get along." He gave her a pleading look.

At that moment, she felt truly sorry for him. "No, I don't have to. And neither do you. But you can if you want. Now, please, I'm asking you nicely. Leave."

He scurried out of the office. She was looking around for something to throw against the wall, when her cell phone rang. She checked the display. *Sasha.*

"Oh, am I glad to hear from you. You're never gonna believe the stunt Preston just pulled," she fumed.

"I want to hear all about it. But, later. Right now, I have a proposal for you. If you're interested, that is."

Sasha's voice blazed with ferocity, determination, and something Maisy couldn't quite place. Whatever Sasha was up to, she wanted in.

"Heck, yeah, I'm interested. What are we doing?"

"We're taking down Ron Botta and Cinco Prescott."

And Leith Delone, Maisy thought to herself. Suddenly, she realized what the third emotion was in Sasha's voice. It was vengeance, and it was coursing through Maisy's veins like blood.

"Just tell me what to do," she said.

35

Friday morning

Ron ate breakfast at his desk while he tried to catch up on all the work that he'd let slide while he'd been preoccupied by the civil rights case. Now that defending the case was Cinco's problem, he could turn his attention to more urgent matters—like approving three weeks' worth of vacation requests. He tried hard not to deny vacation requests during the summer months. Many of his ADAs had young families, and this was prime travel time for them.

Afraid that his frequent heartburn was a sign that his stomach ulcers were getting worse, he'd traded his sausage, egg, and cheese with a large coffee for a bowl of baked oatmeal and a glass of water. He figured he might as well use this unexpected free time to turn over a new leaf in his personal life, starting with his health.

He established a rhythm as he worked and ate. Take

a bite, grant a request. Take a bite, grant a request. He chewed and worked methodically.

He was finishing his last spoonful when someone knocked on his door.

He took a swig of water, and then called out, "It's open."

He wiped the traces of his breakfast off his chin with a napkin as the door creaked open. One of the legal assistants from the pool on the second floor gazed at him with an apologetic smile. "Sorry to interrupt your breakfast, Mr. Botta, but I found this woman wandering around in the hallway and she insisted she needs to speak to you."

Ron frowned and peered around the doorframe at his unannounced visitor. When he saw who it was, he nearly choked. "Maisy Farley?"

The news anchor waggled her fingers at him and smiled her familiar sparkling smile. "Live and in person. Could I just have ten minutes of your time?"

He swept the remnants of his breakfast into the trash and hurried around his desk to the door. "Of course. Please come in, sit down." He ushered her inside and into a chair.

Then he turned to the legal assistant and took a stab at her name. "Thanks for escorting her in, Jamie."

"It's Janie."

"Right. Sorry. Thanks, Janie."

"Uh, sure. Do you need anything else or …?" She hovered in the doorway.

Ron resisted the urge to shove her out into the hall

and close the door. "No, thanks. Oh, unless you'd like something to drink, Ms. Farley? Coffee? Tea?"

"Please, call me Maisy. And it's very kind of you to offer, but I don't need anything but your time, District Attorney Botta." Her emerald eyes danced, and Ron felt as if he were in a trance.

"I'll just close this, then," Janie muttered as she turned to leave the office.

"Oh, Janie," Maisy called in her delightful accent, "thank you for your help, sugar."

"Sure thing." She shut the door behind her.

Ron took the seat across from Maisy and rested his elbows on his thighs. "I can't believe it's really you. My wife isn't going to believe this when I tell her. Julie's a huge fan of yours."

Maisy laughed a tinkling laugh. "Isn't that sweet?"

He cleared his throat. "So, what can I do for you?"

"I realize this is a bit unusual, but I have some questions about one of your cases, and I told myself, well, Maisy, the best way to get clarity is to talk to the guy in charge, the man himself. So here I am."

Ron straightened his shoulders the way the guy in charge might. "I'll help you if I can. But, you understand, there are some limitations about what I can share."

"I understand."

"In that case, shoot. I'll tell you what I can."

She smiled that heart-melting smile and fluttered her eyelashes. "When did Leith Delone first approach you about the settlement?"

The baked oatmeal in Ron's stomach turned into a rock. No, a boulder. "I ... what?"

"The settlement with Max Barefoot, Sam Blank, and Charlie Robinson. You know, the case that you hired Prescott & Talbott to take over?"

"That wasn't my idea," he protested. *Stupid, Ron.* He wished he could stuff the words back into his mouth.

"Oh? Did Mr. Delone make that decision, too?"

"I ... oh no, you're not running a story about this are you?"

She tilted her head and gave him an innocent look. "It seems newsworthy. Why wouldn't I?"

He was torn. He didn't want to tell her anything. But he didn't want her to go poking around on her own and kick over a hornets' nest. He'd feel terrible if anything happened to her.

"These are bad people, Maisy. Powerful, bad people."

She blinked. "You mean people who might do something like this?" She took her phone out of her bag.

"What are you doing?"

"I'm going to play a video for you, Ron. Come closer so you can see it."

Gut churning, Ron leaned forward. The video had been filmed in low light and was somewhat grainy, but he had no trouble recognizing the woman whose face filled the screen. Sasha McCandless-Connelly. He reached for the water and gulped it down.

On the video, Sasha said, "Evening, officer. Is there a problem?" Then a stern, masculine voice ordered, "Ma'am, turn off the engine and step out of the car."

"Turn it off," Ron begged. "Please."

Maisy hit the pause button and gave him an expectant look. "Are you ready to talk to me, now?"

"It was Cinco's idea," he told her. "You have to believe me."

"We do," she said. "Here's how this is going to go."

Twenty minutes later, Maisy stepped out of the Milltown District Attorney's Office and crossed the street. She sat on a park bench and pulled her phone out of her bag. She felt just a tiny bit sorry for what she'd put Ron Botta through. Then she thought about the video Sasha had sent her, and her smidgeon of guilt disappeared as if by magic. Watching the way that police officer had tried to intimidate and threaten her friend had made Maisy sick to her stomach and had sparked a fire deep inside her. These men weren't going to get away with this. Not if she could help it. And, as it happened, she could.

She hit Sasha's number on her speed dial.

"Hello?" Sasha whispered.

"He'll play ball."

There was a pause. Then Maisy heard the soft click of a door and Sasha spoke at a normal volume. "You're sure?"

"I'm positive. I've got a camera crew on the way now to record the piece."

"Won't that tip off Delone?"

"No. Jocelyn's going to film it herself. She's solid. She's not going to tell anyone."

"There's still time for you to back out, Maisy. You don't have to do this."

"Back out for what? An eyelift and the graveyard shift of local television?"

"What are you babbling about?"

"I never told you my story last night. Once we get this mess wrapped up, I'll tell you all about it. Are you still at home?"

"Just left."

Maisy nodded to herself. Sasha hated to lie to Leo, so she'd decided to leave before he and the twins woke up, thereby obviating the need to lie.

"Are you going into the office first or straight to P&T?"

"Straight to the Seventh Circle of Hell. I drafted the settlement agreement last night and sent it to the guys to sign. As soon as we hang up, I'll forward it to Ron from my phone."

"You didn't sleep last night, did you?"

Sasha was silent. Maisy got it. She hadn't slept either. Just watching the video had kept her up. She couldn't imagine living through it.

"Listen, sugar. The hard part's over."

"I know. We've got this."

"Yeah, we do." A white van pulled up in front of Ron Botta's office and the driver beeped the horn. "Jocelyn's here. Show time."

"Break a leg," Sasha told her.

"You, too. As long as it's Cinco's."

Maisy hung up to the sound of Sasha's laughter.

36

L ettie Conrad was a woman of habit. Sasha banked on those habits not having changed in the past eleven years. Her belief in Lettie's steadfast nature paid off. At 7:28 on the dot, a blue sedan slowed to a stop near the side entrance to Prescott & Talbott, and Lettie emerged from the back seat. Sasha pushed off the wall she'd been leaning against and fell into step next to her former secretary.

"Morning, Lettie."

Lettie looked up in surprise, then arranged her expression into a smile. "Sasha! What are you doing here?"

"You're still in the same carpool, huh?"

"Well, sure." She waved goodbye to her commuter friends, then turned back to Sasha. "Were you waiting for me?"

"I was. Lettie, I need a favor."

Lettie eyed her and pushed her glasses up on the bridge of her nose. "Is this about Ellie?"

Sasha blinked. "What about Ellie?"

"Well, she was assigned to that case with her dad. You know the one."

"Oh, I know the one," she confirmed.

"She came back from court yesterday, banged around in her office for a bit, and then swept out with a banker's box full of her stuff."

"She quit?"

Lettie nodded. "Marlena in Human Resources said she came in and gave her two weeks' notice. Marlena wasn't sure, but she thought Ellie had been crying. When Marlena told her she had six weeks' accumulated vacation, Ellie laughed and said, 'see ya, suckers.' Then she cleared out her desk and left while I was in training to use this new billing software they installed." A small grin crept across Lettie's face. "And here I thought you would always have the most epic quitting story at the firm."

Sasha laughed. "I like her. Ellie. She's going to be a good attorney."

"Yes, she is, now that she's out from under her father's thumb." Lettie blinked at her. "So, what's the favor?"

LETTIE BADGED SASHA into the building and took her to the nearest stairwell. "Okay, as soon as I get to my desk, I'll call Darcy. She'll unlock the door to the inner sanctum for you and then I'll tell her to go to the ladies' room so she'll have plausible deniability."

Sasha gave Lettie an approving look. "That's a solid plan."

"You think you're the only badass around here?" Lettie said primly.

Sasha nearly choked. "Don't make me laugh, someone's going to hear us. Are you sure Darcy will do it?"

"That woman's been working Cinco's desk for eight-and-a-half years. She'll do it, and she won't even ask why."

"Perfect." Sasha did love it when a plan came together.

"Now, scoot." Lettie shooed her up the steps.

Sasha climbed the stairs at a quick clip. She peered through the small window cut in the door until she spotted Darcy strolling along the hallway, headed for the restroom. Then she eased the door open, slipped into the hall and raced to the outer door to the inner sanctum. She tried the handle. Open.

Bless you, Darcy.

She hurried through Darcy's office, noting as she did that Darcy had redecorated, but had kept Caroline's little touches like piped-in classical music and big vases bursting with fresh flowers. She pressed the handle to Cinco's private space. Also open.

A double heap of blessings for Darcy.

Sasha stepped inside and surveyed the orange room. It was as disconcerting as ever. The same nude painting hung over the same white couch where she'd sat to turn down partnership. She eyed the pair of white captains' chairs. Surely there was a mechanism to lower the seat so her feet could touch the floor. There had to be.

37

Cinco strolled into his office suite. "Good morning, Darcy," he said.

No response. He turned toward Darcy's empty desk and frowned. Just then, Darcy scurried into the room.

"Hi, Mr. Prescott. I'm sorry, I was in the ladies' room." She handed him a cup of coffee. "I stopped and got this for you on the way back."

"Oh. Thank you."

She was being unusually solicitous, even for her. Had she heard about Eleanor? He immediately berated himself. Of course, she had. Even the most mundane gossip spread like fire in this place. And Eleanor Anderson Prescott up and quitting without so much as a goodbye was anything but mundane. He was certain the associates would be murmuring about it for years to come. Well, he'd weathered worse.

He pushed open the door to his office and nearly spilled his coffee onto his snowy white carpet. Sasha

McCandless-Connelly was sitting in one of his captains' chairs. She'd dragged a four-thousand dollar end table across the room and was currently using it as a foot rest.

He placed the coffee on the table just inside the door with great care.

She waved. "Hi, Cinco."

"Sasha. I see your feet still don't touch the ground in that chair."

She scowled. "What kind of custom-made chairs don't have levers to make adjustments?"

"The kind that are custom-made to fit my frame, not yours. Do you need something? Are you here to accept the settlement offer? I knew you'd see reason, but you could've just picked up the phone." He was babbling, and he knew he was babbling. Why did this miniature-sized lawyer make him so nervous?

She leaned back and cracked her knuckles.

"That's a vulgar habit," he told her.

"Do you think so? Do you know what I think is vulgar?" She didn't wait for a response. "I think conspiring with a district attorney who is already under fire for professional misconduct to have a police officer abuse his authority and threaten a civilian all while doing the bidding of a sociopathic billionaire is vulgar. I doubt it's a habit, though." She widened her eyes. "It's not a habit, is it, Cinco?"

He sputtered. "I have no idea what you're going on about."

She gave him a disappointed look. "Oh, come on. That's your defense? You can do better than that."

A thought struck him. "Did Eleanor speak to you?"

"Eleanor? Your former associate? No, not since we saw each other in Judge Cook's chambers." Her expression tightened. "Why?"

Of course she hadn't. What was he thinking? "No reason. I genuinely don't know what you're talking about. Are you feeling okay?"

"Well, I was a bit rattled last night after my run-in with one of Milltown's finest. But then I thought to myself, who knew that I was going to be in Milltown? Oh, that's right, you did."

"I don't know—"

She hopped off the chair and stalked toward him.

"The thing about you, Cinco, is you always assume you're the smartest person in every room. And, I'm sure that's true often enough. But not always. Do you know why you knew I'd be at Max Barefoot's house from seven until nine last night?"

"Because you told us?"

"Right. And do you know why I told you?"

"So Eleanor could reach you if we had any movement on the settlement?" He knew he was walking into a trap, but he couldn't see it, so he didn't know how to evade it. It was an unpleasant, unmoored feeling.

"No. It didn't matter where I would be. That's the beauty of cell phones. I wanted you to know because you're predictable, Cinco."

He didn't like her tone. "This is growing tiresome, Sasha. What did you predict?"

"I figured you'd seize on that piece of information and try to turn it to your advantage. And you did. You called Ron Botta and asked him to get a police officer to shake me up."

"I did no such—"

"Careful. Ron already gave you up."

He closed his eyes and sighed deeply. Of course Ron did. That was the problem with conspiring. You never knew if your co-conspirators were going to squeal. He opened his eyes and gave Sasha a resigned look. "What do you want?"

She smiled. "So, you're right. My clients have decided to settle. I sent a signed counter-offer to Botta this morning. He's certainly signed it by now. You'll submit it to Judge Cook as your last official act before you retire from the practice of law."

He scoffed. "You're holding me up. So unnecessary. I was authorized to go higher, you know."

"I know. Fifteen million. But our counter was for a court-appointed monitor to supervise the district attorney's office for a period of four years, a public admission of guilt, and nine hundred thousand dollars—the approximate amount of Ron's insurance kitty. The plaintiffs have each agreed to donate a hundred thousand dollars split evenly between two criminal justice reform organizations. That leaves them two hundred thousand apiece." She stopped and laughed. "Funny. I just realized that's the exact amount Naya guessed Botta would offer to settle—before we knew."

"Before you knew what?"

"Before we knew that Leith Delone was funding the settlement."

Cinco's heart fell with a thud and hit his stomach.

That's what it felt like, anyway. She knew everything. But how?

"Sasha, listen to me. Leith Delone is a dangerous man. You don't want him as an enemy. Believe me."

"No, Cinco. You listen to me. Ron Botta has already given an interview that's going to air tonight. If you do what I tell you to, that interview will consist of Ron explaining the terms of the settlement, expressing his regret, and announcing his resignation so that the office starts fresh with a clean slate."

"And what if I don't?"

"If you *don't* do what I say, a longer version of the interview will run. That'll include the whole mess—proof of Delone's involvement, your request that Ron have a police officer shake me up, all of it. And then WACB will air an exclusive video."

Cinco had a sinking feeling he knew what this video would be. And if he was right, he had no options. "What video?"

"The cell phone video I recorded when I was pulled over last night. It's pretty damning. Definitely disbarment material for you and Ron. And probably criminal charges, too. Followed by a protracted and expensive civil case."

Cinco focused on his breathing. If he just kept breathing, he'd make it through this. "So I need to submit the settlement to the court?"

"Right. We need the judge to sign off on the court-appointed monitor."

"And that's all I have to do."

"No. You'll also resign. Effective immediately."

"Sasha, be reasonable. I need to make arrangements. I can't simply leave a leadership vacuum."

"Cinco, you *are* a leadership vacuum. You have been for years. You're miserable, and everyone knows it. Just walk away. Quit and go be a tortured artist somewhere instead of just being tortured. Really, it's easier than you think."

"You should know."

"I do. So does your daughter."

He nodded. "Yes, I suppose she does."

"So, you're going to do what I said?"

He met her blazing green eyes with a defiant look of his own. "Yes, I'll resign. But you can't possibly think Delone's going to stand for this."

"Actually, I do. I don't know exactly why he decided to meddle in the case, and it doesn't much matter. Paying three men to settle a civil rights case certainly wasn't his end game. But it's the part I care about. And he should be pleased. He gets the settlement and he gets to keep his fifteen million dollars. It's a win-win for America's least favorite billionaire."

She brushed past him and left him standing there, much as she had eleven years earlier.

38

L eo dried his hands on a kitchen towel then hustled through the house to answer the door. He looked through the glass to see his friend and boss standing on the porch with a courier's envelope tucked under his arm.

"Hey, Hank," he said as he unlocked the door. "You want to come in?"

"No. I can't stay. I got a call from the office. You got a package, and the delivery service said it was urgent. It was supposed to be delivered yesterday, but ..."

"But nobody was there," Leo finished for him.

"Right." Hank smiled. He handed the envelope to Leo.

Their 'office' was, for lack of a better word, a front. A cover story for what they really did, which was a step or two beyond classified. Its highest and best use was as a mail drop. They never went there, either of them. Hank was single parenting six kids and Leo had the twins and the pets, so they hired a crusty Army vet to check the mail once a week and make a show of turning the lights on for a few hours at a time every now and then.

"Did Benny bring it to you or did you have to go out there?"

"He dropped it off."

Leo gave him a look.

"It's okay. He knows where I live because he saw me in the yard once, playing catch with the kids."

"Still. It's sloppy op sec, Hank." Leo frowned.

"I'm not worried about Benny. I also don't have a wife who attracts trouble like it's her superpower."

It was a fair comment. But he felt compelled to defend Sasha's honor anyway. "She hasn't been in a fist-fight in ... almost a year."

"You must be very proud," Hank cracked. He looked behind Leo. "Where's the terrific twosome?"

"Slime camp this week. Today's the last day. They get to bring all their creations home."

"Good luck with that." Hank clasped him on the arm.

"Thanks. You sure you can't come in? Have a beer?"

"No, the youngest two have archery camp next week. Which means I found out today I need to source child-sized bows and arrows."

"Good luck with that. And thanks for bringing this by." He tapped the envelope.

"No problem. What is it?"

Leo glanced down at the package. "I have no clue."

"Give everyone my love," Hank said as he turned and jogged down the stairs.

"You, too," Leo said absently, staring down at the package.

He went inside and closed the door. The envelope was thick and rectangular. It was addressed to Agent Leo Connelly at the office address that appeared on one iteration of his business cards and marked 'hand-delivery.' He sank down on the couch and turned the package over in his hand.

Mocha trotted over and sat at his feet, looking up at him with his head cocked.

"I don't know either, boy," Leo told him.

He stood and reached up to the mantle where Sasha had left the letter opener she'd stolen, quite reasonably asking what else she was supposed to do with it. He slit the envelope open and removed a notecard. Landon Lewis' letter opener clattered to the floor.

The card in his hand was eerily familiar. It was written in the same elegant script, on the same expensive stationery as the one Sasha had shown him on her phone two nights ago. He'd just opened a letter from Landon, using the dead man's letter opener. He scanned the letter, it was similar but not identical to the one Sasha had photographed. Almost as if the one on his desk had been a draft, not a suicide missive.

He read the card again, more slowly this time:

Agent Connelly,

I must apologize for my behavior earlier. I was reeling, having realized that I have made a grievous mistake.

I have made other mistakes in my life. Lord knows I have. But I have always tried to do the right thing. I may not always have succeeded, but I did try.

Everything I did, I did in Josh's memory, as an effort to honor him. Please bear that in mind when you judge me. But all my work is about to be used for ends that are dishonorable at best, dangerous for certain, and dystopian if they prevail.

I must find a way to make amends for my recent errors of judgment. If you're reading this, then I have failed, and I must ask you to pick up the task. I don't know where else to turn, and I feel seeing you out my window was a sign of some sort.

Enclosed is a program that you can use when the time comes to stop Mjölnir. It will not complete the task, but it will get you in the door.

Best regards,

Landon Lewis

Leo stared down at the gibberish. Mjölnir? As in Thor's hammer? He may have found the note on Landon's desk to be oddly nonspecific, but he found this one to be the rantings of a delusional man. He peered into the envelope. A small, rugged flash drive with a raised physical keypad on its slim body rested at the bottom. He took it out and turned it over in his hand.

He'd seen drives like this before. He'd used them. The keypad was used to set a PIN that had to be entered to unlock the drive itself. Any data transferred to the drive for storage was automatically encrypted at the level of military-grade protection. The aluminum-reinforced drive was coated with a hardened epoxy as a defense against physical tampering. And if this drive was the same as the ones Leo had used, any attempt to extract the flash chips from within the body of the drive by physical means would initiate a destruction process whereby the epoxy would destroy the data. Landon had gone to considerable length to protect whatever was on this drive.

He turned the drive over and over in his hand as he read the letter for a third time. It was no more coherent on third reading. And he didn't even have the PIN in the event that ... what? Thor showed up?

He returned the notecard and drive to the envelope and, as an afterthought, dropped in the letter opener. Then he took the envelope upstairs to his home office, opened his fingerprint-secured safe, and placed them inside. As he looked at the safe, his watch alarm beeped.

Time to leave for slime camp pick-up. Landon's cryptic message would keep. Meanwhile the late pick-up clock was ticking. He turned out the lights and left the office.

39

After an early Friday dinner of takeout pizza from the Neapolitan joint off Walnut Street, Finn and Fiona ran upstairs to their playroom to enjoy their collection of slime creations and Sasha and Connelly retired to the living room to enjoy the rest of a bottle of red wine and the relative calm.

When the kids were halfway up the stairs, Connelly shouted, "Halt!"

They halted, giggling.

"One more time, the rules," he said.

Fiona ticked them off on her fingers, "Keep it on the tarp. Don't take it off the tarp. Don't let Mocha eat it. Don't let Java roll in it." She frowned. "There's one more. Finny?"

Finn leaned over the railing and bellowed, "Stay on the tarp!"

"Carry on, slime warriors," Connelly said, saluting them with his wine glass.

Sasha snuggled into his side. "I feel like at least one of those rules should have mentioned the tarp."

He chuckled. "I don't ever want to try to get that stuff out of a carpet again."

"I'll drink to that." She clinked her glass against his and rested her head on his chest.

"How was your day? Scratch that, how were the past two days? I feel like I haven't seen you since ..."

"Date night. Yeah. It's been an eventful couple of days for sure. How about you?"

"Hank stopped by today."

She pushed herself up on her elbows. "Everything okay? Do you have a new case?"

"Not exactly. It's ... involved."

"Eventful and involved. It sounds like we have a lot to talk about."

"We do," he agreed.

She gave him a sheepish smile. "But not right now, okay? I promised Maisy we'd watch the news."

He raised an eyebrow, but stretched over and grabbed the remote. He pointed it at the tv. "Do you know why?"

"Maybe." She smiled a mysterious smile and sipped her wine.

On the television, a beautiful, but harassed-looking strawberry blonde shouted into her microphone, "So despite the record-breaking heat and humidity, today's free day at the Pittsburgh Zoo smashed all attendance records." The camera panned across the parking lot, testimony to the sea of sweaty humanity.

Maisy appeared on the screen. "Thanks to Summer

Reed for that live report. The zoo is one wild place this evening, isn't it, Chet?"

Maisy's co-anchor fake laughed. "And to wrap up our broadcast we have …" he glanced to his side as if the teleprompter were playing a trick on him. After a beat, he recovered, "…an explosive story that our own Maisy Farley broke earlier today. Now, for an exclusive report, here's Maisy interviewing Milltown District Attorney Ronald Botta." Chet turned in his seat to stare at Maisy.

"Thanks, Chet," she chirped.

On the couch, Connelly elbowed Sasha in the side. "Did you know about this?"

"Maybe. Shh. Watch."

Maisy stood next to a sweaty, pale Ron Botta. She smiled encouragingly at him then began, "This is Maisy Farley. I'm at the Milltown District Attorney's Office with Ronald Botta, the Milltown District Attorney. District Attorney Botta, I understand your office entered into a groundbreaking settlement agreement today in the case of Barefoot, Blank, and Robinson versus your office. Is that correct?"

Ron smiled, but the effect was more of a grimace. "That's right, Maisy. As you may remember, in early 2021, this office was sued in federal court for civil rights violations. The complaint alleged that the three gentlemen named in the complaint had had their civil rights violated by law enforcement."

"Attorney Sasha McCandless-Connelly represented the plaintiffs, isn't that right?"

"Yes, that's right."

"And you've settled?"

"Yes. Earlier today we entered into a settlement agreement with the three plaintiffs in the amount of nine hundred thousand dollars, three hundred thousand of which is to be directed to Project Innocence and the ACLU. The remaining funds will be shared equally among the three plaintiffs."

"And attorney's fees?" Maisy prompted.

That sly minx, Sasha thought gleefully.

Ron looked constipated as he said, "Attorney McCandless-Connelly represented the three men *pro bono*, that is for free. So there is not an attorneys' fee component to the settlement."

"Is there any non-monetary component?" Maisy asked.

"Uh, yes. As part of the settlement, which has been filed with the court by my attorneys at Prescott & Talbott, Judge Cliff Cook will appoint a monitor to supervise the district attorney's office for a period of four years. This court-appointed mentor will report directly to Judge Cook. While I wholeheartedly support this oversight, I have also decided that my continued leadership will be a distraction and a deterrence to healing. So, I am announcing my resignation. Deputy District Attorney Melody Jordan will be stepping into my role until a special election can be held."

"This is certainly a ground-breaking settlement, Mr. Botta."

Botta flashed another sickly smile. "It certainly is, Maisy. I'd like to close by addressing Maxwell Barefoot, Samuel Blank, and Charles Robinson directly. On behalf of the Milltown District Attorney's Office and on my own behalf, I want to apologize for the miscarriage of justice that you experienced at the hands of this office in conjunction with the police department. It was wrong, it never should have happened, and I am deeply sorry. I hope that this settlement and the reforms that will be put in place will allow the community to move forward and heal. Thanks, Maisy."

"Thank you, Mr. Botta. And best wishes to you in your retirement. This is Maisy Farley reporting for WACB."

Back in the studio, Chet eyed his co-anchor. "Wow, Maisy. That's quite a story."

"Yes, Chet, it is. And in late-breaking news, I learned that Mr. Botta's private counsel, Charles 'Cinco' Prescott, managing partner of Prescott & Talbott, a Pittsburgh institution, also announced his retirement today. When reached, Prescott & Talbott confirmed Mr. Prescott's resignation from the firm, effective immediately, but had no further comment."

"Double wow, Maisy."

Back on the couch, Connelly turned to Sasha. "How much of a hand did you have in this?"

She pushed out her lower lip and waved her hands in a terrible Marlon Brando impersonation. "I made him an offer he couldn't refuse."

"That's so bad it's good." Connelly leaned in to cover her mouth with a kiss, but on the screen, Maisy said, "I have one more piece to add to this story."

Sasha pushed Connelly away. "Wait!"

40

The technical director in the control booth was yelling into Maisy's ear through her earpiece. "Maisy, we're going to cut your mic."

Then, also in her ear, even louder, Preston yelled, "No we are not. You have ninety seconds, Mais. That's all I can give you."

That's all I need, sugar.

Maisy took a deep breath, pasted on her best smile, and said, "Chet, when I set out to report this shocking development, I was concerned because just days earlier the new management here at WACB tried to use a very junior reporter to place an unsourced piece claiming Attorney McCandless-Connelly was interfering with settlement talks. Do you remember that?"

Chet mumbled something indistinct. Maisy rolled on. "When management interferes with a newsroom to insert a piece with no sourcing or fact-checking, that's commonly called propaganda. And, I'm afraid that as WACB was recently purchased, through a series of intermediaries, by the well-known billionaire Leith Delone, such propaganda and interference with independent news will become more commonplace. Did you know, Chet, that Mr. Delone is a noted critic of the First Amendment? The one that guarantees the freedom of the press? Curious that a man who doesn't believe in a free and independent press is going around the country gobbling up news stations and local papers, isn't it? Surely there's another moon he could buy instead. This is Maisy Farley signing off for what I have a feeling could be my last broadcast. I love you, Pittsburgh."

Jocelyn pulled in close for a shot of Maisy's eyes, brimming with tears.

"Outro music. Chet, you do it tonight," the technical director said.

The credits rolled and the cameras stopped recording.

"Geez, Maisy, a little warning next time?" Chet groused.

Maisy spotted the two uniformed security guards standing shoulder to shoulder behind Jocelyn. "Not so sure there's going to be a next time, Chet."

She took off her mic pack and wrapped it up neatly. Then she took a deep breath and walked off the set. Preston pushed his way between the security guards, snapping, "I'll tell her."

He came to a stop in front of Maisy, out of breath and more disheveled than ever. "I'm sorry, Maisy. It was out of my hands. You're ..." he looked away.

Say it.

"You're fired."

Maisy looked over his head at the woman standing quietly in the corner with a 'guest' pass affixed to her blazer. "Naya, I'm fired!"

Naya pumped her fist and whooped.

Maisy turned back to Preston. "It's okay, Preston. I know I had it coming. You tried to push me out gently, then not so gently. I wouldn't quit. It's not your fault."

He gave her a confused look. "But why? Why make them fire you?"

She leaned in and whispered in his ear, "Because I have a one-million-dollar golden parachute in that contract I never bothered reading. It kicks in if I'm fired, and only if I'm fired. Even if it's for cause."

He gaped at her, apparently at a loss for words.

She pulled back and smiled at him. "You take care now, sugar."

He stared at her. "Your eyes—they're brown tonight."

"They always were."

She patted him on the shoulder. Then she ran over to Naya, who wrapped her in a huge hug.

"So, what's next for you?"

"I don't know," Maisy said slowly. "Maisy Farley, Independent Investigative Reporter, has a nice ring. Don't you think?"

THANK YOU!

Thanks for reading *Independent Sources!* At the end of this book, Maisy practically demanded (in her polite Southern way) that I give her a book of her own. I know better than to argue with Maisy. *Steeltown Magnolia* follows Maisy as she digs into her first story as an independent investigative reporter: Why would Landon Lewis, a brilliant but troubled tech genius, jump to his death when he was on the cusp of receiving a one-hundred-million-dollar windfall? It doesn't add up, and Maisy's determined to get to the truth.

Meanwhile, Leo has his own questions about Landon Lewis. Namely, what's he supposed to do with the package Landon sent him the day he died? In *Insidious Threats (Sasha McCandless Legal Thriller No. 16)*, Sasha and Leo unravel the truth about the powerful and dangerous Mjölnir network and work together to dismantle it without being detected.

To get updates about release dates and other book

news, sign up for my newsletter on my website where you can always find an up-to-date list of the titles in this series, as well as my other books on my website, www.melissafmiller.com.

In addition to new release alerts, newsletter subscribers receive notices of sales and other book news, goodies, and exclusive subscriber bonuses.

Share it. This paperback book is definitely lending-enabled; so please lend your copy to a friend.

Review it. Please consider posting a short review to help other readers decide whether they might enjoy it.

Connect with me. Stop by my Facebook page for book updates, cover reveals, pithy quotes about coffee, and general time-wasting.

Keep reading. Check out the first book in one (or all) of my other bestselling series:

Critical Vulnerability (Aroostine Higgins Thriller No. 1):

Aroostine relies on her Native American traditions and her legal training to right wrongs and dispense justice. She's charmingly relentless, always dots her *i*'s and crosses her *t*'s, and is an expert tracker.

Dark Path (Bodhi King Forensic Thriller No. 1):

Bodhi is a forensic pathologist and a practicing Buddhist who's called upon to solve medical mysteries and unexplained deaths while adhering to his belief system. He's thoughtful, unflinching, and always calm in an emergency.

Rosemary's Gravy (We Sisters Three Humorous Romantic Mystery No. 1):

Rosemary, Sage, and Thyme are three twenty-something sisters searching for career success and love. Somehow, though, they keep finding murder and mayhem ... and love.

ABOUT THE AUTHOR

USA Today bestselling author Melissa F. Miller was born in Pittsburgh, Pennsylvania. Although life and love led her to Philadelphia, Baltimore, Washington, D.C., and, ultimately, South Central Pennsylvania, she secretly still considers Pittsburgh home.

In college, she majored in English literature with concentrations in creative writing poetry and medieval literature and was stunned, upon graduation, to learn that there's not exactly a job market for such a degree. After working as an editor for several years, she returned to school to earn a law degree. She was that annoying girl who loved class and always raised her hand. She practiced law for fifteen years, including a stint as a clerk for a federal judge, nearly a decade as an attorney at major international law firms, and several years running a two-person law firm with her lawyer husband.

Now, powered by coffee, she writes legal thrillers and homeschools her three children. When she's not writing, and sometimes when she is, Melissa travels around the country in an RV with her husband, her kids, and her dog and cat.

Connect with me:
www.melissafmiller.com

Made in United States
Orlando, FL
11 August 2022

20859498R00182